CYNERIC

OTHER BOOKS BY ANNA DURAND

The Mortal Falls (Undercover Elementals, Book One)
The Mortal Fires (Undercover Elementals, Book Two)
The Mortal Tempest (Undercover Elementals, Book Three)
The Janusite Trilogy (Undercover Elementals, Books 1-3)
Obsidian Hunger (Undercover Elementals, Book Four)
Unbidden Hunger (Undercover Elementals, Book Five)
The Thirteenth Fae (Undercover Elementals, Book Six)
Echo Power (Echo Power Trilogy, Book One)
Echo Dominion (Echo Power Trilogy, Book Two)
Echo Unbound (Echo Power Trilogy, Book Three)
Passion Never Dies: The Complete Reborn Series
The Notorious Dr. MacT (A Hot Scots Prequel)
The British Bastard (A Hot Scots Prequel)
Dangerous in a Kilt (Hot Scots, Book One)
Wicked in a Kilt (Hot Scots, Book Two)
Scandalous in a Kilt (Hot Scots, Book Three)
The MacTaggart Brothers Trilogy (Hot Scots, Books 1-3)
Gift-Wrapped in a Kilt (Hot Scots, Book Four)
Notorious in a Kilt (Hot Scots, Book Five)
Insatiable in a Kilt (Hot Scots, Book Six)
Lethal in a Kilt (Hot Scots, Book Seven)
Irresistible in a Kilt (Hot Scots, Book Eight)
Devastating in a Kilt (Hot Scots, Book Nine)
Spellbound in a Kilt (Hot Scots, Book Ten)
Relentless in a Kilt (Hot Scots, Book Eleven)
Incendiary in a Kilt (Hot Scots, Book Twelve)
Wild in a Kilt (Hot Scots, Book Thirteen)
Unstoppable in a Kilt (Hot Scots, Book Fourteen)
Lachlan in a Kilt (The Ballachulish Trilogy, Book One)
Aidan in a Kilt (The Ballachulish Trilogy, Book Two)
Rory in a Kilt (The Ballachulish Trilogy, Book Three)
Brit vs. Scot (A Hot Brits/Hot Scots/Au Naturel Crossover Book)
The American Wives Club (A Hot Brits/Hot Scots/Au Naturel Crossover Book)
One Hot Chance (Hot Brits, Book One)
One Hot Roomie (Hot Brits, Book Two)
One Hot Crush (Hot Brits, Book Three)
The Dixon Brothers Trilogy (Hot Brits, Books 1-3)
One Hot Escape (Hot Brits, Book Four)
One Hot Rumor (Hot Brits, Book Five)
One Hot Christmas (Hot Brits, Book Six)
One Hot Scandal (Hot Brits, Book Seven)
One Hot Deal (Hot Brits, Book Eight)
Natural Obsession (Au Naturel Nights, Book One)
Natural Passion (Au Naturel Trilogy, Book One)
Natural Impulse (Au Naturel Trilogy, Book Two)
Natural Satisfaction (Au Naturel Trilogy, Book Three)

CYNERIC

Undercover Elementals, Book Seven

ANNA DURAND

JACOBSVILLE BOOKS JB MARIETTA, OHIO

ISBN: 978-1-958144-08-4 (paperback)
ISBN: 978-1-958144-09-1 (ebook)
ISBN: 978-1-958144-10-7 (audiobook)

Manufactured in the United States.

Jacobsville Books
www.JacobsvilleBooks.com

Publisher's Cataloging-in-Publication Data
provided by Five Rainbows Cataloging Services

Names: Durand, Anna.
Title: Cyneric / Anna Durand.
Description: Marietta, OH : Jacobsville Books, 2023. | Series: Undercover elementals, bk. 7.
Identifiers: ISBN 978-1-958144-10-7 (paperback) | ISBN: 978-1-958144-09-1 (ebook) | ISBN978-1-958144-10-7 (audiobook)
Subjects: LCSH: Vampires--Fiction. | Magic--Fiction. | Dragons--Fiction. | Older women--Fiction. | Romance fiction. | BISAC: FICTION / Romance / Paranormal / Vampires. | FICTION / Romance / Paranormal / Shifters. | FICTION / Romance / Fantasy. | GSAFD: Love stories. | Occult fiction. | Fantasy fiction.
Classification: LCC PS3604.U724 C88 2023 (print) | LCC PS3604.U724 (ebook) | DDC 813/.6--dc23.

Chapter One

THE SCENT OF HUMAN BLOOD AROUSES MY SENSES, BUT THE TASTE OF IT enthralls me, and I cannot stop myself from surrendering to its call, sinking my fangs into the pliant flesh of a mortal. When I break through a vein, the taste is delicious. But when I pierce an artery, a high like nothing else in the multiverse consumes me, bringing with it the sweet, spicy, exquisite flavor of the freshest blood.

"Oh God, yes, don't stop."

The voice of the woman I'm devouring, in the most literal sense, pulls me out of the blood trance. I retract my fangs from her flesh and glide my tongue over my teeth and lips to lap up every iota of this woman's essence. Yes, blood is the essence of life—and of death.

"Do that again," the woman pleads, her tone breathless and her breasts heaving. "That was incredible. Please, do it again."

My lips are still teasing the skin of her inner thigh, where I had gorged myself on the femoral artery, though I had stopped before I took too much. Now, I lick the blood away from the wound, slowly, sensually, while the woman writhes and moans beneath me. I have no desire to kill this mortal by drinking too deeply. As I drag my tongue over the fang marks, her skin seals up.

Sometimes I do want to drain a mortal completely, but that would mean death for the one I devour. I could drink until my lover is near that point, but I won't do it tonight, with this woman. Never again, if I can't find the one woman I've sought for so long. Have the Four Winds hidden her from me? They know the sweetest blood of all still calls out to me.

As I lap up the last bit of this mortal's blood from my lips, I slide off the bed onto my feet. Then I stretch and groan with deep gratification, though not complete satisfaction.

My lover crawls toward me on hands and knees, then rises to kneel inches away from me. The nameless female skates her hands up her belly and over her breasts before settling her palms on my chest. "Let's have sex again. You can bite me as many times as you want. Never knew anything could feel this good. Wasn't it incredible?"

"Yes." But not for the reasons she believes. The taste of human blood makes me hard, and I needed the release of taking her body after the first time I devoured her.

She tries to kiss me, but I shove her backward. The woman falls onto the bed on her back. And she pouts. "Come on, baby. You know you want me."

"Once was enough." With a single thought, I summon my clothing onto my body. "I have no more need of your flesh."

I teleport away before she can beg me to fuck her again. The lust has dissipated, and my hunger is satiated—for now. No matter how many mortals I drink from or how many lovers I take to bed, never again will I experience true satisfaction.

Unless I can find *her…*

But Riley Jordan is beyond my reach. The Four Winds ensured that. They fear my power, and perhaps all I need to do is employ my heightened sense of smell to sniff her out. No being in any world could smell as delicious as Riley. Once, I had sunk my fangs deep into her carotid artery. The flavor of her has stayed with me ever since. With one taste, I became helplessly addicted.

Stop, Cyneric, you're killing Riley.

The memory slams into me so hard that I stagger sideways and bump into a brick wall. I'm standing in an alley—where on earth, I have no idea—and my heart has begun to pound with a ferocity that makes my head spin and my breaths shorten. Tris of the copper fae had been begging me to stop, but I could not.

Take her. Have her. Devour her.

I clutch my head with both hands and sag against the wall while the words Drakon had spoken months ago echo in my mind. The crown prince of the Western Kingdom of Dragon Shifters had bade me to give in to the craving, to the searing lust that demanded I drink Riley dry. I'd wanted to do so much more than that with her, but the seductive call of blood had taken control.

Imagine what she will taste like, how good it will feel to feast on her blood.

Drakon had said that. Or was it Tris? No, it must have been the dragon prince.

If you don't stop now, she will die.

Tris had snarled those words. Something about the tone of his voice had triggered a pang of…regret inside me. I had gently retracted my fangs from her throat, but it was too late. She would have died if not for the powers of a healing vortex and the being who controlled it—Triskaideka of the copper fae.

The whirling in my head subsides. My pulse returns to normal.

I drag in a deep breath and exhale it slowly. Drakon died months ago, destroyed by Tris and Riley. Why can I not cease to remember those days? Why do I still crave the woman whose blood I drank of deeply? Ever since, I have been suckling from the veins and arteries of woman after woman but never find what I need. Perhaps because I don't know what I need.

Except for *her*.

I push away from the wall and survey my surroundings. I've landed in an alley, and I hear the sounds of revelry further down the narrow passage between two buildings. Perhaps there is a drinking establishment down there. I believe mortals call it a club. Before my emancipation, I had only used a club to bludgeon my enemies, but humans turned that word into something else. They are strange and incomprehensible. But then, all beings in every realm seem that way to me.

As I stride down the alley, the noises from the club grow louder. A low, rhythmic thumping emerges from inside the building, and I can hear the faint sounds of screeching music. Yes, mortals believe tuneless noise is music and the louder it is, the better. My elemental ears can handle the noise without incurring damage. The mortals in clubs must all be half deaf.

I walk straight past the club with its thundering racket. Places like that one are not appealing to me. Seduction requires that my target can hear my voice.

At the street corner, I glance left and right. None of the garish establishments in the vicinity appeal to me. I jog across the intersection and into the alley on the other side. The deeper shadows here provide cover for me, and my dark clothing adds an extra layer of anonymity.

Up ahead, the rear door of a building swings open. A man and woman exit, their features obscured by the shadows as the door shuts behind them. But I can see a head of long blonde hair. The woman wears denim shorts and a tank top while hiking boots cover her feet.

My pulse accelerates. *Riley*.

I stride swiftly down the alley to reach whatever establishment she had come out of, arriving just as the woman throws her head back and laughs. Her companion is not the leprechaun Tris, and perhaps the absence of her copper fae lover should stop me. But it doesn't. I clamp a hand down on the woman's shoulder.

She jerks and swivels her head to stare at me with wide eyes. Fear radiates off her.

The woman is not Riley.

Her companion pushes the girl behind his body and gives me a strong shove. "Back off, perv. The BDSM club is two blocks east."

I tip my head to the side. "What is BDSM?"

"The twisted shit freaks like you love." He scans me up and down, his lip curling. "You went all in for that garbage, didn't you? Leather coat, leather pants, black T-shirt. What, you couldn't afford the whips and chains?"

Despite knowing the blonde girl is not Riley, I experience a strong urge to touch her, to gaze into her eyes, to sink my teeth into her throat. I grasp the annoying male and hoist him off the pavement. His shoes hang several feet off the ground. "You are in my way."

I hurl him down the alley.

The man smacks down on the pavement, rolling three times, and winds up flat on his back.

As I stride toward the woman, she cowers against the wall of the building.

"Please," she says, her voice shaky. "Please don't hurt me."

I halt a few paces away, canting my head to study her. I can smell her fear. The air is redolent with it. I dislike that stench, but I cannot stop myself from leaning in to sniff her throat.

"Please don't kill me."

That soft plea, half whispered with a hiccup at the end, snaps me out of my trance. No, this woman is not the one I seek. Riley Jordan would never beg for her life in such a manner.

I march down the alley, stepping over the man who still lies prone on the ground. He moans when I pass by but does not rise. He will survive, though his bruises might make him wish he had not. His injuries have no meaning to me. At the next intersection, I veer down the sidewalk. Why? I made no conscious decision to do so. But as I wander down the concrete path with grumbling vehicles rushing past on the street, I experience an odd sensation of…anticipation. Perhaps I subconsciously sense another woman whose blood I might drink. But no, this sensation is like nothing I've felt before.

The doors of a closed shop fly open, and a woman stumbles out onto the sidewalk. She gestures rudely at the man who just shut the door. I've learned that flicking one's fingers across the chin is a crude gesture in the mortal world, though I still cannot fathom why.

"Your crap is overpriced," she hollers at the man. "Only a moron would pay that much for a pair of pawned earrings."

The woman straightens her clothes and squares her shoulders, then walks away—toward me.

I quickly duck into the shadows under the awning of a shuttered shop.

The woman ambles down the sidewalk, posture slumped, and struggles to keep her large bag hooked over her shoulder. A lock of hair keeps falling over her eyes, and she continually swipes it away. A filthy man wearing tattered clothes crashes into her, and she nearly falls down but catches herself at the last moment. As the vagrant flees, she throws her arms up and shouts, apparently to the sky, "Oh, come on. Is this really what I deserve?"

She bows her head but does not move.

The scent of her wafts over me, sweet and redolent with flavors I cannot describe. No woman I have ever tasted smelled as delicious as her, not even Riley Jordan.

I clench my hands and my teeth. No, I do not want *this* female. Only Riley.

But the aroma of this woman…

No. I seek Riley. She belongs with me, not the leprechaun.

The woman freezes. With her head still bowed, she rotates only her eyes to stare into the shadows where I hide.

I smell no fear from her, which does not make sense. A stranger hides in the shadows to watch her, yet she feels no trepidation. Though I have no idea why I do it, I find myself walking out of the darkness to approach the woman. The glow of a neon sign reveals me.

She straightens and lifts her brows, raking her gaze over me from head to toe. "Do you always skulk in the shadows? That's not very polite."

"Why do you not fear me?"

"Trust me, hon, I've seen worse things than you on the streets at night."

Her voice reminds me of Riley, but only because of her accent. She must be American, though I still do not understand what that means.

The strange mortal eyes me up and down again, then shakes her head. "A kid like you shouldn't be out alone this late. It's after midnight."

What is a "kid"? I won't ask her. It doesn't matter.

She smiles, and the expression tightens wrinkles around her eyes. "You seem confused. Are you lost, sweetie?"

Her smile, her scent, her voice… They confound me. I feel oddly drawn to her, against my wishes, but I will not allow the Unseen to hold sway over me here in the mortal world. I do not want this woman.

So, I whisk myself away.

Chapter Two

I EMERGE FROM THE DARK VOID INTO THE SUNLIGHT. TELEPORTATION ALways involves traveling via the void, a dark and treacherous tunnel that winds its way through the empty spaces between particles. The journey takes less than an instant. I had left my previous location seconds ago, yet it seems as if hours or even days have elapsed. Perhaps I have landed on the other side of this world where night has not yet fallen, or perhaps I've come to a different world altogether.

Fortunately, my aversion to the sun has gone away, a recent change that I cannot explain. The reasons why matter little to me. I am free to go wherever I choose. But I did not choose this location. I was either pulled here by an outside force or my targeting had failed.

Where am I?

Glancing around, I realize I stand alongside a wooden structure of some sort that only vaguely resembles a house. A grassy plain stretches out in all directions. I can see other buildings far in the distance, though I can't discern their purpose. Even my enhanced vision doesn't help me see objects that far away.

A strange odor wafts over me.

I sniff the air, turning in a circle, trying to determine from which direction the stench came. It seems to be the building directly in front of me. I stride into the structure where several large animals reside. They emit odd groaning noises and have organs that drop down from their bellies as well as what seem like multiple fingers protruding from beneath their bodies. I approach one of the creatures. It looks up at me with large brown eyes but does not pause in chewing the strands of vegetative matter that stick out of its mouth. The strands appear to be dead grass or weeds.

As I gaze into the creature's eyes, I begin to feel…relaxed. An inexplicable urge seizes me, and I stretch a hand out to touch the creature.

"What the hell are you doing to my cows?"

The angry voice originated behind me, near the doorway to this structure. I ignore the voice and stroke the hairy beast before me.

A hand seizes my arm and attempts to pull me away from the brown-eyed creature.

I do not move.

"Get away from my cows," the voice growls. A noise that sounds like *ka-chunk* follows. "Move now or I'll blow your damn head off."

Mortals can be so tiresome. This one speaks with an accent I recognize because I have met an elemental who once lived in Texas when he was human, before his forging, though his accent has now changed.

I turn toward the being, who I can now see is a human male. He holds a long stick of a sort I have seen before. I believe it's known as a shotgun. The man aims it at me. I wave my hand, and the weapon vanishes.

"What the—" The stranger turns his palms up as if studying the empty space where his shotgun had once been. "How did you—That's impossible."

"It is entirely possible. I teleported your weapon away." Turning halfway toward the animal, I watch it chewing the dead grass in its mouth. "What variety of creature is this?"

The man does not speak.

Swiveling my head toward him, I ask the question again in case he believes I was speaking to the grass-eating beast. "What sort of creatures are these?"

His lips work for several seconds before he speaks. "It's a cow."

"What is the purpose of cows?"

"They, uh, make milk and can be killed for their meat."

I gaze at the cow again, but its appeal has waned for me. I whisk myself away again. This time, I've landed in a city. Is it the same one as before? I can't tell. The answer hardly matters to me since I seek only to find another mortal to drink. I should not have become weakened, even slightly, from transporting myself twice. The nourishment I received from that woman earlier should have sustained me, yet I already feel peckish.

Horns blare out on the street, but I wander down a narrow pathway where the street noises are somewhat muffled. Sunlight filters down to me, muted by the structures at either side of the alley, and the stench of refuse sifts into my nostrils. I wander back to the street and head down the sidewalk. Mortals give me strange looks, though some females clearly appreciate my attire.

Ahead of me, a woman crouches on the sidewalk, attempting to gather up the items she had dropped. I hesitate a short distance from her, cocking my head to the side as I watch the woman and listen to the half-mumbled words she speaks.

"Damn, damn, damn. Frigging jackass. Knock me down like a domino, then run off."

None of her words make sense. She believes no one heard her, but my supernatural senses allow me to detect sounds that no mortal could hear. The scent of her envelops me, and I recognize the aroma. This is the woman who had called me "hon" and "a kid." I can't resist inhaling a deep draft of her scent. It makes my cock rouse.

She gives up on gathering her possessions and drops her face into her hands. Her shoulders quiver.

Her plight should not bother me. Yet I find myself walking up to the woman and kneeling beside her. "May I assist you?"

She jerks her head up, and her brows draw together. "It's you again."

When she looks into my eyes, I become frozen to the spot where I kneel. I cannot tear my focus away from her amber eyes, and her husky voice sends a shiver of lust through me. I was not this close to her the last time we met. Now, hovering inches from her shapely figure, I seem to have lost all my ability to move or speak.

"You okay, hon?"

This female is nothing like Riley, yet I experience a similar need to possess her. Riley had never allowed me to claim her. Might this woman permit me to possess her body and her soul? No, I do not want anyone but Riley. I had once worshiped Larissa, the mortal who had formerly been the goddess Hathor, but I had not craved her the way I hunger for this woman. Perhaps her scent reminds me of Riley. That would explain my attraction to her.

But no, she smells nothing like that. Her scent is stronger and more intoxicating.

The strange woman touches my cheek. "You look pale, sweetie. Probably got low blood sugar. When was the last time you ate something?"

"I do not know. It was night the last time I fed."

She keeps her hand on my cheek, the warmth of her palm seeping into my flesh. "Why don't you come with me to the diner down the street? I haven't had lunch yet either."

"You do not speak the way others in this city do."

"I could say the same about you. I'm originally from Pennsylvania." She winks at me. "And I'm guessing you're originally from England."

"Am I? Others believe I am British."

"Because that's what English people are called—British." She pulls her hand away, robbing me of her soft skin. "Do you have amnesia?"

"I do not know. What city is this?"

"Amarillo. That's in Texas, hon, in case you can't remember." She once again attempts to gather up her belongings, but she still can't carry all of those items. "Damn. I'm so clumsy today."

I teleport her belongings into my arms and rise. "I will carry these for you."

She tips her head back to stare up at me with wide eyes. "How did you do that? You just made all that stuff go poof and…appear in your hands."

"Yes." I tip my head to the side. "What did your ex tell you?"

When she struggles to get up, apparently hindered by her high-heeled shoes, I offer her my hand. She accepts my help, and I pull her close. She gazes into my eyes as if she has never seen anyone like me before. She has not, that is for certain. "I think we'd better go to my apartment instead of a diner. You might cause a panic if you poof things away again. Your blue eyes are so pale they seem unearthly, and they swirl too. That would definitely scare the shit out of most people."

"You do not fear having me in your home?"

"I should be afraid, but I'm not. How strange is that? I feel I can trust you."

Have I ensorcelled her without consciously trying? I doubt that's possible. Yet she does appear slightly dazed. "Where do you live?"

She recites an address, and I teleport us directly into her home. We land in the living room beside a sofa. Over the past several months, since I fled the Unseen and came to the mortal world, I have learned many of the terms that humans use. Many more still elude me.

I release the woman.

She backs away from me, but only a short distance. "What's your name, hon?"

"Cyneric."

"That's unusual. I've never heard that name before."

"It is more ancient than any civilization you have encountered." I cant my head, studying her. "What is your name?"

"Amanda Nelson. Don't you have a last name?"

"No."

She wanders over to the sofa and sits down, then pats the cushion beside her. "Have a seat. I think we should talk before I make lunch for us."

I shuffle toward the sofa, my footsteps halting, and stare down at the cushion beside Amanda. I cannot move one step further. This woman confounds me more than anyone, even Riley, has ever done before. But my body seems to have a mind of its own, because I settle onto the sofa.

Amanda turns slightly toward me. "You aren't like other people. Are you, hon?"

"You are correct."

"Either I'm having the wildest dream, or you can actually take us to another place in an instant."

"I can do that."

She leans back and folds her arms under her bosom. The action lifts her breasts and draws my focus to them. "Thank you for carrying my stuff for me. But I need to know one thing. What are you?"

"I don't understand the question."

"You aren't human, right? You're something else." When I nod, she narrows her gaze on me. "So tell me, hon, what are you?"

"An elemental vampire."

She stares at me while remaining completely still. Even her eyelids don't move. Then she blinks rapidly. "Oh. Is that all?"

A hiccup of nervous laughter had interrupted her words. I've spent enough time in the presence of mortals to know they often laugh when confronted with my true nature. But none of them know what I really am.

Amanda tightens her arms around herself, which hoists her breasts even more. That makes me hunger to devour them, to devour her, but I experience a strange impulse not to do that. I need to know more about this human female who does not fear me.

"Do you believe that I am a vampire?"

She bites her lips and studies me for a moment. "Yes, I believe you. Like I said the first time we met, I've seen worse things than you."

"I doubt that."

"You have no idea what I've witnessed, and you're too young to understand." She lowers her hands to her lap and roves her gaze over me. "How old are you, sweetie? Can't be much more than your mid-twenties."

She has no conception of how ancient I am. And I suddenly realize that I do not want to tell her. I need to keep her with me, to possess her, to erase the memory of Riley by claiming this woman.

Amanda's gaze flicks down to my groin, and her lips tick upward at one corner. "You are way too young for me, hon."

I am developing an erection, and she could see that. Despite her statement that I'm too young for her, I can smell her desire. She wants me. I would love to fuck her, but something about this woman makes me feel...protective of her. Still, I experience an oddly powerful need to explain. But I resist that urge. If she knew my true age, she would run away.

So instead, I ask, "How old are you?"

"Did nobody ever tell you it's rude to ask a woman that question?" She smirks and pats my cheek. "Luckily for you, I'm not sensitive about my age. It's a badge of honor for me. And to answer your question, I'm fifty-three years old."

"Is that meant to be shocking? Most of the beings I have met are far older than that."

And no, I will never tell Amanda how long ago I was created.

The world shifts around me with dizzying speed and force, dragging me through the abyssal tunnel headfirst. I drop face-down onto cool, damp earth.

"There you are, you naughty vampire."

I push up onto my hands and knees, rotating my head to glare at the being who had spoken. "Why have you summoned me, Janus?"

"Because you need an intervention."

Chapter Three

NTERVENTION?" I RISE AND BRUSH DIRT AND GRASS OFF MY CLOTHING, then survey the area in which I find myself. "This is the Unseen. You must have required the cooperation of many elementals to summon me back to this world. I do not wish to remain here, and you cannot stop me from leaving."

"Perhaps not. That is why this is an intervention and not a destruction ritual."

His accent has always irritated me. The ancient Romans had worshiped Janus as a god because he *is* a god. Not in the sense that he created the multiverse. Only in the sense that he is not an elemental and possesses power beyond that of any other being in the Unseen—except for me. Yet even with my exceptional abilities, I can't destroy Janus or even hurt him.

Not yet.

"Your powers continue to expand," Janus tells me as if I don't know that already. "This is an issue of concern."

"For whom? I have no concerns about my powers."

The god strides closer to me, so close in fact that his breaths reflect off my face. His golden, metallic eyes shimmer but don't swirl as those of elementals do. They seem like disks of actual gold. "You are unstable, in many ways, and the imbalance within you threatens to destabilize both worlds."

"Not my concern."

Janus takes two steps backward and waves his arm in a flourishing gesture.

Metal chains appear, wrapping themselves around my body so that I can't move at all.

"You must be dealt with, Cyneric, and the decision of how to do that lies in the hands of the Four Winds."

"Release me now," I snarl. "You have no right to restrain me."

"I have every right." Janus raises his arms. "Four Winds, open your temple doors for Cyneric and judge him as you must."

My breath catches as magics tug at me, attempting to haul me away to the Temple of the Four Winds. I will not go there. I refuse to be judged by them. No master controls me any longer, and I will never become a prisoner again.

The ground begins to tremble.

Another being appears beside me—Brennus, the raven shifter who had once served the sylph kings Notus and Skeiron. Is he to take me away? No, I will not allow it.

Beneath my feet, the earth quakes with more force, ramping up toward a cataclysm that I can feel in my bones. *Yes, destroy the Unseen*, a voice inside me urges. *Destroy every being in this world.* No one in either world has welcomed me. Why should I not annihilate the multiverse?

But that would mean eradicating Riley—and Amanda.

I do not care for that woman. Only for Riley.

A burst of power erupts inside me, hot and sharp like a knife dipped in lava. I roar and throw my arms out, shattering my chains. Brennus and Janus both crouch and cover their heads as the fragments fly far and wide, disintegrating everything they touch.

I teleport myself away.

Darkness envelops me as my feet touch down on a hard surface. My vision requires a moment to adjust. Where am I? Not in the mortal world. The two moons that glow in the sky tell me this must be the Unseen. Yet a moment ago, it was daylight here. Now, it's night. I can see the outlines of structures up ahead along the trail on which I stand. When I try to walk, I can only stagger down toward my destination. My head pounds. My muscles feel weak.

I need to feed.

As I stumble toward the buildings, I suddenly realize where I am. This is the village of the copper fae. I have been here before, though not for months.

Riley lives here.

My strength returns quickly as I bypass the fountain in the village square and sniff the air to search for a sign of Riley. No one is outdoors at this time of night, so I'm not forced to engage in conversation with any of the residents. As I wander the streets, at first I detect no sign of Riley. Then, I finally catch her scent in the air. Sweet, savory, unlike any other being in any world. I veer down an alley to emerge directly beside a home that lies dark and silent now.

Riley has moved into a different house. But I have found her at last.

I pause on the doorstep and inhale deeply. The drugging scent of her suffuses me, and my pulse beats faster. My breaths come faster too, and I cannot wait any longer. I teleport myself directly into the bedroom, to the foot of the bed. Riley lies under the covers with Tris, the redheaded leprechaun who stole her away from me. He lies behind Riley with his body cradling hers.

My fingers curl into my palms. At the sight of her, my cock begins to thicken, and the blood lust rushes through my veins.

I approach the side of the bed, careful to make no sound, and slant toward Riley. The scent of her is stronger now, so intense that my head begins to swim, but I don't care. I need to taste her again. To experience the incredible flavor of her life force. I stretch out one hand toward her face.

Another hand, one much larger than Riley's, grasps my wrist to stop me. "What the hell do you think you're doing, Captain Fang?"

He spoke in a soft voice as if he doesn't want Riley to awaken.

I shake his hand away from my wrist.

"Get out of here," Tris growls, "before I grab my endued sword and ram it into your chest like you did to Larissa."

"Riley belongs to me."

"Like hell she does."

The slumbering woman rouses and sleepily glances between me and Tris. "What's going on?"

Tris glowers at me. "Cyneric was just leaving. Go back to sleep, baby."

Riley sits up and rubs her eyes. "What are you doing here, Cyneric? We haven't seen you in months."

"I wished to make sure you are all right."

Tris snorts. "Sure you did. If 'all right' means 'drink her blood.' You need to scram right now before I make good on my threat."

He conjures his endued sword.

I could steal Riley away from him and take her to a place where neither he nor anyone else could find us. But I've suddenly lost my desire to do that. Another place and another woman calls to me. But no, I will never visit Amanda again. Something about her disturbs me.

Instead, I whisk myself away to the mortal world but on the opposite side from where Amanda lives. I sit down on the summit of a tall sand dune, watching as a storm approaches. The wall of sand will draw closer and closer, but I don't care. Let it rush over me and dessicate my flesh. I will regenerate, no matter what happens.

No one wants to be in my presence. No one except for Amanda.

But I need Riley.

The ground begins to shake, and the sand falls away down the slope, erasing itself little by little as I slide lower and lower. The sand threatens to swallow me, but I teleport away from the disaster despite the fact it would not have killed me. I am immortal and unkillable, that is what Tris and his cohorts have said. They fear me, though they try to hide it. I do not care how they feel about me.

I emerge in another location where trees with long leaves are swaying in a temperate breeze. The sand here does not form high dunes, and waves lap against the shore. This must be the ocean. I've heard of that but never attempted to visit such a place place. As I walk toward the shore, the ground begins to quake and the trees begin to sway wildly. I struggle to remain upright, but even my elemental powers can't stop me from tumbling onto the sand face-down.

The world around me shifts again.

And I land flat on my back this time, gazing up at the twilight sky. Shades of pink and purple fan out across the horizon, growing darker every moment until, soon, they will vanish altogether. I seem incapable of moving, even after the sunset has disappeared. Where am I? I don't know or care.

Suddenly, I'm whisked away to yet another location—one that I recognize.

Amanda sits on the sofa in the living room of her apartment. She wears different clothing than she had earlier. Or was it on a different day? I've lost track of time in the most literal sense. She wears loose-fitting clothing that I have learned from past experiences is known as "sweats." I still cannot understand why mortals refer to their clothing that way since sweat is a substance the human body produces, not something woven in a factory.

With her auburn hair held back in a ponytail—another term I've learned of late—she seems younger than her stated age. Fifty-three does not sound old at all, not to someone such as myself. I had materialized in the corner of her living room, in a shadowed spot that conceals me just enough that Amanda has not noticed me yet. Her gaze is riveted to a book she holds in one hand.

She jerks her head up, glancing around. Then her attention lands on me, and she smiles with what seems like affection. "Cyneric, you're back."

I stride out of the shadowed corner and approach the sofa. When she waves for me to sit down, I do so. Not because she suggested it. I simply wish to sit down so I can recover from my frenzied travels.

Amanda skims her gaze over my entire body. "No offense, hon, but you don't look so hot."

"I am always hot. My body temperature is warmer than that of a human."

She smiles with softness and perhaps affection, causing faint dimples to form in her cheeks. "I meant you don't look healthy and strong. What's wrong?"

"Why do you not care that I keep appearing inside your home?"

She shrugs. "Because I don't. You seem like you need a friend, anyway."

I stare at her for a moment. Then I blurt out words I hadn't meant to speak. "I have never had a friend."

"Never? You poor thing." She clasps my hand. "Well, you've got one now."

The silkiness of her skin has begun to make me feel… I don't know. This is something I've never experienced before. I can't feel…safe. No, never in all my existence have I felt that way.

"Why do you treat me as a child?" I ask. "I have never been such a thing."

She studies me again, with even more intense scrutiny. "What do you mean you've never been a child? Everybody starts out as a baby, becomes a child, and then grows into an adult."

"No, not everyone."

Her brows have drawn together, tightening into wrinkles over her nose. She has the loveliest features I have ever seen, and the lines of age on her face only increase her appeal. I have met other mortals who had far more lines on their faces, but none of them had this effect on me. It is…disturbing, yet also arousing. The natural scent of her drives me mad, inflaming my lust for blood and for her.

I can't control myself. I lay a hand on her cheek and thrust my fingers into her hair, tugging her closer until our lips almost meet. Her pupils grow larger and darker. Her breaths grow shallower. As we gaze into each other's eyes, my breathing becomes shallower as well, and my cock stiffens. I slant closer until my lips graze hers.

She pulls away, clearing her throat. "I'm too old for you, hon."

"I am not as young as you believe."

"Okay, that might be true. I've known people who seem younger than their true age. So tell me, Cyneric, how old are you?"

"I was created before the dawn of humankind, but I lost count of the epochs."

CHAPTER FOUR

EPOCHS?" HER JAW DROPS, AND FOR A MOMENT, SHE SEEMS TO HAVE become frozen in time and space. Her eyes widen little by little, and she seems incapable of looking away from me. At last, she shakes off her shock—quite literally, by shaking her head. "Holy shit, kid. You don't look your age at all."

"You believe me?"

Amanda shrugs. "Why not? I realized a long time ago there are things in this universe that can't be explained. I've experienced those mysteries firsthand." She leans toward me again to stare into my eyes. "But I've never seen anything like your eyes. They're the most incredible shade of bright, pale blue, and they seem to shimmer and swirl too."

"Yes, I know."

She pulls away from me. "I don't think I'll ever be able to reconcile your young looks with how old you claim to be. I will always feel like I'm too old for you, hon."

"Too old for what?"

"Being with you. I'm fifty-three years old, which means I'm not in my prime anymore. I'm not decrepit, but neither am I a nubile young thing." She laughs, but it sounds nervous rather than happy. "I'm post-menopausal, for heaven's sake."

Mortals have the strangest ways of speaking and often say bizarre things that have no meaning to me. Post-menopausal? I haven't a clue what that means. I suspect it has something to do with her age based on her uneasy laughter.

"Years mean nothing to me," I say. "Time is irrelevant to a being from the Unseen. I am immortal."

Her expression goes blank. She simply stares at me for so long that I begin to wonder if someone has cast a spell that turned her to stone. "Are you serious? Immortal?"

"Yes. Immortal and invincible."

Her jaw drops yet again. She covers her mouth with one hand, then lets it fall onto her lap. "Holy shit."

"You don't believe me. No mortal would."

"Oh, no. I believe you." She clasps both hands on her lap and swallows forcefully enough that I can see the movement in her throat. "What do you want with me?"

"I don't understand the question."

"You keep turning up now and then, kind of like a lost puppy. But I can't figure out why. An immortal, invincible vampire could have his pick of the litter when it comes to women. They must beg for the chance to be with you."

"I have tasted and enjoyed many women. But none intrigue me the way you do. I cannot understand it." My gaze drifts down to her breasts, and I can smell her desire for me. But curiosity overpowers my lust, for the moment. "You mentioned that you have seen worse things than me, and that you have experienced the mysteries of the multiverse firsthand. How could that be?"

Amanda turns away from me and stares out the window. She wrings her hands briefly, then jumps up and hurries over to the bar that separates the kitchen from the living area. Stools offer a place to sit. But rather than doing that, she reaches under the bar to pull out a bottle that holds amber-colored liquid. "I need a shot of Jim Beam if we're going to talk about this."

I rise and stride over to the bar, leaning one arm on it. "If we are going to talk about what?"

"My past." She pours the amber liquid into a glass and downs the contents in two gulps. "I meant it literally when I said I've seen worse things than you. I'm not a newbie when it comes to parallel worlds."

Her statement stops me, and I can't think of anything to say. Few mortals ever learn of the Unseen's existence, much less visit it. But I cannot say for certain that's what she meant. She might have heard tales of the Unseen but never visited it. I need more information.

"You must explain," I say. "Your statement was vague."

She pours more of the amber liquid into her glass, filling it to the brim this time, and swigs a large mouthful. "The man I married turned out to be an incubus."

"A salamander?"

"Yeah. He hid his true nature until the wedding night." She laughs, but there is no humor in the sound. "I thought I just lucked out and snagged a guy who was incredible in bed. Mind-blowing, actually. I was such an idiot."

"Hiding his true nature was unconscionable. Even I would not do such a thing."

She has just raised the glass to her lips again, but she rotates her eyes to look at me sideways as she sets the glass down. "What do you mean 'even you' wouldn't do that? Something about the way you said it makes me think you do other bad things that aren't completely unconscionable."

"Perhaps I have. What else did the incubus do to you?"

She folds her hands around the glass and turns it side to side, her focus bound to the liquid inside it. "I know you're changing the subject to avoid talking about yourself. I'll excuse that for now. Balder, my husband, had no interest in our relationship after the wedding. He took me away to another world, literally, and then revealed himself to me. I was shocked, of course. He had coppery skin, gigantic muscles, and swirling eyes."

"If you have seen an elemental's eyes before, why did you seem stunned by mine?"

"Because your eyes are the most stunningly beautiful thing I have ever seen. They're like…gemstones and fire and stardust, like something that was forged in the center of the universe or in the fires of creation. Even Balder's eyes couldn't match yours."

No one has ever described my eyes the way she has done. I feel an odd sensation of warmth spreading through my body even while I feel lighter in a way I cannot describe. Is this pride? Satisfaction? I haven't experienced the sensation before, so I can't determine its meaning.

Amanda climbs onto a stool and pushes her glass away. "Balder had told me he was from Norway. What a joke. He had never left the Unseen until he came up with his master plan."

Though it feels as if my mouth has gone dry, I never suffer from that sort of thirst. It must be something else. "What did his plan involve?"

She crosses her arms over her chest and shakes her head. "Uh-uh. You won't get the whole story from me until I get more information about you."

"I will not share information with you. My story is of no relevance."

"Of course it is. You want to fuck me, and I need to know I can trust you before I let that happen."

Her statement stuns me, though it shouldn't. She knows I wish to fuck her. But I will not give in to the lust. It has a strangely powerful effect on me, and I do not want to become a slave to my desire for her. I should leave and never return to this place or this woman.

Amanda leans toward me. "Come on, Cyneric. Tell me one thing about yourself."

"Such as what?"

"Were you born? Or did you just poof into existence?"

The room seems to spin once, then a familiar voice echoes in my mind. *You were my first son, and I shall always love you above all others.* "I will not discuss my past."

"But you expect me to share everything with you."

I pound my fist on the counter and snarl, "Stop speaking."

My breathing has become labored, and I grip my head in both hands as the room spins once again. When I attempt to teleport myself away, I instead drop to the floor. Darkness encroaches on my vision. My ears ring. I squeeze my eyes shut and command my powers to function, to no avail.

Amanda crouches beside me. "Cyneric? What's wrong?"

You were born of my blood, of my flesh, of my powers. The words Eros had spoken to me long ago reverberate in my mind. *If you betray me, my son, I shall mete out retribution and destroy you.*

A roar of anguish and agony explodes out of me.

"Cyneric! What's going on? Please talk to me."

"No more talking. Leave me alone."

The building begins to shake, faintly at first, then growing stronger with every passing second. Objects hung from the walls crash to the floor. Furniture begins to slide across the living room. The stools at the bar tumble over one by one. I throw my arms around Amanda and roll over, shielding her with my body as various objects pelt my backside. Chunks of the ceiling seem to be crumbling away, and it feels as if the floor might do the same. I want to teleport us away, but I can't be certain that will work correctly. If it does not, Amanda might be harmed.

Outside, the cacophony of sirens and car horns is nearly drowned out by the noise of the earthquake. A large chunk of the ceiling comes crashing down, about to crush us.

I whisk us away.

We land in a grassy field, though I have no conception of where we are in the mortal world. I'm still lying on top of Amanda, so I spring to my knees. She stares at me with glazed eyes, her lips parted, and I know she is alive only because I notice the rising and falling of her breasts. A rumbling in the distance draws my attention to the city we had just left—Amarillo, she called it—and I can see several buildings have suffered damage. None of it seems catastrophic. Perhaps I'm too far away to appreciate the full extent of the damage.

Amanda pushes up into a sitting position and scrambles backward away from me. "You did that, didn't you?"

"Of what do you speak?"

"The City of Amarillo. You wrecked it. All because I wouldn't tell you about my past and my demon husband." She clambers to her feet, brushing off grass and dirt. "You had a temper tantrum, and it nearly destroyed a city."

"I am not a child."

"Maybe not, but you sure as hell acted like one just now." She sets her hands on her hips, apparently waiting for me to respond to her statement.

"Never will I share my past with you."

"So instead, you'll destroy the world. Great plan, kid."

Every muscle in my body has gone taut, and my jaw begins to ache from the effort of clenching it.

Amanda's gaze shifts to the city in the distance. The anger vacates her features, replaced by an expression that seems like...sadness. "I wish you'd never come back. After three weeks, I assumed I would never see you again."

"Weeks? It was only a matter of hours."

She swerves her attention to me. "Hours? You're even crazier than I thought. Missing time is not a sign of good mental health."

I could not have been gone for that long. But perhaps… No, it's impossible. Only Janus has the power to bend time.

Amanda rubs her forehead. "I wish I'd never met you."

She marches off through the tall grass, heading toward the city.

I sweep her into my arms and whisk us back to her apartment. The damage isn't as severe as I had assumed it would be, though a large hole does gape in the ceiling. I can see another apartment above the hole.

Amanda wriggles out of my grasp and stumbles backward away from me. "Leave me alone, Cyneric. I've had enough elemental bullshit for one lifetime. And I sure as hell don't need an unhinged vampire stalking me."

That coldness infiltrates me again, and I can't convince my muscles to function. I simply stand here staring at her while she gazes steadily at me. When she turns away, I teleport myself to another place.

I wind up in the temple precinct of Dendera in Egypt. This was the place where I had seen Larissa for the first time, though I had encountered her alter ego, Hathor, a few times before. This is a temple to Hathor, the goddess. Why am I here? I have no desire to harass Larissa, and besides, she does not live here. I once worshiped the goddess Hathor, after she helped free me from the grip of Eros.

I created you, named you, and molded you, my son. You are my greatest accomplishment.

The words Eros had spoken many epochs ago echo in my mind. As a whirling sensation overtakes me, I stagger through the temple complex and approach the steps of the portico, which leads into the Temple of Hathor. Though I try to climb the steps, I trip and fall to my knees. The world around me gyrates, and my vision has grown blurry. I can't catch my breath either. Never have I suffered symptoms like these, and I do not understand them.

A force latches on to me and whisks me away.

Chapter Five

I'M DROPPED ONTO THE GROUND FROM A GREAT HEIGHT, AND FOR A LONG moment, I can do nothing but lie here and wait for the gyrations to subside. I have never been on a ship or a boat, but I imagine this is what it might feel like to be tossed about on a stormy sea, adrift and helpless to end the wild lurching.

"Hey, wake up," someone says. The tip of a boot nudges my hip. "I said wake up, Captain Fang."

And that book kicks me in the side this time.

"Be nice, Tris. He's having a rough time lately." That voice belongs to Riley, but I am too weak to respond to her presence.

The leprechaun snorts. "Yeah, I feel so bad for the bloodsucker. Why are we helping him, anyway?"

"Because I commanded it."

Janus's voice booms and echoes off some sort of walls or other obstacle, though I cannot see where I am. My eyes remain closed. I feel weak and lethargic, but I never feel that way, not even when I'm starved for blood.

Large hands push under my armpits and hoist me onto my feet. Those arms continue to hold me up while I struggle to shake off the stupor and open my eyes.

"Are we meant to feed him?" Max the incubus asks. He must be the one holding me upright. "Am I wrong, or did this wanker nearly drain Riley dry a few months ago? I thought we frowned on that sort of thing. But I guess it's 'anything goes' these days, eh? Maybe we should ask the gnomes to pitch in. Travis loves those filthy, odiferous tree trunks with mouths."

"I do not love the gnomes," Travis snaps. "Shut your trap, Max, or I'll conjure a vat of sea slugs for you. I know how you love those. When Harper took you to the aquarium, you shrieked when you saw the slugs."

"You bloody liar—"

"Enough!" Janus bellows, and his shout once again reverberates around us. "This is not a playground for childish elementals. We are here for a somber reason."

At last, I manage to open my eyes. I blink many times in rapid succession until the blurriness resolves and I can make sense of my surroundings. We are in the makeshift training ground for vampires. I had once been confined here, until I gathered enough power to escape. I will do so again once my body has recovered, just as my eyes and mind have already done.

Max hoists me higher so that my feet no longer touch the ground. "I'm bloody sick of hugging this wanker. Can I put him down now?"

Janus waves a hand imperiously. "Yes, you may. He is too weak to escape from us."

My feet touch down on the ground. As I survey my surroundings, I realize the other vampires are not here. I see only Max, Travis, Tris, and Riley. My pulse accelerates when my gaze lands on her, and I begin to breathe more rapidly.

Max clamps an arm around my neck. "Don't get any ideas, mate. Maybe I can't destroy you, but I can give you a nasty headache if I snap your neck."

I refuse to respond to his juvenile taunts. Fortunately, the incubus releases my neck and steps away from me. The stench of a salamander is more unpleasant than that of a gnome. They are the whores of the multiverse, after all.

"Where are the other vampires?" I ask. "They cannot leave this place, yet they're gone."

Max rubs his jaw. "Yeah, about that. We sent them out to explore the Unseen. Each vamp has a sylph chaperon."

"Never mind that," Janus commands as he strides toward me. "You did not heed my warning the last time we met. Now, the problem has grown far worse."

He seems to want a response, but I have none to give. These beings would destroy me if they had the power, so I owe them nothing.

Max gives me a hard shove. "Start talking, mate. Right now."

I skim my gaze over the individuals gathered around me, but I feel nothing for any of them except Riley. My focus becomes fixated on her, yet the memories that assail me involve Amanda.

Triskaideka stomps over to me and leans in until our noses almost touch. Then he jabs a finger in my face. "Tell us how you're doing it."

"Doing what? Your demand is too vague."

"You know exactly what I mean." Spittle sprays from his lips as he snarls, "You're trying to destroy the worlds."

"I'm flattered that you believe I have such power. But you are as delusional as all other creatures in the multiverse."

The leprechaun steps away from me and folds his arms over his chest. "You are never going to have Riley as your girlfriend. Get over it, bloodsucker."

I have not tried to seduce Riley, and I suddenly realize I don't want to do that, not anymore. "You may have her. My obsession with her has ended."

Travis walks up to me and eyes me with suspicion. "Right, you're over it. That's so bloody comforting to hear from a vampire who tried to kill me, Larissa, and Riley."

"Believe what you like."

Janus marches up to me, and the others scatter in his wake. He stands tall and majestic like the god he is, but I do not feel awed by his presence. He is nothing more than a gatekeeper for the Unseen.

"You are destroying the worlds," Janus tells me. "Does that not bother you in the least? If you do not end the tumult, there will be no mortals left for you to feast upon."

"I have done nothing."

Janus narrows his gaze and stares directly into my eyes. Then his brows lift, and he shakes his head slowly. "You honestly do not know what you have done."

"Because I have done nothing." I won't mention to Janus that I seduce mortal women and drink their blood. Neither will I confess that I've met a mortal who has become my new obsession. "All of you gathered here understand that you cannot force me to remain in this place. That means I don't need to stay here to listen to your outlandish claims about me."

"Yet you remain here. That suggests you know, at least subconsciously, that you are causing the earthquakes that have been ravaging the mortal world recently."

I freeze as the implications of his statement sink into my mind. No, he can't be right. I have no power to control the earth, the weather, or any other natural element. I might be an elemental vampire, but I cannot summon a storm or an earthquake. My element is blood.

"You do not believe," Janus says. "But you clearly suspect that I speak the truth. Otherwise, you would have taken yourself away from this place."

"I don't have the powers necessary to cause that sort of devastation."

Tris comes up beside Janus, and his brows have cinched together over his nose. "Damn, you really don't know you're doing those things. That's way worse than making earthquakes on purpose. It means you have no control over your new powers."

Riley squeezes between Janus and Tris, approaching closer to me than even the god had done. "You need help, Cyneric. Let us do that for you."

I transport myself away from the training camp.

Lights flash. The screams of mortals fill the air, and panic spurs them to flee.

I make my way down a street in an unknown city, through the crowd of humans. The scent of blood infiltrates my senses and awakens the hunger in me. Even I do not feed off wounded or deceased mortals. But the scent draws me to the edge of the crowd where I can see what has happened. Two mortals lie dead on the ground, apparently having been stabbed. The sight of blood heightens the hunger, and I need to get away from this place before I seize the nearest female and devour her right in front of the bystanders.

I teleport straight into Amanda's apartment.

That's where I intended to go. But I find myself inside a different structure—where on earth, I don't know—one that I believe is known as a motel. I'm inside a particular room, though I see no sign of Amanda. The bed's covers have been thrown back haphazardly, and an open suitcase rests on the floor in front of various types of furniture that are unfamiliar to me. I recognize the bathroom, though it seems to consist of only two sinks. The bathroom occupies the same space as the bed, though it's tucked into the far corner of the room. A door to the right of the sink stands closed, though I can hear water running inside whatever space lies beyond it.

I throw the door open and stalk up to the bathtub, which is obscured by a semitransparent curtain. Then I rip that open.

Amanda yelps and jumps.

Her naked body is on display, and my focus is drawn to her figure and the way the water drizzles down her skin. A soft, low growl rumbles in my throat.

She grabs the curtain and wraps it around herself. "Cyneric, what on earth are you doing? You scared the living daylights out of me."

"I needed to see you. Is that not preferable to the dying daylights?"

"Don't get cute with me. Try knocking next time." She makes a shooing motion with one hand since the other is holding the shower curtain around her body. "Walk out the door and shut it. Wait for me in the bedroom. I'll be right out."

Following her orders, I retreat from the bathroom and shut the door. Then I wander over to the bed, settling onto the mattress at the foot. After a few moments, the shower shuts off. I hear no other sounds until the bathroom door swings open and Amanda exits, wearing nothing but a towel that barely covers her breasts and her groin. She has tucked one corner of the thin cloth inside itself to keep the towel in place. Grabbing another towel from the sink area, she begins to dry her hair while scowling at me.

"You can't just appear and disappear whenever you like," she says, and she sounds rather irritated. "It's rude. You need to knock on the door and ask permission like a normal person."

"I am neither normal nor a person. I'm an elemental vampire."

"Yeah, I know. That's why I said 'like' a normal person. You must be able to fake it pretty well, or else the women you seduce would turn around and run away."

"No woman has ever rejected my advances. I am irresistible. My lovers have told me as much."

She freezes in the midst of drying her hair and drops the towel onto the counter. The other towel still covers her body, unfortunately. Even a glimpse of her figure roused my lust—for sex and for blood. My mouth has begun to water, and I can't stop myself from licking my lips. To taste her… No, I should not do that. This woman confounds me. She's nothing like Riley Jordan, and I cannot explain why my craving for Amanda grows ever stronger.

Perhaps I don't want Riley anymore. Perhaps Amanda has become my new obsession, and I won't be able to fight it any more than I could resist my desire for Riley.

Amanda walks over to the bed and sits down beside me. She still wears only that towel. "Look, hon, you need to go home, wherever that might be. I can tell you're attracted to me, but I'm damaged goods, in more ways than you could possibly imagine."

"I have no home. And I am also damaged goods."

"Who told you that?"

"The ones who freed me."

She studies me for a moment, the way she has done every time I've come to her. "Why did anyone need to free you? That implies you were a prisoner at one time."

"I was not a prisoner, as such. I was…ensorcelled." I wince when she seems confused. "You have never heard of ensorcellment, have you?"

"No, I can't say I have. What is it?"

"Ensorcellment is the most depraved sort of black magic. It strips away the victim's will and their ability to fight back. Only a powerful sorcerer or a god can inflict ensorcellment on another being. The one who is bespelled becomes a willing slave."

"But it's not willing if they're bespelled." She clasps my hand. "If someone ensorcelled you, who was it? Why did they do it?"

"My father did that to me."

"Oh God, you poor thing." She brushes hairs away from my face. "How long were you enslaved like that?"

"I cannot say for certain. Tens of thousands of years, I imagine."

Her eyes gradually widen. "No wonder you're so screwed up."

"What does that mean?"

"That your mind has been warped by what was done to you." She releases my hand, sliding her palm down to my inner thigh, though I doubt she realizes she has done that. "Who is your father, the one who ensorcelled you?"

"Does it matter?"

"Please tell me."

I stare down at her hand, where it lies between my thighs, and struggle to resist the rising hunger her touch has inflamed. "Eros created me, and he also was responsible for ensorcelling me."

Chapter Six

CREATED YOU? I DON'T UNDERSTAND. YOU MUST MEAN IT IN THE SENSE that he and your mother created a baby together, and that baby was you. To 'create' a child means to have sex. The man impregnates the woman during intercourse and then she gives birth to a baby."

"I spoke the exact truth. The god Eros created me to be his gift to the goddess Hathor, but after he created me, he couldn't bear to let anyone else have me." My breaths come more heavily, and when she squeezes my thigh gently, a bolt of lust punches through to the core of me. I should leave this place now. But I can't. "Eros called me his son, but he treated me like a captive."

"You don't need to talk about that anymore. Not right now." She curls her arm around me even while she massages my thigh with her free hand. When she rests her chin on my shoulder, her breaths tease my cheek. "I know what it's like to be enslaved, though I'd never heard the term ensorcellment until I met you."

I turn my face toward hers, and without intending to do so, lower my head until our noses touch. The scent of her arouses me, but the feel of her hand caressing my thigh has incited the blood lust. I don't know how much longer I can restrain myself. Never have I wanted any woman, not even Riley, as fiercely as I want Amanda in this moment. I try to hold back, but I can't stop myself from grazing her lips with my own. Though I get only the barest taste of her, it's more than enough to shatter my willpower. I must fight it. I must leave now.

She leans toward me even more, and our lips meet.

A low growl resonates in my throat. "Amanda, I can't—I must go."

Our lips scrape against each other with every word she speaks. "Don't leave, Cyneric. I haven't wanted anyone since Balder ruined me. But I need you to take me right here, right now, even if that means you drink my blood."

"You can't possibly understand—"

"I was ravished by an incubus. I know exactly what I'm doing." She grasps the button on my pants and unhooks it, then drags the zipper down. "I know you want me. So stop fighting it and give us both what we want."

Might she be trying to trick me? If so, I have no idea why or for what purpose. But I can't believe she is deceiving me, or perhaps I simply don't want to accept that she might. Either way, I have no choice now. The blood lust throbs inside me, and the sexual hunger burns like a roaring bonfire in my veins.

She pushes her hand inside my pants, grasping my cock.

I vanish my clothes and her towel.

Amanda is now draped over me in the nude, with her hand clasping my cock and her breasts rubbing against my chest. I take one tit in my hand and duck my head to swallow the nipple and areola, suckling hard while scraping my teeth over the tip. She gasps and digs her nails into my skin. I shove my hand between her thighs to roughly massage her folds. She throws her head back as a cry is torn from her lips.

"Holy shit," she exclaims. "I'm about to come and—"

Amanda unleashes a cry of sheer bliss that fills the room, just as her body folds in on itself. I keep ravaging her breast and her cleft, punching my longest finger into her opening while she comes harder and the climax rolls on and on. My cock feels ready to explode, but I need to be buried deep inside her body when that happens.

When I release her nipple and remove my hand, she's breathing hard. "Cyneric, that was incredible. I need to reciprocate."

She slides off the bed to kneel between my legs, pushing my thighs apart to make room. Her gaze lands on my lower belly. "That's an interesting tattoo. What is it supposed to be? I've never seen a circular design as complex as this one."

"I don't know what it symbolizes. I had the mark on the day I was created, but my father refused to explain its purpose. He called it a 'grotesque stain' on my otherwise perfect body."

"Let's forget about your jackass father for now. I'm dying to taste you."

I watch in rapt wonder as she grasps the base of my cock and lowers her head toward my groin. But when she seals her mouth around my erection, I stop breathing. I can do nothing except watch her mouth slide over my length so slowly while she gazes up at me with hooded eyes. Her cheeks and chest are dappled with pink. I can smell her cream and hear her soft grunts as she begins to glide her mouth up and down my cock, taking her time, seeming to enjoy the task deeply. I'm breathing so hard that my ears ring, but I don't give a fuck about that. Even if I pass out, I will awaken ready to take her body.

Amanda slips her other hand beneath my cock to tease the flesh behind my balls.

I jerk and cry out. "Suck me harder. I'm a vampire, not a mortal."

Her brows shoot up, then she heeds my command. She devours me so greedily that her cheeks cave in over and over, and her grunts become louder. The noises she makes drive me to the brink of insanity, but I need her to keep going until I come inside her mouth. Her tongue rasps my flesh, and her teeth nip at me, which only makes me hunger for her blood even more. The tension rises like a tsunami rushing toward the shore, about to crash into a sheer cliff and shatter.

A hoarse roar erupts out of me, and I come.

She keeps consuming me while the jet of my release goes on and on, but I know she can't swallow everything I have to give. So I pick her up and toss her onto the bed. She lands on her back. I pump my cock hard and fast until all my seed has been expelled onto her body. Then I watch while Amanda writhes and cries out, her body curling in on itself as if she is coming. Perhaps my seed has a similar effect as a salamander's excretions.

Amanda is gasping for breath, no longer in the throes of pleasure. Her tits heave. I might have reached the heights of pleasure, thanks to her, but I'm far from done with this woman.

Because I haven't tasted her blood yet.

I pick her up and carry her into the shower, yanking the curtain shut behind us. Though I set her on her feet, she seems unable to stay upright without support. I turn on the water and wait until I have it adjusted to the right amount of warmth. Then I grasp her arse in both hands, lifting her off the floor, and wrap her legs around my hips.

"We are not done," I growl into her ear. "This is your last chance to tell me to stop. Next, I will sink my fangs into your flesh and gorge myself on your blood."

"Do it, please. Fuck me while you drink me, Cyneric."

No woman has ever spoken those words to me with such intense passion in her voice—for me, not for the pleasure I can and will give her. "Blood is the essence of life, the one element that no mortal can live without. No vampire can either. But when I take your body, that essential element will flow from you into me, warm and liquid and sensual, a transfer of life and desire like nothing else in the multiverse."

I pull my hips back and thrust into her, penetrating so deeply that I can feel the back wall of her womb. She wraps her arms around my neck. We stand face to face while I pump in and out at a measured pace, letting her feel my full length and breadth before I drink her. Once I pierce her flesh, I will forget about everything else. She gasps and moans, gazing into my eyes all the while, and I quicken my pace just enough to increase her pleasure.

"Cyneric," she breathes, her voice shaky. "Yes, oh, yes. Take me any way you want, please, don't stop."

As I lower my head to her throat, I lave it with one long swipe of my tongue. She whimpers and lets her head fall back against the shower wall. My hearing becomes attuned to her body, and I listen to the pounding of her heart for a moment before I do what we both want and what I need.

I sink my two longest teeth into her flesh.

The first taste of her blood rushes through me like a drug. I groan and sink my fangs in deeper, drinking her at a leisurely pace, needing to experience every moment of this. All the while, I continue pumping my cock into her body. She grips me so tightly with her legs and arms that, if I were a mortal, she would have strangled me to death. But I can handle her passion. I thrust harder and faster while she comes again, her body clenching me in wave after wave of spasms while her scream fills the cramped bathroom.

Once she goes limp in my arms, I give in to the lust and drink her more deeply while I fuck her so hard that she goes off again with even more vigor. I roar as I come inside her, blowing apart like a volcano, searing her with my seed.

For a moment, we remain frozen in place. I brush the backs of my fingers over her cheek and nuzzle her neck, licking at the flesh I had punctured until the wounds have sealed up. Then I fill the bathtub with warm water and kneel with her still in my arms. Carefully, I sit down and position her between my legs. She lets her head fall back against my chest. I fold my arms over her belly.

"Mm, that was…" She fans herself with one hand. "I might not be able to walk for a week after this."

"I hope I have not injured you."

She laughs softly, affectionately. "I'll survive, hon. That's one thing I'm good at."

"You will need to eat and drink soon to replenish yourself."

"I'd like to lie here in the tub with you for a while first."

"As you wish."

Never in all of my existence have I lain with a woman without fucking or drinking her—not in a tub, a bed, or anywhere else. But as I lie here cradling her body with mine, I find myself relaxing in every way, from my muscles to my mind that no longer races with thoughts of what to do next, how to find an anonymous woman who will feed my hunger for blood and sex. Amanda's presence alone can soothe me. It feels very strange. Just hearing her voice calms me.

While I gaze down at her, she closes her eyes and smiles with a sort of calm satisfaction that I have never experienced myself. Have I ever been at peace? Perhaps when I was with my father. But Eros had ensorcelled me to feel that way. He did not truly love me but only used me in his efforts to bring Hathor back into his fold or to alleviate his own loneliness.

Amanda settles her hands on my thighs and twists her head around to gaze up at me. "Tell me more about Eros, please. I want to know you and what you've been through."

"I would prefer not to discuss the topic of my father."

"There are a lot of things I'd rather not discuss either, but I told you about Balder."

"Not everything."

She touches her wet fingers to my bottom lip. "I'll share everything with you, Cyneric, if you'll do the same for me."

I shift uncomfortably beneath her, but despite that, I want to share more of myself with this woman. "What would you like to know?"

"Everything. But we can start with Eros. Why do you call him your father? You said he created you, but when I mentioned the mortal way of making babies, you scoffed at that. So I assume you meant he used magics to make you."

"I do not know how he created me. I was not, and then I was."

She wriggles around until she's facing me with her knees bent at either side of my legs and her breasts crushed to my chest. Her arms are wrapped around my neck. "What did it feel like? Being created, I mean."

"Eros welcomed me with open arms and called me his son. I believed him to be my father because that was what he told me." I suddenly realize I have wrapped my arms around her. The realization doesn't bother me, though. "I loved my father deeply. No matter what he did, nothing could diminish my devotion to him because I knew he loved me best."

"Well, you are stunningly beautiful. Of course Eros loved you. But you aren't with him anymore, and I'm wondering why."

"It is a long story."

She kisses me sweetly. "I'm not going anywhere. Take as long as you need."

"The troubles began when I learned I was not the first or the only being Eros had created. Hathor had come before me, but she fled from Eros long before I existed. I grew jealous, but I feared losing my father's love if I admitted that to him." I close my eyes, and the memories assail me once again, things I wish I could forget or at least change. But I lack the powers of Janus, the only being in the multiverse who can affect the past, present, and future. "I might have been jealous, but at least I knew I was my father's only son. Until he created more of my kind."

"More? I don't understand. Why would he make more beings like you?"

"He thought he could win Hathor back by gifting her with a horde of vampires. They were beautiful too, like me, and my father loved them equally. But the god Setesh grew jealous and cast a curse that made us ugly and vile."

Amanda's lips part, as if she wants to say something.

But the ground beneath us shudders and shakes, and car alarms blare in the parking lot outside while dogs bark and howl. As the earthquake intensifies, I try to transport us away from this place, but I cannot do it.

The bathtub cracks and splits itself in half straight down the middle. Water sluices into the empty space below.

I sweep Amanda up in my arms and race out of the bathroom, leaping over ceiling beams that have fallen and kicking the broken door out of the way. Amanda clings to me with her face buried against my chest. The motel sign, a large and undoubtedly heavy object, comes crashing down on us. The thunderous noise it creates deafens me, and Amanda screams. I shield her with my body, letting the sign fall onto my back. I push up onto my hands and knees to ensure she won't be crushed. Only when the tremors have stopped do I attempt to push the sign off my back. It takes a moderate effort, though for a mortal, it would be a Herculean task.

Amanda lies limp on the shattered asphalt, her eyes closed.

The smell of blood permeates my senses, but I feel no compulsion to feed. I drop to my knees and do what I've seen mortals do in similar situations. I take hold of her wrist and feel for a pulse. It's there, but weak. "Amanda, wake up."

She does not respond. Blood streams from a wound on her head.

I lift her into a sitting position and cradle her to my chest.

Then I roar.

CHAPTER SEVEN

AN AMBULANCE ARRIVES SEVERAL MINUTES LATER, BUT MY ROARING had already scared away the mortals who had been in the vicinity. No one remains to interfere with the work of the paramedics. They give me strange looks, and I assume their reaction to me is because my eyes are glowing and swirling. I cannot see my own face, but I have experienced this reaction before when mortals glimpse my true nature. I could conceal my eyes, but I have no energy or desire to do so.

All I can think about is Amanda.

The paramedics treat her in the best manner they can under the circumstances. When they try to load her into their vehicle on a narrow, wheeled bed they refer to as a "stretcher," I stand between them and their vehicle.

"Where are you taking her?" I demand.

"To the hospital. She's lost a lot of blood, so we'll start an IV to keep her going until we get to the hospital. They'll do a transfusion."

"I must go with her."

The paramedic eyes me with a hint of fear in his expression. "Uh, sure, yeah. You can come with us."

I shouldn't have growled softly, but I can't control my responses right now. Never have I lost control in this way. I don't care how many mortals witness my elemental nature, not now. I climb into the "ambulance" with the paramedics.

Two hours later, I sit in a hard chair alongside a hospital bed on which Amanda lies unconscious but stable, according to the doctors. Wires and needles are attached to her body, though she can breathe on her own. It had taken much longer than it should have for the ambulance to reach the hospital. The earthquake had caused significant damage that blocked many streets.

I drag my chair closer to the bed and clasp Amanda's hand.

A nurse walks in and skims her gaze over me and the woman whose hand I'm holding. A soft smile curls her lips. "You're so sweet to stay by your mom's side."

"Amanda is not my mother. She is my lover."

The nurse's eyes widen, though only for a moment. "Oh, I see. You look so young, and I assumed—Sorry, sugar, that was my mistake. It's none of my business. I'm sure your girl will be just fine. That was some weird earthquake, wasn't it?"

I shrug. A conversation with this woman is not what I want right now. Though a name tag on her uniform identifies her as "Darlene," I don't care to know her name. I don't care to know anyone except for Amanda, but she lies unconscious, and I have no idea when she might awaken.

But I abruptly realize what Darlene said a moment ago. "Earthquake? What is unusual about that?"

She gives me a strange look. "This is Texas. We don't get the big ones, just the occasional four pointer that doesn't cause any damage." She comes up beside me and pats my hand. "You ain't from around here, are ya? Sounds like you're British. Bet you don't see many quakes in England."

"England? I have no idea what that is."

Her eyes widen again, more so this time. "But your accent—"

"I don't wish to speak to you anymore."

"Sorry, sugar, I didn't mean to upset you. Your girl is very anemic, and that combined with her head wound means it might take a good long while before she wakes up."

"What is 'anemic'?"

"It means she lost a lot of blood, more than what her head wound should have caused. It's kind of a mystery. That's why we're giving her a transfusion." Once Darlene has inspected whatever instruments she needed to check, she leaves. As she walks out the door, she says, "If you need anything, hon, just let me know."

A hard mass has settled onto my chest, though it's clearly a phantom sensation. It feels as if the weight of the entire city now rests on me. I hadn't experienced this pain until the nurse referred to me as "hon," the same thing Amanda calls me.

I lean back in my chair, and the memories assail me once again. Visions of my past. Of what I've done, what I could never do, and what others assume I should do. I had wanted Riley and became obsessed with finding her. Yet when I finally saw her again, the desire to claim her as mine sifted away, replaced by a feeling that I no longer belong in the world where she lives or in any world. I am singular, and that is not a pleasant realization.

If you don't stop now, she will die.

The voice that had spoken those words belonged to Triskaideka, but now, I hear it as someone else's voice. Whose? It sounds like mine, but I would not say those things to myself. It makes no sense.

The high-pitched sound of an alarm going off shakes me out of my semi-sleep. I rub my eyes and struggle to make sense of what is happening around me. Darlene and two others are talking in voices filled with anxiety as they fiddle with equipment. One of them begins to pump her chest, then breathes into her mouth, repeating the process multiple times.

I spring out of my chair. "What are you doing to her?"

The nurses and doctor ignore me.

So I seize the doctor's throat and rip him away from Amanda. "What are you doing to her? Tell me now before I tear your throat out."

Darlene punches a button, and another, louder alarm blares. "Call the police!"

I release the doctor and roar.

And I am whisked away against my will.

The sun shines down from a sky bluer than any seen on Earth, and the beings who stand in a circle around me are not human. Janus's friends have encircled me, as if that will prevent me from doing whatever I like to them. They believe I am a vicious and dangerous creature, yet they know nothing about me. Larissa and Riley tried to understand me, but their fear of my power led them to stay away from me.

My attention lands on Riley.

She gazes at me steadily, showing no fear. I can't smell fear from her either. The woman I have coveted since the moment I first saw her stands there studying me, and yet I feel no urge to take her.

The snapping of fingers draws my focus to the leprechaun. Tris crosses his arms over his chest. "Stop staring at Riley. You're here to listen to what we want to tell you, and you will not leave until we've said our piece."

"If I choose to leave, you cannot stop me."

"This is the third time we've summoned you back to the training ground. If you run away again, we'll know you are a damn coward."

Max grunts. "And a bloody psycho."

"We already knew that. It's a given."

"He's not a psycho," Larissa says. "We've all done things we wish we hadn't. Let's not play the blame game, okay? Cyneric is troubled, and I thought we were here to help him, not sling insults."

Max glowers at me, but the expression has no effect. So he turns his attention to Larissa. "He nearly killed you and Riley. Couldn't stop himself from guzzling your blood like it's free beer night at a pub."

"Silence!"

That single word reverberates through the training ground. Only a god can bellow in such a manner, and I know precisely which god shouted that command before Janus even shows himself. He saunters up to the circle of elementals who have caged me, or so they believe. Their attempts to capture me have proved desperate and pointless. No one can stop me.

Janus pushes through the circle of elementals and halts halfway to me. "What did you do to Amanda Nelson?"

I lift my chin and refuse to speak.

"Amanda who?" Travis asks. "Never met any woman with that name."

"She is a mortal," the god explains. "And she was taken to a hospital due to severe blood loss that did not originate from the head wound she suffered during a strong earthquake. So I ask you again, Cyneric. What did you do to Amanda Nelson?"

I still do not respond. I owe no explanations to these beings, yet I begin to feel an itch deep under my skin, one that must be scratched though I would need to tear the flesh from my bones to find the source.

Tris glowers at me, shaking his head. "You screwed her, didn't you? Grabbed a hapless mortal and used your vampy voodoo powers to make her think she wants you, just so you could drain her dry."

I raise one brow at him. "Amanda Nelson is not dead."

"Oh, goody for you. This time you left a woman comatose, but you didn't actually kill her. Not yet, anyway." Tris stalks up to me and stabs a finger into my chest. "You are a threat to every living thing in the mortal world. You can't control yourself, can you? Just gotta fuck and drain every woman you meet."

Fuck me while you drink me, Cyneric.

Amanda had wanted me. I did not coerce her with magics. Did I? No, I do not have the power to ensorcell.

Tris leans closer, searching my gaze. "You're starting to wonder, aren't you? Can't be sure that woman really wanted you to suck her blood or if you might've magicked her into saying yes. Did you even ask her?"

My pulse begins to pound so hard that I can hear it inside my head and feel it thundering through my veins. A veil of red descends over my vision, and I fist my hands tightly. Blood drips from my fingers because I've dug my nails into my palms.

Tris's lip curls. "You are one whacked-out bloodsucker. Look, he's bleeding. That probably means he's about grab one of us and guzzle our blood."

I tip my head to the side. "The blood of elementals cannot sustain me. You know this."

"Yeah, but you're so far gone that you probably would rip our veins open and slurp up the blood anyway."

"Enough!" Janus bellows. "You will listen to me."

He plants a hand on Tris's chest and shoves the leprechaun away, sending him flying through the circle of elementals. Travis and Max fall to the ground, pinned there by Tris's body on top of them.

And every last one of them falls silent.

Janus steps closer until he stands inches away from me. "You have one final chance to redeem yourself, Cyneric."

"I do not need or want redemption."

The god stares into my eyes while his golden irises whorl and shimmer. "You have not killed yet. But you teeter on a precipice, and if you fall over the edge, there will be no coming back from it. Destruction shall be your only option."

"No one can destroy me."

"You are not a god yet. But even if you were, a god can be destroyed. I know this from first-hand experience."

But he's leaving out the most important piece of information. The other gods and the most powerful elementals had conspired to destroy him, but he could not be fully eradicated. His essence and powers remained, housed in a holding cell of sorts until the Four Winds deemed him ready to return and resume his godly duties.

That means even if I am destroyed, I might return.

"Do you, Cyneric, consent to whatever means we deem necessary to ensure you will not harm any mortal?"

I roll my shoulders back. "I consent to nothing."

"Then you leave us no choice." Janus throws his head back and shouts, "Come to us now!"

A violent wind erupts around us, snatching leaves off the trees and forcing the other elementals to fight to remain standing. They fall down one by one, rolling away from the spot where Janus and I stand. The wind has no effect on us. Magics have ensured that, I can feel it.

Janus shuffles backward several steps.

The Four Winds appear and form a circle to stand at cardinal positions around me. One of the beings, Miriella, speaks.

"You are a danger to all beings in the multiverse," she pronounces. "Your powers grow, yet you cannot control them. The mortal world is at the greatest risk, particularly if you continue to visit Amanda Nelson."

"I did not choose to visit her. Someone is employing magics to send me to places where I do not wish to be." I glance at Tris. "The leprechaun and his friends would do such a thing."

"No, Cyneric. You do this to yourself." Miriella steps forward, though she stops short of approaching me. "That is what makes you the greatest threat the multiverse has ever seen."

"You cannot destroy me."

"We know this. Yet you cannot be permitted to go on as you are, causing earthquakes, consuming the blood of mortals, engaging your growing powers without understanding them."

Tris and his friends have re-formed their circle, though they remain behind the Four Winds and Janus.

"What will you do?" Travis asks. "Put him in elemental prison?"

"No," Miriella says. "Something far more drastic is required."

"And that means..."

Miriella rejoins the circle of the Four Winds. They raise their arms in unison, and she declares, "The source of your power and your pain must be uncovered. That means you, Cyneric, must undertake a long and arduous journey that will conclude in one of two ways—your redemption, or your destruction. The quest begins now."

They cannot do that. I am indestructible. "What quest?"

"To find Eros."

You were born of my blood, of my flesh, of my powers. The words Eros had spoken so many eons ago echo in my mind.

Miriella casts her gaze on me one last time. "May the Oversoul guide you, Cyneric."

The Four Winds stretch their arms higher and bend their heads back as they chant in a language none but they can understand.

And everything vanishes.

Chapter Eight

I CRASH INTO THE GROUND ON MY BACK AND IMMEDIATELY BEGIN ROLL-ing down, down, down a steep slope in the center of nowhere. Even as I continue rolling, I can see that nothing but grassy hills extend out toward the horizon. When I finally reach the bottom of the slope and cease rolling, I wind up gazing at the clear blue sky above me.

Where am I?

As I rise and dust off my clothing, I scan the vicinity. There appears to be a city some distance away, too far for me to see any details. I have no idea where I've ended up, but the Four Winds dropped me here for a reason, which they will undoubtedly never share with me. They expect me to figure it out on my own.

I trudge back up the hill and continue down the other slope, toward the city I can see miles away. I do not like cities. They're filthy and overcrowded and full of noise. But I cannot simply "hang out," as the leprechaun Tris might say, here in the hills in the middle of nowhere. I've been commanded to undertake a quest of some sort, but with no instructions concerning what that quest will involve or how I am to initiate it.

As I crest another, smaller hill, I come upon a trail and a mortal man walking toward me on that path. He dresses in the manner I have come to know as "hiking" clothes. It means he walks these hills for personal enjoy-ment. I don't find the terrain enjoyable at all.

I halt, waiting for him to pass by me and leave my sight.

But instead, he halts too. "Hey, there, stranger. Not many folks dress in leather to go for a walk. You ain't the average hiker, are ya? Must not be from around here."

He speaks with some type of accent. I believe it is called "southern." I have heard such accents in various locations within the nation of the USA. But I do not wish to converse with this creature, so I attempt to move past him.

The man steps into my path. "What are you doin' out here dressed that way? Ain't normal. You some kinda freak huntin' for kids to kidnap?"

Nothing this man says makes sense.

I push him out of the way. "Do not bother me again. I must get to the city."

The man's brows rise. "You're British, ain't you?"

Riley and Amanda both had told me, on separate occasions, that I am "British." But I still don't understand what that means.

When I attempt to head down the hill, the man seizes my arm. "Where do you think you're going? I'm talking to you, pal."

"No, you are not."

I grasp his shirt and fling him over the top of the hill. For a moment, I watch him rolling down the other side while shouting and cursing in the most vile manner. Once he reaches the bottom of the hill, he screams more obscenities at me but appears unharmed, considering that he clambers to his feet. I head down this side of the hill, aiming for the city in the distance. No one else accosts me, and I reach my destination quickly by employing my elemental ability to run faster than any mortal on earth could hope to do in their wildest dreams. I'm only mildly winded when I stop at the edge of town.

I stop and read a sign that's posted alongside the road. "Welcome to Nashville," it says. What is Nashville? The name of the city, I assume. Why a sign should welcome me to this place, I don't know. The citizens of this region have no idea whether I am worthy of welcome or not. They may come to rue their decision to offer me their regards.

I trudge down the two-lane road, and cars blare their horns at me. That might be due to the fact that I'm walking down the center line. It seems the most obvious choice.

A particularly rude driver rolls down his window to point one finger at me and shout, "Get off the road, ya dumb-ass!"

His statement seems illogical. Why should I walk on the dirt when a relatively smooth road has been provided for the purpose of traveling into and out of the City of Nashville?

A woman driver also points one finger at me. But she shouts, "The road is for cars, dickwad!"

Several more drivers honk and show me their fingers as I continue on my way. Mortals are bizarre. I try to teleport myself away from this town where everyone seems to have only one finger, but a strange force knocks me backward onto my arse. I break into a sprint instead, dodging around the cars whose drivers seem determined to prevent me from using the road. Today is the first time I have ever attempted to use a street or road or highway, other than to simply jog across a street to reach a destination. Teleporting is faster and far more convenient than driving.

Amanda would know the rules of navigating a mortal city.

I halt in the middle of a four-lane street, where tall buildings cast shadows. *Amanda.* Is she still alive? If she was dangerously anemic because of what I did to her, perhaps she has…died.

I'll survive, hon. That's one thing I'm good at.

She had told me that. But is it true? Mortals are surprisingly fragile creatures. If I drank of her too deeply…

The ground beneath me trembles, though not enough that a mortal would notice. I clench my hands, squeezing my eyes shut, and will the anxiety away before I do any further damage to this world. I still can't quite accept that I might be responsible for the earthquakes in Amarillo, yet I have no other explanation for them. Amanda had said that city never has large tremors.

I'll share everything with you, Cyneric, if you'll do the same for me.

Did she mean that? I need to know everything about her, but I cannot share everything about myself. She would run away if I did.

I should leave her alone. After I've determined that she is still alive. But my second attempt at whisking myself away fails, leaving me alone in the center of the four-lane street. Cars race past me, but at least no one shows me their deformed hands. Did the citizens of this place endure a nuclear disaster? I see no other explanation for why they have just one finger.

A man dressed in dark blue marches up to me. His dark sunglasses hide his eyes. A metallic badge is pinned to one side of his shirt. He holds up a hand to stop me from walking any further, though I could easily slip past him. I decide to find out what this mortal wants from me.

"Good afternoon," he says. "What's your name, friend?"

"We are not friends. I have never seen you before."

"Tell me your name, then I'll know who you are."

I try to walk past him.

But the man attempts to block my way with his body. "You're jaywalking, buddy. Get on the sidewalk and be on your way before you cause an accident and get somebody hurt."

"Nothing can harm me."

"You could hurt somebody else. That's what I just said."

I scan the vicinity. "I see no bloodied corpses."

"Are you trying to make a joke?"

"No, I'm stating a fact."

The man gapes at me while I continue on my way, though I do move onto the sidewalk as the gentleman had suggested. I turn at the next corner, though I haven't a clue why, and meander down the streets of Nashville with no particular destination in mind since I'd never come to this location until today. The noise of cities has always confounded me. Why would anyone want to live in such a loud and overcrowded settlement? The more I learn about mortals, the less I understand them. In the Unseen, we have no "skyscrapers," only towering castles and temples and other such structures.

I prefer the outdoors. And I prefer to have no one else around.

Yet here I am, in a city, traveling to an unknown destination. I've heard mortals call this "meandering." I am growing tired of meandering, though, and wish I could teleport away from this place. But my feet have other ideas, dragging me onward against my will, forcing me to turn down a street called Broadway. The buildings here host garish signs that I suspect would flash brightly at night. The names of the establishments baffle me.

Nudie's Honky Tonk. Crazy Town. Betty Boots.

As I pass by more of the establishments in this quarter, I grow more and more confused by the surroundings and what might go on inside those buildings. My curiosity gets the better of me, and I push open the door of one establishment. The garish sign above me and the door in front of me declare this to be Deva's British Honky Tonk. Aren't people known as British meant to live in England? I still don't understand what those words mean.

I leave the short, cramped entryway of this establishment and walk into a larger yet still cramped space filled with tables and chairs as well as a long, L-shaped bar with a wall behind it. On this side of the bar stand uncomfortable-looking stools where, presumably, mortals sit down to drink. I might not know what a "honky tonk" is, but I'm well aware of the fact that humans enjoy getting drunk while sitting in places such as this.

At the far end of the "honky tonk," a small stage has been erected with bare wood planks. Various types of equipment lie on the stage, but no one is there to make use of the platform. I have heard "music" before and pray no one will arrive to make use of the instruments they had abandoned on the stage. The dark atmosphere does appeal to me. However, the neon signs behind the bar do not. I see many bottles on display, full of liquids of various colors. They are alcoholic beverages, I'm sure. Yes, mortals must need a great deal of alcohol to remain in a place like this.

With nothing else to do, I settle onto a stool.

A dark-haired man emerges from a door at the other end of the bar. The door swings shut behind him. He approaches me and smiles.

"Welcome to Deva's British Honky Tonk." He offers me his hand. "I'm Deva Bakshi, the bloke who owns this joint."

Though I would prefer not to engage in conversation with this man, I decide to try behaving like a mortal. Perhaps that is why the Four Winds have stranded me here. So, I shake his hand. "I am Cyneric."

"Cool name. It's great to meet you, Cyneric."

"Yes, it is not unpleasant to meet you."

He chuckles. "You're strange, but I like it. You'll fit right in. Nashville is a very diverse town where you'll meet lots of wonderful people."

"What sort of name is Deva? I've never heard it before."

"My full name is Kamadeva, but that's a bit of a mouthful. I prefer the shorter version—Deva."

Kamadeva. I know that name. He was one of the gods who enslaved Hathor and later tried to recapture her after she became the mortal Larissa. But this man can't be the same Kamadeva. Surely, whatever tribe he hails from gives that name to many of their children.

Deva picks up an empty glass and begins to wipe it with a white cloth. "It's nice to meet a fellow London boy. Not many of those round here."

"London? I was there once, but only briefly. What is a London boy?"

He freezes. "Uh, it's a man born in the city of London. Like you. Your accent gives it away, mate."

"I have been told I'm British, but I don't understand what that means."

Deva eyes me up and down, his brows lifting. "You're seriously into leather, eh? That's cool. It's a bit warm today for that sort of clothing, though."

"What sort should I wear?"

He shrugs. "That's your call, mate. I'd go for jeans and a T-shirt myself."

Yes, I now realize he is dressed in that manner, though he also wears a strange overgarment that covers only his front and has a slender strip of fabric that's tied around his waist. And he thinks my clothing is unusual.

I attempt to conjure different garments, but I can't do it. The Four Winds have blocked all my powers, apparently.

"Something wrong, Cyneric? You look a bit poorly."

"No, I—"

The room begins to spin around me, and I grip the bar to stop myself from tumbling over backward. Slow clapping echoes in my mind as the present gives way to the past, dragging me downward into the oblivion of memories. Once, I had visited a cinema, and what I am experiencing now reminds me of the moving images on the screen in that theater. It feels like a film, not a real event. The past can't be experienced again, though it can be reenacted.

And I'm about to live through that time once more.

CHAPTER NINE

IN THE MEMORY, I STAND WITH MY FELLOW VAMPIRES ON THE FLAT ground at the base of the temple of Dendera where the ancient Egyptians had worshiped the goddess Hathor. I see her—or rather, Larissa, the human who had once been Hathor. She and Travis the incubus are further away. But we vampires hover between Hathor and the god Eros, who stands tall and proud, almost gleeful in his accomplishment.

The sun-like light that had blinded me a moment ago has faded, and I glance down at my body. Shock ripples through me in icy waves. I am…myself again. The form my father had given me, once corrupted by Setesh, has been restored. I am no longer a slavering, hideous creature. I am Cyneric once again.

The slow clapping has finally ended. Kamadeva saunters toward Eros but halts a good distance away. He smiles smugly at Eros. "Aren't you the clever one? But you can't be stupid enough to believe I'll let you get the upper hand."

He snaps his fingers.

And I burst into flames. I scream and stagger about in search of something, anything, that might douse the fire that consumes my flesh, but I find nothing. While my brethren drop to the ground, rolling in a vain effort to save themselves, I race into the Temple of Hathor. Behind me, I hear Kamadeva laughing uproariously.

"I made them allergic to sunlight," he says to Eros while still laughing, "even the fake version you created."

Eros roars. "You will pay for this, you insipid runt."

Now I am inside the temple, away from the gods and even from Larissa. My fellow vampires writhe and scream on the floor. But I remain standing, gasping for breath and scratching my head as if I can eradicate the memory of being on fire in that manner.

My vision returns to the present and the man who stares at me as if I had burst into flames a moment ago, here in this "honky tonk" bar. And I suddenly recognize him. He is not merely a man called Kamadeva. He is the god Kamadeva himself. The Four Winds had rebuked him along with Eros and Setesh, for what they had done that night in Egypt. Their punishment was to become mortal, or at least have their powers stripped and their memories erased. They were also given new lives in this world as a test to determine if they must be destroyed.

I'm gasping for breath, just as I had back in the temple at Dendera months ago.

"You all right, mate?" Deva asks. "You're sweating like a ruddy pig."

He turns on a faucet and soaks the small towel he had been using to clean glasses. Then he offers me the towel. I rest my elbows on the bar and hold the damp cloth to my face. My pulse gradually returns to normal, and I no longer feel as if I might fall off my stool.

I hand the towel back to Deva. "I do not need this any longer."

"You talk like a medieval bloke or something. Do you teach at uni?"

"At what? I am not a teacher."

The door at the far end of the bar swings open, and a blond girl strides up to Deva. "Want me to sweep the floor now? I know you hate doing that." The girl glances at me. "An early bird, huh? We only just opened fifteen minutes ago."

The woman speaks with some variety of accent. I believe it's "southern," like the other rude people I have met in this area, though I have been told that not all southern accents are the same. I can't tell the difference between them.

Deva lays a hand on the lovely woman's back. "Cyneric, meet my right-hand woman, Margo. She's the real brains behind this operation. I just chat to the customers and serve them drinks."

"Cyneric?" Margo says. "I've never heard that name before."

"Yeah, neither had I. It's kind of cool, though."

"Sure is. I'll go start up the jukebox."

While Margo ambles over to the strange, massive contraption in the corner, I study Deva. Does he sincerely not remember who he once was? Can a god who wanted to destroy Egypt become…reformed? I cannot believe I was drawn to this place by accident. I was dropped off in the hills beyond Nashville, then led into the city where I wandered without purpose until I happened upon this honky tonk, where the former god Kamadeva now works.

Did the Four Winds guide my journey? Or did fate bring me here?

The "jukebox" abruptly comes to life, blaring the most irritating music I have ever heard. It's loud and abrasive, and I can't remain here if it means I must listen to that so-called music. Fortunately, Margo lowers the volume just enough that my eardrums won't shatter. Then she smiles at Deva in a manner I recognize. It means she is attracted to him.

Deva waves to Margo as she heads toward that swinging door. Once it shuts, he turns to me. "Margo's a great business partner, but she has a bit of a crush on me. She knows I don't roll that way, though."

"Roll what way?"

He grins. "I'm gay, mate. That's what I meant."

"What does 'gay' mean?"

"That I prefer men."

"Oh. I see." I had known that about the god Kamadeva, but the term gay had confused me. No one in the Unseen uses it.

While Deva gets to work, I sneak out of the honky tonk and swiftly leave the area of Broadway. Once again, I wander aimlessly since I have no idea where to go or what I should do. Meeting Kamadeva, realizing he is the god who abused Larissa when she was still Hathor, all of it has left me…shaken.

I stop at the corner where two dreary streets converge. I do not want to remain in this city. Where is Amanda? Did I end her life when I drank from her artery? She had seemed unharmed afterward. But Darlene, the nurse at the hospital, had said Amanda was very anemic and that it meant she had lost too much blood. Because of me. She begged me to drink her while I fucked her, but I should have refused that request. Am I a monster?

Kamadeva had done terrible things, much worse than what I've done, yet he was granted a second chance. Is that what the Four Winds are offering me? If so, I cannot comprehend what they mean for me to do.

I suppose that is for me to determine.

"Move your ass, pal," someone shouts from behind me. "You're blocking the corner."

As I move my arse, crossing the street, I can't stop thinking about Amanda.

Halfway across the intersection, I am whisked away.

And I'm plunged into darkness. I lie on my stomach on a soft surface that gives a bit with my every movement. Is it a mattress? Before I have time to consider the answer, my focus shifts to the scents around me. One specific aroma captures my attention and makes my cock rouse. But it can't be. She was in the hospital, on the verge of death. Yet I swear that the scent enveloping me comes from Amanda.

A soft moan escapes her lips, and she rolls over as if she wants to lie on her stomach, but my body prevents it. My eyes have adjusted to the darkness as much as they can in the pitch black inside this room. Even my heightened elemental senses have their limits. The natural scent of her becomes infused with the aroma of her desire, and she snuggles up to me to drape on arm across my back. I'm wearing my clothes, which means she feels my leather jacket instead of my skin.

"Cyneric?"

Her query sounds rather sleepy and confused. I can tell it's her when the room is pitch dark, yet she isn't sure if the body beside her is mine. I shouldn't be offended by that. Amanda is, after all, a human and not an elemental. Still, I can't help feeling somewhat…wounded by the fact she isn't certain of my identity.

I roll onto my back. "It's me, Amanda."

"Oh, I'm so glad you're back." She fumbles around until she finds the top button of my shirt. "I missed you, hon."

"What are you doing?"

"Trying to get you naked. You could help me out a little here."

"Should we not turn the light on?"

"Mm-mm." She unhooks three buttons in swift succession. "Missed your body, hon. Let's do it in the dark this time."

The hungry tone of her voice causes my cock to begin to swell. I know that, within a moment, I will be fucking her. But the first time I took her, I clearly drank too deeply and left her weak and unable to awaken after the injuries she had suffered during the earthquake. My heart pounds. A cold sweat has broken out on my brow. At any moment, I might trigger another quake without intending to do so.

Amanda frees the rest of my shirt buttons, then unhooks the one on my waistband. Once she has torn the zipper down, she pushes her hand inside my pants to clasp my cock. "I love the way you fuck me, Cyneric. Need you inside me while your fangs are sunk into my throat, just like last time."

I spring upright and flail my hand out, searching for a lamp or some other type of light. I manage only to knock something off the bedside table. The object thunks onto the floor.

A light clicks on.

"What's wrong?" Amanda asks. She is just pulling her hand away from the switch on the table that turned the light on. Now, she shimmies closer to me and grasps my face with both hands. "Talk to me, Cyneric. What happened?"

"I knocked a glass onto the floor."

"You know that's not what I meant."

My pulse still beats faster than normal, but it has slowed considerably. "Why did you want me to ravage you again? I nearly took your life."

"What? That's crazy." She wraps her arms around me, linking her hands to hold me tightly. "I've been so worried about you. When I woke up in the hospital, they told me you were gone and they didn't know where you went. I doubt they tried very hard to find you, considering that they thought you were a lunatic."

"Perhaps I am."

"No, sweetie, you're not. I bet you panicked when I got injured and passed out."

I cannot look her in the eye, so I turn my head away. "I do not panic. But I was…concerned. Darlene told me you were very anemic, and that it was more than could be accounted for by your injuries that happened during the earthquake."

"Yeah, I met Darlene. She's nice, and a competent nurse, but she was wrong about that. My injuries did cause most of the anemia."

"Most?" I can't stop myself from swerving my head to stare at her. "That means I was responsible as well. You should have told me if you felt unwell after I—" I clear my throat but the lump I feel refuses to go away. "After I consumed your blood. I took too much."

"No, hon, I felt fantastic after that."

"But that makes no sense. When mortals lose that much blood, it leaves them weak and exhausted." I try to break free from her embrace, but I can't do it. I'm capable of shaking off her arms, but I simply can't convince myself to do it. "When I drank from Riley's throat, she would have died if Tris hadn't intervened."

"Who are Tris and Riley? You haven't mentioned friends before."

"They are not my friends. No one would wish to spend time with me unless it's a woman I'm fucking."

Amanda rests her cheek on my shoulder. "I want to spend time with you. And I'd like to get to know you better. So, please tell me about Tris and Riley and anyone else you know."

She wants to know about my life. How can I share that information without mentioning my beginnings? I doubt she will be as understanding when I tell her the story of my life.

Amanda kisses my throat. "Maybe you should tell me while we're having sex. You won't be able to hold back then."

"Sex is not the answer. I would lose control and drain you."

"Way to be positive, kid."

That lump has re-formed in my throat, harder and larger than before. "I am not a child. You have no conception of what I truly am or the things I have done to please my father."

She nuzzles my ear while whispering to me, "I want us to get to know each other. But maybe I should start things. I wasn't very forthcoming when you asked me about Balder. It's time I told you everything."

"Only if you truly want to tell me."

"I do truly want you to know everything." She peels her arms away from me and sits cross-legged beside me, facing me. Her sleeping garment is flimsy, almost translucent, and it barely covers her bottom. The slender straps that hold it up seem as if they might snap at any moment. One strap slides off her shoulder, and she pulls it up again. "I told you how Balder seduced me and whisked me away to the Unseen as soon as we'd said our wedding vows. He only cared about one thing after that."

"Sex. That was all he cared about."

"Mm, no. That wasn't the main thing he wanted from me." She rubs her arms as if she's cold. When I remove my jacket and drape it over her shoulders, she gives me a sweet, if small, smile. "Thanks, hon. You're very considerate."

"No one but you would say such a thing about me."

"I bet you haven't let them see the real you." She tugs my jacket closed, holding it that way with one hand. "Balder wanted to screw me, for sure. But his main goal was to get me knocked up."

CHAPTER TEN

I FIND MYSELF ONCE AGAIN STARING BLANKLY AT A MORTAL BECAUSE I don't understand the terms they use. I've learned some of their idioms, but far from everything. Maybe I should ask Amanda to explain to me the idioms I've heard in this world, but right now one phrase alone matters to me. "What is 'knocked up'? I have never heard that term."

"You really are from another world, aren't you?" She holds up a hand to silence me when I open my mouth to respond. "That was a rhetorical question, which means I don't need you to answer it. The term knocked up means that Balder got me pregnant."

"But an elemental cannot impregnate a mortal without consciously trying to do so."

"Really? I had no idea. I assumed my birth control pills were working great and that's why I didn't get pregnant until after the wedding." She laughs, but it's not a happy sound. "How dumb was I? A few days earlier, I'd stopped taking the pills because I wanted to have a baby with the man I loved. Balder thought it was a great idea."

"He should not have done that." My hands ache, and I glance down at them to find I've been clenching my fists tightly. "A hybrid pregnancy is extremely dangerous and nearly always fatal to the human mother."

"I know that now. But back then, I had no idea. I actually thought it was sexy that I'd married an incubus. My personal sex machine." She shakes her head while tears form in her eyes. "I was such a damn idiot."

"The salamander is to blame, not you. He employed his powers of seduction to make you want him."

She seems completely unfazed by the snarl in my voice, as if nothing could convince her to run away. She takes hold of my hands, carefully uncurling my fingers one by one. Then she massages the palm of one hand in the most delicate and soothing manner that causes my muscles to soften and my jaw to relax. How she does this to me, I cannot fathom. But I…enjoy the sensation.

"Maybe I shouldn't tell you the rest," Amanda says. "It upsets you, and that's the last thing I want to do."

"I must know. Please." When I realize what I've said, my body goes rigid, immobilized by shock.

"Cyneric, are you okay?"

"Yes. But I said—We're fortunate this is the mortal world and not the Unseen."

Her brows draw together, creating a dimple over her nose. "I don't understand. Why is it fortunate?"

"Because using that word in the Unseen would seal a debt between us. The magical sort."

"Using what word?"

"It, ah, begins with the letter P."

She stares blankly at me for a moment, then laughter erupts from her. "You are such a sweet, confused vampire. It's adorable. You can't say the word please in the Unseen, and you were afraid even to say it here in this world. But you already said it a minute ago. The cat's out of that bag and hunting mice."

"What mice? I will destroy them if they attempt to hunt you. Where is the bag they emerged from?"

She throws her head back and laughs with such fervor that her eyes water. Once she's done mocking me, she lays a hand on my cheek. "It's a metaphor, hon. Or maybe a simile. I get the two confused. Anyway, the cat-and-mice thing was just a joke. Does the Unseen have giant, terrifying mice? In this world, they're cute little buggers."

"I see. You must think I'm an idiot."

"You aren't familiar with this world, that's all."

Wincing, I scratch behind my ear, though I can't explain why. "What is a 'mice'?"

"Mouse. Mice is plural. It would be too hard to explain. But if I see one, I'll point it out to you."

"How large are mice?"

She shrugs. "Maybe five inches, including the tail. Do you know what an inch is?"

"Yes." A breath rushes out of me. "At least they're small."

"But still terrifying. A lot of people scream when they see mice."

"If I see one, I will not scream."

She smiles with her lips closed and winks at me. "Good to know I've got a big, strong mouse hunter on my side."

I feel strangely good whenever she teases me in such a way. It should irritate me. Shouldn't it? But I feel nothing like that. "Tell me more of your story."

"Okay." Her fingers twitch in a restless manner, and she gazes down at her lap. "Balder took me to his lair and screwed me for three days, giving me occasional breaks to make sure I'd be able to keep going for as long as he wanted. By time time he was done, I could barely move. Took me weeks to recover. He was kind enough to drop me off at an emergency room in Philadelphia."

"That was not kind at all. He is a bastard."

"I was being sarcastic, sweetie. Of course it wasn't a nice thing to do." She rubs the back of her neck and sighs. "The doctors didn't know what was wrong with me. I told them I'd been in a car wreck. They believed me. A few months later, I found out I was pregnant. That's when the horror began in earnest."

A chill washes over me. I can't speak, though I feel the rage burning inside me again, hotter and more powerfully with every new detail she provides.

"Balder visited me not long after I found out I was pregnant. He told me he didn't care if I died as long as the baby survived." She waves her hand in a dismissive gesture. "He had some crazy idea that a hybrid baby would grow up to be the most powerful salamander ever. No idea why he wanted that."

My hands clench into fists yet again, and I grit my teeth, forcing words out through them. "He had no right to do such a thing to you."

"Balder pointed out that I willingly had sex with him. It's sort of the truth. I did initially want him, before I found out what he really was. I don't know exactly when he ensorcelled me, so maybe I never did genuinely want him."

"Does the salamander still live?"

She shrugs one shoulder. "No idea. I never want to see him again."

"What about—" I hesitate to ask the question, which is not my normal behavior. I still feel the fire of anger burning inside me, though my body temperature remains normal—for an elemental. We always burn hotter that mortals. Yet the fire I experience now has nothing to do with my body temperature. I do not understand my responses at all.

Amanda leans back against the wall, stretching her legs out, and sighs. "Go on. Ask me."

I hesitate again, yet only for a heartbeat. "What happened to the baby?"

"The pregnancy was a nightmare, and both I and my baby were going to die. The doctors knew it, though they couldn't explain why it was happening." She hugs herself as if she is cold. "But a being who called herself Miriella came to me one day and offered to end the suffering. The baby was only a fetus at this point, but it was my child. I didn't want to terminate the pregnancy. Balder might have been an evil bastard, but my child was innocent."

"But you did not have a child."

She bites her bottom lip hard enough to turn the skin white. "Miriella said that if I wanted to keep the baby, she would do everything she could to protect me and my child—from Balder and from the perils of a hybrid pregnancy. But she couldn't promise either of us would survive. Six weeks before

I gave birth, Miriella came to check on me. By then, I knew I couldn't keep the baby. What if Balder found out? He might kidnap my child and do horrible things to the baby. So, I gave my son up for adoption."

"That must have been painful for you."

Amanda closes her eyes. "Yeah, losing my son gutted me. But the pregnancy itself damaged me in more ways than I can count. That's why I never married again and never had any other children, not even adopted ones. Ever since, I've spent my life working for charities that help families stay together or provide assistance for people who want to adopt children."

"Why would you do that? Your chance to have children was ripped away from you."

"Because I get a lot of satisfaction from helping other people start families. That's why I do it."

I remember what she said a moment ago, and I need to know the answer. "Did you attempt to get pregnant again? With another man? You said the hybrid pregnancy damaged you in more ways than you can count."

"No, I never tried again. It was impossible. My womb had been so horribly damaged by the pregnancy that I had no choice except to have a total hysterectomy." She almost smiles, probably because I seem confused. "That means all the organs in my body that made pregnancy possible are gone."

"You should never have been abused in that way." To hear what she has endured triggers a sort of anger I've never experienced before. It seethes inside me, hot and viscous like the flaming waters of the poisonous river that surrounds the castle of the dragon king. "If I ever meet the salamander who did that to you, I will tear him apart so thoroughly that there will be no need to destroy him. There will be nothing left but a mound of bloody entrails."

Her eyes widen. "You're serious, aren't you?"

"Yes."

She opens her mouth but seems incapable of speaking.

I have shocked her, haven't I? Understanding the way mortals will react to anything is still beyond my ability. I offered my undying fealty to Larissa and later to Riley, and though both said they appreciated the offer, neither wanted to accept it. I have sworn to avenge the horrific treatment Amanda suffered, yet she seems horrified rather than grateful.

Then she blinks rapidly, and her lips curl into a small smile. "You are so sweet in a bloodthirsty way. Literally bloodthirsty, in your case."

"Are you not angry with me? I meant what I said. It was not a metaphor."

"Oh, I understand that, sweetie. You would dismember Balder just for me." She grasps my face with both hands, then kisses me. "Thank you, Cyneric. I'm grateful I have you on my side."

"You might not feel that way after I tell you my story."

"Don't be such a worrywart. Just get it off your chest. You'll feel a lot better after you've done that."

I doubt that will be the case, but I trust Amanda. She wouldn't lie. Yet she could easily be mistaken.

She lies down on the bed with her head resting on a pillow and pats the other pillow beside her. "Lie down. Then you can tell me everything. Confession is easier when you're comfortable."

I don't accept that hypothesis, but I won't share my opinion with Amanda. She wants to help me, for reasons I cannot understand. So, I lie down beside her and clasp my hands over my belly.

She lifts her head to study me. "Why do you always wear leather? You would seem less intimidating if you dressed casually."

"Do you find me intimidating?"

"No, of course not. I meant that you have this air of untouchable-ness, which I think you cultivate on purpose, to protect yourself emotionally."

"Maybe you're correct that I keep others at a distance. But I haven't consciously done that. In fact, I only began to dress this way after Tris the leprechaun annoyed me by conjuring ridiculous clothing for me." I smirk. "And I responded by exchanging the garments he chose for black leather. I've continued to dress that way ever since."

"Don't you get hot in this getup? I mean sweaty hot, not the sexy kind."

I arch one brow at her. "I am an elemental. It takes an enormous amount of energy before I produce any perspiration."

"Right. That makes sense." She eyes my clothing again. "Just out of curiosity, what did your friend conjure for you to wear?"

"Tan pants that were too large for me and had pockets all over them. I've since learned that means they were 'cargo' pants, though their pockets don't seem large enough to carry freight." I shift about while remaining in this spot, but the action stems from annoyance rather than discomfort. "Tris also provided me with a pink T-shirt that included the image of Mickey Mouse. But the mice you described to me do not resemble the one on that shirt. Mickey Mouse appeared to be badly deformed."

She flattens her lips and snorts repeatedly while her shoulders quiver. Then she bursts out laughing. She doesn't stop until her eyes are watering and her cheeks have turned pink. "Damn, I needed a good laugh. I know you didn't mean to be funny, but you were, hon. Your confusion over everything in the mortal world is adorable."

"I have heard women use that word before. 'Adorable' and 'sweet' both mean that a woman wants me to fuck her."

Amanda bursts out laughing once again.

I frown at her. "Do you want to hear my story or not?"

She ceases laughing and wipes at her eyes, then grabs a tissue from a box on the bedside table and finishes drying her eyes and cheeks. "Yes, I do want to hear it. Sorry. I'll be quiet while you tell me about yourself."

Mortals will never cease to confound me.

"I told you that Eros created me and ensorcelled me so that I would love him above all others, remaining faithful to his commands. But then Setesh made all the vampires hideous, and everything changed."

Chapter Eleven

To help Amanda understand me, I must tell her a story. That means I must return to the past in my mind, going back to a time not long after Eros had created more vampires and Setesh had made us all hideous. My brothers and I still spoke with Germanic accents too. On this day in the distant past, I stride out onto the peristyle of the Temple of Eros and survey the landscape before me. The temple lies atop a high mountain where clouds never gather and the plant life perpetually flourishes, always verdant and succulent.

Eros lies stretched out on a chaise, in the nude, gazing out at his domain with a satisfied smile on his lips. When he notices me, his smile broadens. "Discard your clothing, Cyneric. It is too beautiful a day to hide yourself from the sun's warmth. Besides, you are too pale. Stretch out and let the sun burnish your skin."

"I do not wish to expose my body." My voice has become raspy and harsh ever since the day Setesh cast his curse upon the vampires. My father doesn't realize that I'm not fully ensorcelled. "Everyone recoils from me, Father, because I am hideous."

He rakes his gaze over me. "No, my son, you are still beautiful to me. But do not fear, for I shall return you to your original state—eventually."

"When, Father? I cannot go out into the world in this condition."

"Of course you can. Don't be so sensitive." Eros rises and stretches his entire body, groaning with satisfaction. "Let's go out and look for someone for you to drink and fuck. You'll feel much better when you have a full belly and have satiated your other needs."

"I dislike feeding. The taste of blood is revolting."

"Naturally." He walks over to me and sets a hand on my shoulder. "I couldn't have you and your brothers draining mortals or elementals to the point of death. Of course, elementals would survive it. Humans would perish."

I stare at him as a chill washes over me. He can't mean—No, my father loves me and would never do such a thing. But the way he smiles... "The fact that we despise drinking blood was an accident, yes? You swore to me it was."

He shrugs and smirks. "Yes, I told you that. You are so sensitive, and I didn't wish to watch you cry and wail. But yes, I intentionally made it so that all my vampires find blood to be repulsive. It was a security measure. I need mortals to worship me, and letting my vampires drain the blood from their bodies would kill my worshippers."

Eros leads me down the peristyle steps to the pool where he often bathes. Never has he allowed vampires to swim in these waters. Not even me. He prefers to cavort with females who perform sexual acts with him, acts of a sort that make my stomach turn. He abuses them. Their devotion feeds him more power, and their orgasms provide the most intense energies. Never has he invited me to join in his orgies. I wouldn't wish to do so, but I know he has invited other vampires to join in his erotic games.

Why does he exclude me? I would do anything for my father, even after he created more of my kind and began to treat them as well as he had treated me. I was no longer special. When had he last told me that he loves me above all others? It has been millennia since he spoke those words. Yet I worship him above all others and still would do anything for him. Why? He hasn't shown me his love in such a long time. But I must adore him. I feel compelled to do so.

This was the day when I had realized I was ensorcelled.

Despite knowing what he had done, I continued to do whatever he asked of me, anything to earn his approval. Even ensorcellment could not coerce me to forget my revelation.

I remembered. For tens of thousands of years.

"Oh God," Amanda says, her voice hushed. "I can't imagine what it must have been like to be enslaved to Eros, unable to leave him, while also knowing that he had lied to you and used you."

"You don't need to imagine it. I wouldn't want you to understand the full extent of Eros's depravity. All the gods of the Unseen are equally depraved and ravenous for power."

I glance down at my leather trousers and jacket, and suddenly, I do not want them anymore. With a single thought, I replace my unfriendly clothing with blue jeans and a long-sleeve shirt. I've seen mortal men dressed this way, and women seemed to like it.

I look at Amanda. "Do you approve of my new clothing?"

She raises herself with one elbow and scans me from head to toe. "Yeah, this definitely suits you. I like the brown leather shoes. The laces make them seem classy but casual. And the blue shirt goes with your eyes."

"I am glad you approve."

"What really matters is how you feel about your new outfit. If you did this to impress me..."

"No, I did this because I wanted to."

She kisses me. "Good. You should never change yourself to please me or anyone else."

"You have no reason to be kind to me. Riley and Larissa tried to befriend me, but I wound up nearly killing them both, at different times. The safest choice would be for you to run from me."

She shakes her head. "You can't scare me away. I've told you that before. After the way Balder abused me, I grew an ironclad skin. That means you're stuck with me, unless you can convince me that you're sick and tired of me."

"I do not contract illnesses, and I rarely grow tired."

"You know what I meant."

"Perhaps I do." I avert my face for a moment, then sigh and give in. "Shall I tell you more about my past?"

"Only if you're ready. We can always wait awhile." She snuggles up to me, and the scent of her has the usual effect. It arouses me. "If you need a break, we can have sex. I'd love for you to sink your fangs into me again. When you did that before, I came so hard I swear I actually left my body for a minute."

"I might injure you without intending to do so."

She begins to unbutton my shirt. "But you didn't hurt me. And I know you never will. I want you, Cyneric, right now."

"And I want you like mad. But—"

She seals my lips with her fingers. "Stop worrying and show me what an elemental vampire can do. Unless you're already tired of me."

"Never. I'm certain I could spend millennia fucking you and never grow tired of doing so."

Amanda has unhooked all the buttons on my shirt, and now she lowers her head to lick my chest. She moves lower and lower with every swipe of her tongue, the velvety texture of it teasing my flesh and arousing me even more. My cock swells. My breaths shorten. When her chin bumps into the waist of my jeans, she uses her teeth to free the button there so she can grasp the zipper and drag it down so slowly that I realize I'm fisting my hands in the sheets.

As she carefully pulls my cock out, she lifts her gaze to mine. "I love taking your dick into my mouth so I can suck until you come."

"If you swallow my seed, it might have an effect similar to when a mortal ingests the excretions of an incubus. The first time you did this to me, you came despite the fact I hadn't touched you. That is what salamanders can do. When swallowed, their excretions cause a woman to come repeatedly for hours."

"Vampires are like salamanders? Hmm, that's fascinating. Are any other elementals that way?"

I gasp because she has just clasped the base of my erection. "I don't know. There are many, ah, species of elemen—Fuck, Amanda." I glance down at her face just as she takes me fully into her mouth. The sensation of her lips gliding along my shaft had surprised me, but to feel her swallowing me... It's like nothing I've ever known before. Libidinous mortal women and elemental females have wanted to suck me off in the past, but I declined their offers. Loss of control bothers me—but not with Amanda. I can't imagine any woman could perform this act with the sensual delight that's evident on her face. Her eyes are half closed. Soft moans escape her lips while she pulls me deep into her mouth, so deep in fact that I can feel it when the head of my cock nudges the back of her throat.

But she doesn't pull away. She continues to lavish my erection with delicate swipes of her tongue even while sucking in a manner that slowly grows more ravenous.

The searing pleasure of an impending climax builds inside me, shortening my breaths even more, making me growl like an animal, and I grip the sheets with such ferocity that the fabric rips apart. I throw my head back, arching my neck, and then my back bows up too—and I come. A spluttering sound emerges from me while my release jets into her mouth, but she keeps devouring me until she has swallowed every last drop.

I'm breathing too hard to speak.

Amanda rises to a kneeling position between my thighs. She wipes her mouth with the back of her hand, then glides her tongue over her lips to lick away the last vestiges of my seed. "Mm, hon, you taste incredible."

"How do you feel? I've never had a woman go down on me in this way."

"Mmmm." She smiles, her eyes half closed, and runs her hands up and down her belly, from her tits to her mound. She does that over and over while she speaks. "Holy shit, I've never felt anything like that in my life. The more of you I tasted, the more turned on I got. I'm so damn wet right now that it's dribbling down my inner thighs, and just feeling a draft on my skin makes me almost come. If we screwed right now, I think I'd have an out-of-body experience because it would feel so fucking amazing."

"But I don't want you to leave your body. That would mean you died."

She sets one hand on the mattress beside my shoulder and leans in to feather her lips over mine. "That's not how an out-of-body experience works. You don't die. You sort of...hover above yourself. That's what I've heard. But you can relax, hon, I don't actually want to leave my body."

Her tits dangle above my mouth, swaying gently while she rocks up and down—to tease me with her breasts, I'm sure.

I catch one nipple in my mouth and suck on it fiercely.

She gasps. "Please fuck me, Cyneric. Do it like the last time."

"Do what like last time?"

Amanda dips her head to nip my throat. "Fuck me while you drink me."

The need to do precisely that throbs inside me. My cock is as hard as granite, and I can't stop myself from growling again. I hunger for her with such ravenous need that I know I won't be able to resist her request for much longer. Do I need to resist? She wants me, and I want her. But I need to make certain of one thing first.

"It's only been a few days since the last time I tasted your blood. That combined with your head injury—"

She jerks upright, sitting back on her heels. "A few days? Sweetie, it's been three weeks."

I stare at her, unblinking. "Three weeks? But it couldn't have been that long. I haven't even slept since the last time I saw you."

She bites her lip as she studies me with her head tipped to the side. "Is it possible that you time traveled?"

Her question stops me for a moment as I consider the ramifications of it. Could she be right? I sit up and gaze directly into her eyes. "I was taken into the Unseen against my will. Time can behave differently in that world for each individual who enters the Unseen, especially if magics are involved. They summoned me there, so—"

"Summoned you? Who did that?"

"The ones who fear my power. The Four Winds joined them this time and sent me on a quest to find Eros."

"Why would they do that?"

"Because my growing powers frighten them. They view me as a threat." I bow my head. "And they are correct to feel that way. I nearly killed two women—three, including you—and I caused earthquakes that injured who knows how many mortals. I am dangerous."

"You don't know that you're the cause of the earthquakes. Maybe your friends sent you on a quest to find Eros because they think the journey will be good for you." She pushes a hand into my hair, cradling my head. "You need answers, don't you? About yourself, your powers, the god who made you."

"That might be true." I lift my head to meet her gaze. "But I have no idea how to find Eros. I stumbled onto Kamadeva, but not my father. The Four Winds deemed Kamadeva, Eros, and Setesh to be too dangerous to be allowed to roam free. As gods, they were indestructible in the truest sense. Only the Four Winds had the power to punish them, but they could not destroy them."

"Don't you think they did that on purpose?"

I nod.

"Then they must have sent you on a quest for a purpose too. Find Eros." She kisses me. "I'll go with you. Finding your father will make you feel better."

"What if it doesn't?"

"Try to think positive, sweetie."

My erection has deflated. Even the sight of her nude body can't rouse it again. Find my father? Once I was no longer ensorcelled, I wanted nothing but to get away from Eros. Yet the Four Winds insisted that I must track him down. As I consider what to do, I experience a sudden realization. "How did my ensorcellment end? All the vampires became free at the same time."

I hadn't meant to speak the words aloud, but the question remains.

Amanda puckers her lips in a strangely endearing expression of confusion. "You don't know how that happened?"

"No."

"Well, I sure as hell don't either." She puckers her lips again, this time while tapping her fingers on her thighs. "When did you first notice that you weren't ensorcelled? You told me about the day when you realized Eros didn't really love you, but you were still under his spell then."

"Indeed I was."

This might be the quest the Four Winds had sent me on—not simply to find Eros, but to understand myself too. But will that lead to freedom or destruction?

Chapter Twelve

"GET DRESSED," I COMMAND. "WE NEED TO SEARCH FOR EROS AND DE-termine how I became immune to sunlight and free from my father's ensorcellment. I still don't know how to accomplish those tasks. But with you by my side, I believe I can do it. Will you come with me?"

"Of course I will." She hops off the bed. "But I need to get dressed first, like you said."

I wave my hand. Clothing appears on her body.

She sets her hands on her hips and shakes her head. "Damn, kid, you are very handy to have around. And you know how to dress me too. These are my clothes, but you picked the items that would go together best and compliment my complexion. I'm impressed."

"You shouldn't call me 'kid.' I am not a child. In fact, I'm far older than you."

"I know. But you look young, and that's confusing." She leans over to kiss the top of my head. "I'll get used to it. You're sweet and so hot in bed that I don't care how old you are."

"Do you mind that I didn't fuck you?"

"Your quest is more important right now." She slides her tongue across my bottom lip. "Besides, we can get it on anytime, anywhere. Just whisk me away to wherever you want."

"What about your job? Your family?"

"My parents passed away years ago. I don't have any family, and I'm sick of my job being my whole life. It's time I took a sabbatical." She smirks. "After all, I've accrued three months of unused vacation time." She hunts around on the floor until she locates her purse. Then she moves her fingers over the small screen. "There. I just told my boss I'm on vacation for three months, and if he doesn't like it, he can fire me. I called it a family emer-gency."

I do not understand why she cares about helping me find my father, or why she cares about me at all. Mortals have always confounded me, but Amanda is the most confusing of all.

Ten minutes later, we walk out of the motel room and head for Amanda's vehicle. It's an old car that seems to have been gnawed on by metal-eating insects. When I speak those words aloud, she laughs.

"Relax, hon, it's rust. No insects did it. Just natural decay."

"Nevertheless, we don't need to travel this way." I sling an arm around her waist to pull her close. "My method of traveling is much faster."

"Where are we going?"

"I don't know. When I found Kamadeva, it was seemingly by accident. The Four Winds deposited me on a hillside near the city of Nashville. Perhaps if I teleport, they will guide me to my next destination as well."

"All righty. Whisk us away."

I attempt to do that while keeping my mind relatively calm, so I won't interfere with whatever the Four Winds might have in mind for me. If they purposely left me on that hill near Nashville.

We touch down in a place where night has already fallen. Either I have somehow lost time again or we've traveled so far that it's nighttime in this region. With my superior vision, I can detect that this is a barren landscape, similar to a desert, with scrubby vegetation. We stand in the middle of a dirt path that has many tire tracks etched into the earth as if mortals often drive through the area.

"Where are we?" Amanda asks. "I can't tell. It's too dark."

"I can see more than you, but that doesn't help me determine where we are."

Noises in the distance draw my attention, and I tip my head to the side to listen. Music. That's what it sounds like. Music and laughter. I hold Amanda's hand as we walk down the trail toward the sounds and gradually begin to see lights in the distance too. Soon, the lights grow large enough that I can discern what must be a building, probably a house based on its shape and size. I am hardly an expert on mortal architecture, but I've seen enough to have an inkling of what lies ahead of us.

Amanda has begun to shuffle her feet.

I halt and turn toward her. "Are you tired? I've tried to teleport several times since we arrived in this land, but it won't work. The Four Winds do not want me to go anywhere yet, and they expect me to walk to my destination. But I could carry you."

"No, I'm okay."

"Is that the truth? Or are you obfuscating for my benefit?"

Her lips twitch, apparently because she's trying not to laugh at me. "You are the first person I've ever heard use the word obfuscate in conversation. It's cute. And okay, maybe I am 'obfuscating' a little bit. I'm tired, but I can make it to that house down there."

"No, you cannot." I sweep her up in my arms. "Since you insist on lying about how tired you are, I will carry you."

"Cyneric, put me down. I have legs. They function pretty well and get me wherever I need to go."

I begin walking again with Amanda in my arms. "If that's true, then why did you need a car? Clearly, your legs are not sufficient for all your transportation needs."

She buries her face against my chest, her shoulders quivering, and I can hear hints of the laughter she tries to suppress.

I scowl, though she can't see that. "You think I'm being ridiculous, don't you?"

"No, I think you're the most chivalrous man I've ever met." She raises her head. "But I don't have a car because I'm incapable of walking. Vehicles are for traveling to places that are too far away or too hard to get to on foot."

"I see. Transportation has never been an issue for me. I can teleport to wherever I wish to go."

"But not anymore. You're grounded and can't travel any faster than the rest of us."

"Yes, it's true I am 'grounded.' However, I can move much faster than any mortal." I burst into a full-speed run, racing down the dirt road so swiftly that the landscape around us blurs. Then I halt approximately thirty yards from the house. And I set her down. "We are here."

She seems a touch dazed and simply stares at me. "That was impressive. You're an incredible runner."

"I'm glad you appreciate my running skills. I've been told I am also an impressive jumper."

"Uh-uh." She sways a little. "I don't think high-speed transit sits well with my tummy."

"What does that mean?"

Amanda bends over and vomits. Fortunately, it lands atop a rock and not on her shoes or mine. "That's what it means when I say something doesn't sit well."

"If you need to vomit again, I won't be offended."

She pats my chest. "Thanks, hon. I appreciate that."

I suspect she is teasing me again, but I don't care. I take her hand as we stride up to the house. The music is even louder now, almost deafening, though it doesn't bother my ears. Amanda winces, only a little and only for a second or two. As we halt at the door, I knock three times, rapping hard enough that I feel certain creatures hiding miles away will hear it.

What awaits us here? My last voyage took me to Kamadeva, who had no memory of his godly status or who I am. If Eros is here...

The door swings open.

And I can do nothing but gape at the man who stands there. I have seen him before and met him on several occasions when I was with Eros. He no longer has reddish-brown skin, but instead a dusky complexion quite common to mortals who live in certain regions on earth. His eyes are an exceedingly pale shade of golden brown with darker veins of onyx and sandstone red roiling within them. His hair, once a shade of glistening black no mortal could achieve even with hair dye, has become a more human color. This is Setesh, the former god once worshiped by the ancient Egyptians and one of the primordial gods of the Unseen.

He seems depressingly human now.

"Who are you?" he asks in his Egyptian accent. "I didn't invite you, but what the hell? The more the merrier!"

Setesh steps aside and waves for us to enter with a grand gesture that seems slightly off kilter. Based on the stench of alcohol I detect on his breath, even from a distance, I can safely assume he is drunk.

We enter the house, and he slams the door shut. With a hearty laugh, he announces, "I am Seth Gamal. Welcome to my home. We have plenty of booze, drugs, and orgies in this house, so don't be shy. Join us."

Orgies? I lean closer to Amanda and whisper, "Have I misunderstood the meaning of the term orgy? Or does he want us to fuck him?"

"Us and everybody else in this house, I think."

Seth joins the crowd of people who seem to be trying to consume beer by opening their mouths wide and pouring the beverage into their throats from six inches above their heads.

"Do you know that guy?" Amanda asks. "He doesn't seem to recognize you."

"That is Setesh, a former god of the Unseen. I believe the Four Winds erased his memories before they dropped him off in this world. Kamadeva and Eros would have suffered the same punishment."

"He must've done something really bad to deserve that treatment."

"Yes, he did. Setesh, Kamadeva, and Eros misused mortals for their own pleasure for as long as the human race has existed. But I believe it was the battle they fought here in the mortal world that sealed their fates."

Seth is now kneeling with his arms spread wide and his mouth gaping. While someone else pours beer down his throat, he guzzles enough to make him drunk several times over, yet he seems unaffected when he gestures that he's done. Everyone cheers and whoops. I've learned that means mortals approve of what someone has done, but I see nothing noteworthy about dumping beer down your throat.

"Would anyone care to challenge me?" Seth shouts. "Or am I still the reigning king of chugging?"

The other people in this house begin to shout in unison, "Seth is king! Seth is king!"

What am I meant to learn from watching a former god participate in "chugging" beer? I'd assumed the Four Winds sent me to Kamadeva so I could learn a lesson from how he has changed since his powers were stripped. But I cannot learn anything from Setesh.

A familiar smell reaches my nostrils, breaking through the aromas of human sweat, food, and sex. I sniff the air to separate out the other smells from the one that makes every hair on my body stiffen. My nostrils flare.

"Cyneric, are you okay?"

I glance at Amanda without moving my head. "I am unharmed. But someone else here is not."

"What does that mean?"

"Someone is dead and has been for quite some time."

While Setesh and his friends strip off their clothes and begin fucking each other en masse, I lead Amanda toward the direction from which the smell of death originates. She wrinkles her nose but does not complain about where I'm taking her. Since she remains as close to my side as possible, I think she realizes we might be walking into danger. But I will never let anyone harm her. She belongs to me.

At the end of a short hallway, we reach a door that stands mostly closed. A small gap allows the stench of death to seep out. I set my fingertips on the door and slowly ease it open.

The stench is overwhelming now.

Amanda lifts her shirt's hem to cover her nose and mouth with it. She glances at me with fear in her eyes.

I need to go into the room to see what has happened, but I don't want to take her in there. I can't leave her alone in this hallway, though. Since the moment I entered this house, I have sensed something dark and dangerous lingering within its walls. Despite my misgivings, I keep Amanda's hand firmly in mine as I push the door open and carefully walk into the room.

"Oh God," Amanda says, her voice hushed and filled with horror. "Who would do this? Why? It's—It's evil."

"Indeed it is."

She stays so close to my side that it hinders our movement, but I don't need to go further into the room to understand what transpired here. An elemental of the worst sort has been using this house as their playground, and death is the game they play. Only one as powerful as a god, or nearly so, could create a deadly tableau like the one we face now.

A dozen bodies of mortals, lifeless and bloodied, lie in a heap in the far corner of the room. Their eyes are wide open yet dead. Based on the intensity of the stench, I assume they died recently.

"Can we get out of here, please?"

I glance at Amanda and nod. As we exit the death room, I carefully shut the door but leave it open the same amount as when we had found this place. Someone created that death room. But who? We stand inside the home of a former god. Could Setesh have done this? I had contact with him when I was still ensorcelled by Eros, yet I never knew him to be this despicable. His sexual depravity was notorious, yes, but nothing compared to the level of depravity required to mutilate and murder mortals.

This was not what I had expected to learn from visiting Setesh's new home.

As we enter the living room, I try not to look at the mortals who writhe atop each other—two, three, four at a time. Amanda also avoids watching them. We've just reached the front door when a man accosts us.

He staggers into us and attempts to grab Amanda. "Come on, join the party. We've got drugs that make shagging even better."

I thrust an arm out to prevent him from touching Amanda. "We are not interested. Return to your friends."

The man seizes Amanda's wrist, then tries to haul her away.

And I seize his throat, hoisting him off the ground. Spittle sprays from my lips as I snarl, "Try that again, and I will rip your head from your body."

He giggles.

And I sink my fangs into his neck.

CHAPTER THIRTEEN

"CYNERIC, NO!" AMANDA SHOUTS. "STOP! LET HIM GO."

I feel her hands on my arm as she struggles to make me release the bastard who had tried to take her from me, but I cannot see, hear, or understand anything. The only thing I know is that I must rip this man apart. A blood lust of a different sort has taken hold of me. I don't want to fuck this man while I drink his blood. I want only to drain him dry and leave him in a crumpled heap on the floor where he belongs.

All because he dared to touch Amanda.

Cyneric, no. Amanda's cry echoes in my mind and mingles with another voice, that of Riley Jordan, the mortal who had tried to stop me from drinking the blood of an ensorcelled succubus. Her master, Drakon, had forced her to do his bidding, but she willingly let me consume her blood and even enjoyed it—much the way Amanda enjoys it when I drink her.

A wave of cold rushes through me. Am I as vile as Drakon? I had let him seduce me into doing things I should never have done, things that resulted in Riley nearly dying. Only Tris's healing skills had saved her.

Let her go, Cyneric!

The memory of Riley's cry, when I had devoured the succubus Anthea, echoes inside me. I freeze briefly, then retract my fangs from the bastard's throat little by little, allowing the enzymes in my saliva to seal up the wound. By the time I have freed my fangs completely, the wound is visible as only a red scar. I set the man on his feet.

He wobbles, but then, he'd been doing that before I bit him.

Amanda gapes at me.

While the man toddles away, Seth approaches us. "Am I higher than a kite on Mount Everest, or did you guzzle Andy's blood?"

I cannot speak. The blood I just consumed contained who knows how many illicit substances, and I feel its effects creeping into me like the sap of a tree dripping into my veins. I sway slightly. The room does too.

Amanda grasps my arm and rotates me toward her. "Cyneric? Are you okay?"

Seth chuckles. "He's feeling the buzz, *neferet*. Considering how many substances Andy enjoyed before your friend imbibed his blood, I think the vampire will be on a fuck-and-suck binge tonight."

What did he just say? I heard something I should not have. This version of Setesh is not meant to remember his past and therefore shouldn't know the Egyptian word *neferet*. Yet I swear I heard him say... I sway again as the pleasure of intoxication pulses in my veins. What had I been thinking a moment ago?

Amanda still has hold of my arms. Now she shakes me hard. "Snap out of it, Cyneric. We need to leave this place *right now*."

"No, don't leave," Seth says. "The party has only just begun."

The woman who has hold of my arms drags me into the corner nearest to the front door. Peripherally, I can see Setesh watching us with an expression that's too lucid and canny for an intoxicated man. But the rush of drugs in my system clouds my mind. I can't hold on to a thought for more than a second or two.

Amanda pulls me close and whispers, "We need to get out of here. Something about that Seth guy gives me the creeps. And I'm worried about you, sweetie. What the hell did you ingest when you drank that man's blood?"

"I...don't know." My gaze drifts to her throat, where I can see her pulse throbbing in her carotid artery. I can hear her pulse too. My nostrils flare. The scent of her suffuses my senses, and I feel my fangs emerging, ready for my next taste of blood. "I need to fuck you. Right now. Fuck and suck."

"That's what Seth told you. He's trying to seduce you into ravaging me, though I can't figure out why. Maybe he's just a sicko." She clasps my face with both hands, our mouths millimeters apart. "Listen to me, Cyneric. You don't want to hurt anyone. I know that. You were trying to protect me, and something about this place pushed you over the edge. We need to leave *right now*."

I can't think clearly enough to understand the ramifications of what she said. Is she correct? I don't know. The room has begun to spin, my heart pounds wildly, and the scent of her is overpowering.

"Yes, that's right," Setesh says. "Go on, give in. Shred her clothes and ravish her body for your own pleasure. You know you want to do it. Together, you and I can enjoy her body for hours or days, however long we want. Imagine sinking your fangs into her flesh while you bury your cock inside her."

The room no longer spins, but my focus remains locked on Amanda's throat, where the carotid artery throbs in the most erotic rhythm. I'm breathing hard. My cock has begun to harden. I curl my fingers into loose fists and blow breaths out through my nostrils.

No, I won't do it. Not again.

Seth comes up beside me. "In this house, you can do anything you want. These people give themselves to me willingly, and they will do the same for you."

Amanda kicks him in the shin, then knees him in the groin. But Seth only laughs. He seizes her arms, pinning them behind her back. As he tugs her into his body, he lowers his head to sniff her throat. "Mm, delicious. Go on, Cyneric. Take her, have her, devour her."

"Don't listen to this creep," Amanda says, spitting the words. "He's a goddamn liar. Don't fall for his bullshit. You could tear him apart with your bare hands, and he knows that."

Seth drags one fingernail down her throat. "Imagine what she will taste like, how good it will feel to feast on her blood."

Everything inside me goes perfectly still. Even my heart ceases to beat for a moment. The quiet inside me provides an opening that my mind takes—and a memory barrels through me. Riley, pinned to a wall in the sex club owned by Drakon the dragon shifter. I, standing right next to her. Drakon, speaking the precise words that Seth just uttered. The seductive tone of his voice coupled with my obsession for Riley had pushed me to do the unthinkable.

I had sunk my fangs into Riley's throat.

"No!" I shout. "I will not do this."

And I clutch Seth's throat with both hands, tearing him away from Amanda. He flies across the living room to smack into the wall so hard that the wall cracks. As he slides down to the floor, I sweep Amanda into my arms and kick the front door open with so much force that it flies out into the darkness of the night. Then I race away from Seth's home as fast as I can go. It isn't as fast as usual. The effects of the drugs I inadvertently imbibed might have waned considerably, but I'm not yet back to normal.

Can I sweep us away from here yet? There is only one way to know the answer. I stop and attempt to use my teleportation power.

Nothing happens.

I let out a wordless snarl.

"Calm down, Cyneric." Amanda sounds reasonably calm, but I detect a faint quiver in her voice that only an elemental would notice. "You're still drugged. Put me down so you can rest."

I set her on her feet.

She backs away, creating a considerable gap between us.

"You are frightened of me now." I struggle to regain my breath, but running at high speed had affected me adversely, thanks to the drugs in my system. "I will not hurt you."

"I believe you mean that. But what just happened proved you aren't as stable as we both hoped."

"The man who calls himself Seth is in fact the god Setesh. He hasn't forgotten who he is. The Four Winds might have stripped his powers, but he remembers everything."

"How do you know that?"

I squeeze words out between my clenched teeth. "Because he recited verbatim what Drakon had said months ago, when he seduced me into drinking Riley's blood."

"The exact words?"

"Yes. But Setesh was not present when Drakon said those things. I don't understand how he could know those words, and it seems rather irrelevant at the moment."

"No shit. We're trapped in the Australian Outback."

"How do you know where we are?"

She rubs her arms as if she's cold. The night is chilly. "I know because that guy whose head you wanted to rip off had an Australian accent. So did the other people in that house. Once I heard their voices, I realized the terrain around here matches what I've seen of the Outback in travel documentaries."

For a moment, we gaze at each other without speaking or moving. Then Amanda rubs her arms again and hunches her shoulders. "I need you to get me home. But after that, I can't see you ever again. I care about you, Cyneric, but you've brought nothing but pain to my life."

She wants to leave me. But I need her. Desperately. Without Amanda, I might lose control and give in to the mistakes that I have fought against repeating for so long. Do I have the right to make her stay with me?

I take half a step toward her. "Don't leave me yet. We need to talk about—"

A flapping sound above our heads draws my attention, and I tip my head back to study the night sky. A blanket of stars glitter there, thanks to the lack of light pollution in the Outback. It's beautiful. But as I admire the sky, a dark shape races across the heavens to pause directly above us, obliterating the stars. The flapping noise begins anew, and I can see the movements of the large, birdlike creature that hovers over us.

No, he will not take her.

I rush at Amanda, tackling her to the ground because I can't think of any other way to protect her from the winged creature. With all my mental strength, I concentrate on whisking us away to anywhere else. Admittedly, my mind is not as sharp as usual. But I squeeze my eyes shut and will us to be sent to the other side of the world.

Our surroundings shift.

I can't see it, but I can feel the change. Bright light burns on the other side of my lids. Warmth toasts the back of my body. I have succeeded in bringing us to a safer place, away from the creature that sought us.

"Get off me, Cyneric. You're crushing me."

Amanda sounds annoyed. I ease myself off her body and rise onto my knees. The midday sun blinds me for a moment, but I recover from the change faster than she will. Or perhaps she will recover faster than I imagined.

She scrambles to her feet and scuffles backward away from me, swiveling her head left and right. Then she turns in a circle, clearly not yet certain of where we have landed. I can't provide any clues. The landscape offers no concrete evidence of our location. I see arid mountains in the distance that encompass the valley in which we stand as well as sand dunes and smatterings of scrubby brush. Dark, narrow lines cut across the desert.

I take a step toward Amanda.

She holds up her hands, palms out. "Stay there. I can't—Just don't come any closer."

Her hands are shaking, though only enough that I can detect it. No mortal would notice.

"Amanda, I must take you to a safe place. This unknown desert doesn't seem secure."

"I think we're in Death Valley." She shakes her head slowly. "I'm not safe with you, Cyneric. All it took was for one slimeball to urge you to bite someone, and you did it. Maybe I've been wrong about you all along."

"I cannot leave you here. At least let me transport you to somewhere else, where you can find food and water and shelter."

She lowers her hands but keeps shaking her head slowly. "I need time to think. Away from you. Getting involved with one elemental bastard was enough for me. I can't go through that again."

"But you said you trust me."

"Guess I was wrong to do that. Wouldn't be the first time." She turns in a circle once again, this time holding up a hand as a visor, presumably to help her see better. Then she points at something in the distance. "There. See that? I bet it's a road."

"Even if it is, the road is too far away for you to walk. At least allow me to teleport you there."

She wrings her hands, her expression pinched. But finally, she nods.

A dark shape swoops down between us. The dragon shifter's black wings and scaly, greenish-black body tower over us both. His wings block my view of Amanda, but he doesn't turn to grab her or even to face her. No, his attention remains focused on me.

He narrows his yellow, slitted eyes on me. "Surrender to me now, and perhaps I'll let the woman go."

"No, you won't let her go. You are not the first dragon shifter I've met, and I know how deceptive your kind are." The drugs are still affecting me somewhat, but I manage to stand straight and tall in the face of the shifter. "Who are you? And what do you want with me?"

His chest puffs up, and he flutters his wings. "I am Thirío, King of the United Kingdoms of the Dragon Shifters. And you are Cyneric, the supposedly unkillable vampire."

"It is a fact. No one can destroy me."

Thirío laughs. "You are amusing, tiny vampire. But I will find a way to destroy you, or at the very least, corrupt you so thoroughly that your woman will not want to fuck you ever again."

"Explain your vendetta." The one thing I have learned from Tris and his friends is that villains always want to brag about their accomplishments. But doing so slows them down and distracts them.

Thirío surges forward, clamping one mighty hand around my neck. "That trick might have worked on Drakon, but I am not a lowly crown prince of one pitiful kingdom. I am the lord of all dragons." He lowers his head until his nose almost touches mine. "And you are about to be obliterated."

Chapter Fourteen

Obliterated? Even the Dragon King cannot do that to me. The Four Winds couldn't accomplish that feat, and they are far stronger than any shapeshifter. Thirío suffers from the same weakness as all dragons—arrogance. I suppose being able to fly and blast fire from their mouths has made them that way. But I dislike them for that very reason. At least I have subtlety.

"Why should you want to murder me?" I ask. "We have never met before, which means you cannot have a vendetta against me. Unless you are insane or incredibly stupid."

"You are the idiot in this conversation, little vampire." He stretches his wings out to their full breadth. "You might not have met me before today, but I know all about you. And I know what you did to my nephew."

"I have no idea of whom you speak."

"Of course you do. Or is your mind so addled that you can't remember meeting Drakon?"

I freeze, my gaze locked on the dragon who still has me in his grip. He blinks his slitted eyes and growls softly. The stench of his breath reminds me of the dead mortals in Seth's home, which makes me wonder if he ever gets a leg over. Perhaps female dragons enjoy the stench of decay when they are being kissed.

Thirío taps my nose with one claw. "You know of whom I speak. Don't you, little vampire? You met my nephew several months ago in London. At the gambling club that Drakon owned."

Yes, I do remember Drakon. He hadn't bothered me in the least, though he must have frightened many other elementals and mortals too. Why would Thirío come for me? I did not destroy Drakon. Tris and Riley did that.

"I'm curious, King Thirío—"

"You will call me Lord Thirío. Dragons don't use the term king."

"But you declared yourself to be the King of the United Kingdoms of the Dragon Shifters."

He bares his teeth in a blatant, and futile, attempt to unnerve me. "That is my official title used only for ceremonial purposes. In everyday parlance, I am Lord Thirío. Do you understand now? Or would you rather nitpick everything I say? I don't mind if you do that. Your death will come sooner, and I'll have more time to debauch your woman."

"I'm not his woman," Amanda announces, though I can't see her. The dragon's body blocks my view. "I don't belong to anyone. And Cyneric's pissing match with you is none of my business. You two can finish measuring your dicks later."

As Amanda walks away, she finally comes into view. I need to rush after her. She will die of thirst and starvation before she reaches those roads in the distance. But Thirío has a hold on me, and I find I cannot move. He must have used magics to restrain me. His hand alone couldn't do that.

Thirío bares his teeth, hissing like a ruddy snake. "This is no fun without an audience."

He hugs me to his body with one wing, spins around, and leaps high above the ground to thump down directly in front of Amanda. She yelps and stumbles backward. Thirío wraps his other wing around her and draws her close. We face each other, each restrained by one of the dragon's wings. I should be able to move my legs, but I can't. What magics does Thirío wield that allow him to circumvent my powers? No one can do that because no one has that kind of power.

Until now.

But I have broken free of such restraints before. Janus attempted to bar me from leaving the Unseen, but my magics proved far more powerful than even those of a god. That must mean I can shatter Thirío's hold if I summon all the magics inside me to do so.

Amanda makes a chomping motion with her teeth, then rolls her eyes toward Thirío.

She can't want me to... No, it would be too dangerous—for her.

The dragon king bends his knees, a sure sign that he intends to fly up into the air and whisk us away, either by flying or by teleporting, I can't tell which one he might choose. The danger is great, but I have no choice. Amanda's life is at stake.

I clamp my teeth down on Thirío's wing.

He roars and thrashes his entire body. Amanda tumbles to the ground, rolling across the sand. I hit the ground a second later, flat on my back. Thirío stomps toward me, snarling and roaring and cracking his knuckles. Just as he reaches me, I spring up to latch on to his throat and sink my fangs deep into whatever vein or artery lies in that spot. I'm not well-versed in dragon anatomy.

Thirío roars again and shakes his entire body.

But I have a solid grip on him now, with my fangs as well as my arms and legs. I have wrapped myself around him while I begin to consume his blood, sucking swiftly in the hopes I can weaken him that way. The blood of elementals cannot sustain me, but I don't need nourishment right now. I need only to drain this winged bastard until he passes out from blood loss.

Something else begins to happen, though. Something…electrifying.

As I drink his blood, I realize I am relishing the flavor of it, so much that I want to devour every last drop of it. The weakness brought on by drinking the blood of a mortal who had taken illicit substances has evaporated. I feel stronger than ever, buoyed by whatever this dragon shifter has in his veins. It's like nothing I've ever tasted, from mortals or other elementals. The energy rushes through my veins, sizzles down my nerves, and invigorates me so intensely that I feel as if I could lift a mountain and toss it onto another continent, perhaps another world altogether.

Thirío grasps my throat and squeezes hard enough that I hear bones cracking in my neck. The only reason I give up drinking his blood is because he has choked off my esophagus.

The dragon king vanishes.

And I slump to the ground on my back, struggling to breathe.

"Cyneric!" Amanda shouts, as she sprints over to me and drops to her knees. "No, no, no, I don't want you to die."

"I will not die." My words emerge as hoarse, choked syllables. "Indestructible, remember?"

"But he crushed your throat."

"It will heal."

But I need to get Amanda away from this place. As I sling an arm around her and attempt to teleport, I can feel that I don't have the energy to do it. I'll need to settle for a more mundane method of transportation. I scramble to my feet without releasing Amanda.

I suck in a rough, shallow breath. "Need your help."

"Anything. Just tell me what to do."

"Give me the kiss of life."

"Okay."

Without hesitation, she pinches my nostrils shut with two fingers and seals her open mouth to mine, then blows. Her breath forces my throat to open. The oxygen, combined with the blood of Thirío, gives me the strength I need. I leap into the air, soaring across the desert to land in the middle of the black strip of road I had seen earlier. The moment my feet touch down, I crumple to the ground.

Amanda kneels beside me. "What now?"

"Wait for a car. Hitch a ride."

"I can't leave you like this."

"You wanted me to leave you alone. Now, you have your wish."

She bites her lip. "I didn't mean for it to happen this way."

The distant rumble of a vehicle engine tells me she won't need to wait long. I stumble off the asphalt track and into the sand, then halt there. The power boost I received from Thirío has given me more than enough strength to cloak myself. Amanda can still see me, but whatever driver picks her up will not know I am here.

She flags down the car. It turns out to be driven by an elderly man whose equally elderly wife sits in the passenger seat. Amanda tells them quite the tall tale, blaming a mythical boyfriend who got angry with her and drove off, leaving her in the middle of nowhere. The couple offers her a ride to the nearest town. She accepts, climbing into the backseat.

And I watch her ride away.

Her face remains visible as she gazes out the rear window at me. But then the vehicle drives too far away for me to see her or vice versa. Amanda has her wish now. She is free of me.

I trudge down the road, though I have no idea where I will go. I need to move, that's all I know. Every woman I have ever wanted for more than sex and blood has rejected me and thought of me as a monster. Maybe I am that. I have done monstrous things, after all. I tore out the throat of the salamander Travis and attempted to gut him with a sword, though wound up thrusting the blade into Larissa's heart by mistake when she attempted to stop me from hurting Travis. Then I allowed Drakon to seduce me into nearly killing Riley.

Yes, I am a monster.

The loud growling of multiple engines approaches me from behind. I halt and turn to look. A group of bikers approach, all riding motorcycles that I believe are called Harleys. The group slows as they reach me, and the man in front shuts off his bike. His black T-shirt features an ornate skull-and-crossbones design. The short sleeves reveal many tattoos of varying colors.

He lifts his sunglasses to eye me from head to toe. His brows lift, undoubtedly because he noticed the blood stains on my clothes and arms. "Damn, pal, you look like you just got in a brawl with a *Tyrannosaurus rex.*"

I suppose in a way I did experience something like that. A dragon shifter isn't hugely different from a dinosaur. "I am in need of transportation."

"No shit." The biker waves for me to approach him. When I do so, he holds out his hand to me. "I'm Mateo Casales. You got a name, pal?"

"Cyneric."

"No last name? Or is that your first name?"

"It is my only name."

"That's cool." Mateo twists his head around to see his gang. "Listen up, hombres. This guy needs a lift. Who wants to cozy up to him?"

A hand rises near the rear of the biker caravan. I can't see who has offered to "cozy up" with me.

Mateo slaps my arm and grins. "Looks like you get to ride with Kiana. Go on, she's waiting for you."

I walk to the end of the line of motorcycles, where a lovely woman dressed in leather smiles at me. All the bikers are wearing leather, actually. I climb onto the bike behind her, and she instructs me to "hold on tight, sugar." Then the bikes take off down the long, desolate road to who knows where.

Maybe I'm being escorted into Hell.

The bikers have reservations at a hotel, so I say goodbye to them in the parking lot. I should have worn my leather clothing today. Then, I would have blended in with the bikers who allowed me to travel with them. As we're saying goodbye, Mateo comments on the pallor of my skin and jokes that I must be a vampire, though he can have no idea that his joke is true.

Where is Amanda?

I at last recover from my encounter with Thirío enough that I can once again whisk myself away to wherever I like, not wherever the Four Winds decide to send me. I need to find Amanda. She told me to stay away, but I can't do that. I need her. Maybe this is my obsession driving me to search for her, but I don't care what the reason is for my behavior. I must find her.

She isn't at the motel where I had found her last night.

And she isn't at the motel where she had stayed after the earthquake.

Neither is she at her apartment, which still lies in ruins.

I should be able to find her simply by thinking about her, but no matter how many times I attempt to discover her whereabouts, I fail. She has no family, and as far as I could tell, no friends of the sort who would visit her or worry about her well-being. What can I do now? Giving up is not an option. That means I need help.

And that means a trip into the Unseen.

With only a thought, I take myself to the one place where I know a doorway to the other world exists and is relatively easy to reach. I materialize in the rock garden behind the shop where elementals gather because they are friends with the owners of the rock shop—Lindsey and her husband Nevan, a former sylph. But I will not visit the shop. Instead, I traipse through the rock garden and down the dirt path that leads past the healing vortex and straight to the waterfall. Behind the curtain of water that tumbles into the pool below, I know I will find a gateway to the Unseen. I've traveled through it before.

Janus might have tried to block me from accessing the portals, but he cannot stop me now.

I approach the wooden railing that hems in the waterfall and the pool below it. Then I leap over it, sailing so high that I easily reach the rock ledge on the cliff, touching down lightly. The cascade rumbles beside me, too loud for me to hear any other sounds. I rotate toward the falls, bend my knees in preparation for jumping through the water into the cavern behind, and...

"What do you think you are doing, vampire?"

The sound of Janus's voice makes me fist my hands and clench my teeth. I do not look at him. "I am going into the Unseen. You cannot stop me."

"Perhaps not. But I can make it more difficult for you to cross the veil."

He lets out a short, piercing whistle.

Three beings appear on the ledge in front of me with the cascade pummeling them. Travis, Max, and Tris all cross their arms over their chests as if they believe they can prevent me from crossing the veil this way.

I teleport myself into the cavern.

And they reappear in front of me, blocking the portal that resides in this cavern. It remains idle, invisible, waiting for a command to open.

"We know what you did," Travis declares. "Thirío was royally cheesed off when you used his artery as a sippy cup. Assaulting the dragon king isn't a clever thing to do."

Tris shakes his head. "Captain Fang always did have a tub of loose screws in his head. But I didn't think even he would do such a reckless, dumb-ass thing."

"Yeah, he's a pillock for sure. Might have the accent women love, but I bet he has to ensorcell the birds to make them screw him."

"Shut up!" I shout with so much volume that the words reverberate off the rock wall behind me. "I have no time for useless morons like you or your pitiful attempts at humor."

Triskaideka sighs. "At least we know what the word joke means. You wouldn't know humor if you got slapped in the face with a banana peel."

Is that meant to be humorous? Their jokes never seem entertaining to me.

Since these creatures refuse to move out of my way, I teleport myself past them. Or I try to do that. But I wind up in the same place where I had started, facing these bloody annoying creatures. They all smirk as if they know with absolute certainty that I cannot get past them by any means available to me. They don't know what the dragon's blood has done to me. I've never felt stronger or more energized in all my existence.

I rush at them while roaring with all the frustration I've kept pent up inside me. The three wankers move out of my way.

And I smack into an invisible wall, landing face-down on the pockmarked stone floor. My face is buried in a water-filled hole. I push up onto my hands and knees. The roar of the falls is quieter here thanks to the magics that dampen it.

Max leans over to pat my cheek. "We tried to tell you, mate. There is no way in the multiverse that you can cross the veil."

I roar again as I spring to my feet. "I don't have time for your bloody stupid games. Get your arses out of my way, or I'll drain each and every one of you faster than you can scream for help."

Tris grins. "Hey, did you guys notice that? Captain Fang finally learned some of the British words."

"Took him bloody long enough," Max announces. "But not as long as Travis, the former Texas sheriff. I guess it would be harder to go from Texan to British than from German to British."

"Why would it be harder?" Travis asks. "The Texas twang is much closer to a British accent than German is."

"Shut your fucking mouths!" I roar, even louder than the previous times. "I need to get into the Unseen. Right now. I must find out where Thirío is and why he tried to capture me, not to mention how Setesh has retained his memories. But most of all, I need to find *her*."

Max's brows furrow. "Who do you need to find?"

I glower at him. "Amanda."

"Anybody here know some bird called Amanda? Can't say I do."

Travis thumps his fist on Max's head. "Is it hollow in there? Of course you know who Amanda is. We all talked about her that day when Janus had us try to catch Cyneric and lock him up."

"Oh, yeah, now I remember." Max folds his arms over his chest and taps one finger on his chin. "Did Amanda actually shag you? Can't see any woman wanting to do that. You must taste like blood when you kiss a girl."

His lip curled when he spoke the word blood, as if it's a vile substance when in fact it is the reason these infants are alive. He is a child—in terms of how young he is compared to me and in how juvenile he is.

I suddenly realize I have begun to growl as if I'm a rabid animal. If these creatures don't let me through the portal immediately, I will lose my mind. Quite literally.

Max raises his hands. "Calm down, Cyneric. We're here to help, I swear it."

"Then open the portal."

He winces. "Can't do that."

Max and the others abruptly go stiff, their gazes trained on something behind me. They back away slowly, halting inches from the pummeling water of the falls.

"How did he do that?" Travis whispers out of the corner of his mouth.

Tris shakes his head and speaks in an equally soft voice. "No frigging idea."

I turn toward the rear of the cavern.

The portal has opened. Its glow causes veins of copper embedded within the sandstone walls to glisten. The entrance to the Unseen hovers like an enormous bubble, just above the cavern's floor and not quite touching the ceiling. Within its fathomless darkness, pinpoints of diamond-like brilliance shimmer, appearing and vanishing over and over. Colors emerge in the blackness too, swirling in shades of iridescent blue, green, and deepest purple.

Janus appears beside me. "It is beautifully terrifying, is it not?"

"Nothing terrifies me."

"We both know that is not true." He turns sideways to me. "The portal opened for you of its own volition, because it sensed you waiting for it."

The spell the portal had cast upon me shatters. I blink rapidly and wait for the trance to fade away. "Why would it wait for me? The portal is a tunnel filled with magics, not a living thing."

"Is it? You may change your mind after this experience."

"Why are you here? You cannot stop me from entering the Unseen."

"Perhaps not. But someone did. A great deal of magics were required to circumvent my powers and the wishes of the Unseen itself." Janus moves closer to the portal and pushes his hand inside the seething darkness. "The portal is neutral. It cares nothing about what you have done or might do because its purpose is to transport elementals, and occasionally mortals, into and out of the Unseen."

"But you prevented me from coming and going through the portal."

"Yes. But that worked only because the Four Winds ensured it would. Now, they realize you must go into the Unseen. The fate of both worlds depends upon you doing precisely that."

CHAPTER FIFTEEN

JANUS AND OTHERS LIKE HIM SEEM TO ENJOY SPOUTING VAGUE PROPHE-cies. But since what he wants meshes with what I want, for once, I won't argue with him.

"You, the wise and wonderful god, are just going to let him traipse about in the Unseen?" Max huffs. "He nearly killed two women."

"And you slaughtered how many men and women during your time as a centurion in the Roman legions? You would do well not to imply that you are more honorable than Cyneric."

I have had enough of their conversing with these beings. I take a step toward the portal.

Janus thrusts an arm out to stop me. "I was not done. When a god speaks, elementals listen."

I compress my lips and bluster a breath out through my nostrils.

Undeterred, Janus gazes straight into my eyes. A tingling sensation sweeps over my skin. "Amanda Nelson has been abducted by Thirío."

Another tingle sweeps over me, this time infused with a frigid chill.

"The dragon king?" Tris says. "Holy moly. How did you manage to tick him off, Captain Fang?"

"Never mind the details," Janus declares. "Those are for Cyneric to learn and not to satisfy your curiosity."

I glare at the shimmering portal. "I have met Thirío. He attempted to abduct me, or perhaps murder me. His motivations were unclear."

Janus veers his gaze back to me. "The Four Winds failed to mention that to me. You must go now, before the portal grows weary of waiting for you."

I take a deep breath and march through the portal. It telescopes shut behind me, and I can no longer see it at all. In its place lies a boulder, positioned at the edge of a small pool. The landscape of the Unseen bears only a passing resemblance to the mortal world. Here, the trees do not have leaves. Instead, a stringy green substance hangs from the branches and almost seems to ooze from the trees. The sky above shimmers in a shade of blue never seen in the mortal world, and the sun glimmers like a polished diamond. At night, twin moons cast their milky glow on the landscape.

Despite its ethereal appeal, I have never thought of the Unseen as beautiful. The mortal realm offers far more variety of landscapes, yet I do not consider that world to be beautiful either. I know of only one thing of true beauty.

Amanda Nelson.

Where has Thirío taken her? Janus failed to mention that, and I had forgotten to ask. My rage had taken over and obliterated reason. I had never experienced anger like that until now.

Two beings appear in front of me.

I clench my teeth.

"Aren't you happy to see us?" Travis asks. "We did irritate Janus by coming here to help you, so you could at least pretend to be grateful."

"Without actually expressing gratitude," Max points out. "Ah, Travis, you're still such a newbie about the rules of the Unseen. You should spend more time learning about this world and less time shagging Larissa."

Travis rolls his eyes. "We're salamanders. That means shagging comes before everything else."

I glance around the clearing. "Tris did not come with you?"

Max shakes his head. "I know you two are best mates, but Janus wanted Tris to take care of something else first."

"What must he do?" The answer is irrelevant, so I can't understand why I asked the question.

"You'll find out soon," Travis tells me. "We're the advance team. Don't worry. Tris will be along soon."

This conversation is quite annoying. "I don't care if he does or does not. And I have no need of your help."

I teleport myself away from the aggravating salamanders, willing the Unseen to take me to the place where Amanda is. Though I enter the abyssal tunnel, I end up back in the spot where I had been in the first place.

The salamanders both give me long-suffering looks. But Max is the first to speak. "Could've told you that wouldn't work. Thirío isn't your average dragon shifter. He's the sodding king of all dragons, you moron."

"But I bested him once. I will do it again."

"Not if you can't find the castle."

"What castle?"

Travis folds his arms over his chest and sighs. "Thirío's castle. It's where the King of the United Kingdoms of the Dragon Shifters lives. Did you think he slept in a gnome's hollow? They might like sleeping in a hole in the ground, but no one else does."

Max aims a smug smile at me. "The only way you're getting into that castle is with our help. We know where it is. You haven't got a bloody clue."

Needing help is not something I would have ever believed could happen to me. Yet if they are correct, Amanda needs me—and I need their assistance. I have no illusions that I can convince these two copper-skinned idiots to tell me the location of Thirío's castle.

Though I want to slump my shoulders, I instead roll them back and lift my chin. "You may accompany me, but only to the castle wall."

Max wags a finger at me. "Uh-uh-uh. We have strict orders to escort the bloodsucking fiend to the castle and accompany you inside the walls. We're meant to stick to you like ruddy glue."

"Tris told you those things."

"No. Travis told me. I would never call you a bloodsucking fiend, and neither would Tris." Max strides up to me and slaps my arm. "I prefer the term alternatively fed individual."

I don't care what the salamanders or the leprechaun call me. "Take me to the castle. Do it now, before I get hungry and decide to drain you both of all the blood in your useless bodies."

Max nods appreciatively. "Gotta say, you craft the best death threats of anyone I've ever met. Don't you agree, Travis?"

"Definitely," his mate says. "Nobody does it quite like the fiendish bloodsucker."

"It's bloodsucking fiend, Travis."

My lids narrow to slits, and I compress my mouth into a slash. My nostrils flare.

"Better get the vamp to the castle," Max declares, "before he goes post office on us."

Travis rolls his eyes. "The phrase is 'go postal,' not 'go post office.' That doesn't make any sense."

"Whatever."

At last, the salamanders take hold of my arms and whisk us away.

We touch down inside a dark forest of the sort mortals like to read about in fairy tales. Inches from our toes, a precipice plummets thousands of feet down—to what, I can't yet tell. Fairy lights dance below us, probably not as close as they seem since such orbs are rarely large. The sky has a bluish-black hue. It seems to generate its own energy, since the clouds that scud past seem to glow only until they drift away from this precinct. In the eerie light, I can see structures far below us on the floor of a flat basin.

The largest structure by far is the castle. It towers above all other buildings in the basin, and the spires on its towers have jagged edges unlike any temple or fortress I have ever seen in this world.

"How should we get down there?" Travis asks. "Looks like a long ways to jump. I know none of us can die from falling, but we would need time to recover afterward."

I lean forward, craning my neck to see down the face of the sheer cliff. "Perhaps there are footholds."

Max makes a rude noise. "You want us to free-fall down…for how many feet? Millions, it looks like."

"Thousands at most." I straighten and raise my brows at him. "If you are frightened, feel free to remain here. I will go to the dragon king's castle alone."

"No, you won't. We've got orders." Max sets his hands on his hips. "And besides, the powers that be have arranged things so you can't go anywhere without us, your vampire minders."

"Who are the powers that be? I've not heard of them."

"I meant Janus and the Four Winds."

"You should have simply said that in the first place. It saved you no time to be coy about it."

Travis whistles loudly. "Listen up, girls. Playtime is over. Let's find a way down to the basin floor."

A horde of fairy lights ascend en masse and swiftly corner us. We cannot go backward, and leaping off the cliff does seem rather ill-advised. Besides, the orbs have surrounded us from all sides.

"Bollocks!" Max shouts. "Bloody fairy light singed me."

"Suck it up, Maxie-pie," Travis tells his friend. "I know that's what your wife calls you."

I jerk my head around to glare at the salamanders over my shoulder. "Shut up. You're acting like children."

Max shrugs. "At least we've never eaten anyone for breakfast—or lunch or dinner."

A flash of movement draws my attention to the nearest spire of the castle, from which a winged creature has just taken flight. The beast flaps its wings casually as it soars ever closer to us.

"Should we, ah, get out of the way?" Max asks. "Don't think the dragon cares if he knocks us off the cliff."

The dragon tucks his wings back and dive-bombs straight toward us, his body soaring at high velocity.

I scramble backward, pushing Max and Travis backward too, but we can't go far. The fairy lights, which I had always thought of as benign, pinch us with electrical bursts of magic that do more than sting us. They prevent us from trying to flee.

The dragon spreads his wings as he lands at the edge of the precipice. Then he folds them back again. "You are coming with us, vampire."

I peer around both sides of his body. "Us? I see only you and your tiny fairy lights."

"My king demands that you meet with him in the castle. Lord Thirío does not like to be kept waiting."

"I don't care about his feelings. What has he done with Amanda?"

The dragon smirks. "She is well cared for in Lord Thirío's quarters."

Well cared for? If that scaly cretin has laid one finger on her, I will drain him dry and rip his body to shreds.

The dragon throws his head back and lets out several high, sharp cries.

More winged beings launch themselves off the spires in various locations atop the castle. At least a dozen of them swoop through the air, crossing the basin within seconds to hover just behind their leader.

He spreads his arms. "As you can see, I am far from alone. Do you wish for your woman to become Lord Thirío's plaything? You have three seconds to decide. Three, two—"

"What do you want us to do?" I snarl. "We can't fly."

The dragon spreads his wings and holds his arms out to me. "You may ride with me. Your friends will have their own escorts."

Max comes up beside me and curls his lip. "You want us to hug you?"

The dragon growls. "Salamanders are all sissies."

He folds his wings around me, shoving Max aside in the process, and dives backward off the cliff while flipping over to face the ground far below us. I could bite this beast and injure him enough that he would lose his hold on me. But it serves my purpose, for the moment, to let him carry me to our destination. I will arrive at the castle faster.

When I glance back at the salamanders, they are being ferried across the basin in the arms of two other dragons.

The bluish-black sky grows lighter as we draw nearer to Thirío's castle. It has a moat, though the liquid seething within it does not resemble water. It seems more like acid. The shapes I had taken for stone gargoyles attached to each corner of the temple and the top of each spire now turn out to be dragon shifters, as evidenced by the fact that they unfurl their wings and screech at us. The gargoyle shifters have smooth gray skin like their mythical counterparts, but otherwise resemble the dragons who are delivering us to the king.

As we fly over the center of the castle complex, I notice elementals in human form wandering down the streets, going about their daily lives. Perhaps prisoners being flown in are a common occurrence.

Finally, we reach the castle proper. The dragons begin their descent, slowing down for landing. Once their feet touch the stone-paved avenue in front of the main gates, they rise to their full height while keeping us in their clutches. Our feet hang just above the ground.

The gates open, seemingly of their own volition.

Our captors drop us on our feet, then herd us into the castle courtyard. No one awaits us. We cross the expansive open area while the gates glide shut behind us, and we climb the wide steps that seem to be fashioned from a type of white stone. We halt at the top of the steps, where a closed door prevents us from going any further. Nothing happens for several minutes. I glance at Max and Travis, but they only shrug. How long will we be made to wait? In all my existence, I have never known the leader of any elemental tribe to open their doors quickly. They always make visitors wait. I assume they believe doing so will make them appear more regal and powerful.

The tactic never impresses me. Instead, it annoys me.

After eight minutes and twelve seconds, which I counted on the clock positioned above the entrance to the palace, someone finally deigns to open the doors for us. Our guards herd us inside, and the doors shut again.

I tip my head back to gaze up at the circular hole in the ceiling. It lies directly above the dais that holds the king's throne. I would assume that hole exists to let sunlight beam down on Thirío, but no such direct light comes from the opening. He wouldn't use it simply to make a grand entrance. Not even a dragon would be that pompous.

A shriek echoes from high above the ceiling, and a shadow falls over the opening. The dragon folds its wings and sails down to land flat on its feet in front of the throne. Thirío shifts into humanoid form, now standing nude before us. He stretches and makes noises that imply he is contented. "I regret making you wait, but a king has many duties he must complete every day."

Two servants rush out from behind the enormous throne. They carry a large fur cloak, which they drape over Thirío's shoulders. The hem drags on the floor as he drapes himself over the marble seat that waits for him, letting one leg hang over the arm so he can swing it slowly. If he intended to disgust us with his display, showing off his genitalia, he has succeeded. Now that he has shifted out of dragon form, he resembles myself and my mates, except that his tanned skin has a faint emerald sheen.

Did I just think of Max and Travis as my friends? No, I would not have done that. I dislike them.

Thirío snaps his fingers, and another servant appears. "Fetch the woman."

Chapter Sixteen

OWING DEEPLY, HEAD DOWN, THE SERVANT SHUFFLES BACKWARD away from the dragon king.

"I have summoned your woman," Thirío says to me. "Maybe I'll make you watch while I defile her body in every way I can think of. My imagination is boundless."

"Your nephew also enjoyed issuing threats of defilement. It doesn't impress me."

He smirks. "We shall see."

Thirío continues to swing his leg, but now he rests his chin in one hand and taps it in time with the movements of his leg. The dragon king turns to Max. "Tell me, Maximus, why are you aiding a vampire? They are the most revolting creatures in the multiverse."

Max shrugs. "I used to be a Roman solder. Bloodletting was basically an Olympic sport back then. If Cyneric wants to swig your blood, I have no problem with that." He glances at me. "Have at it, mate."

Thirío smacks his palm down on the throne's arm. "Silence! This is my moment, not yours. Shut your mouths and listen while Lord Thirío, King of the United Kingdoms of the Dragon Shifters, tells you what is going to happen."

Max gives Thirío the thumbs-up sign. "Sure thing, mate."

The dragon king blows out a fiery breath through his nostrils. "I despise the salamanders. They are the most irritating degenerates in the Unseen."

Travis chuckles. "You haven't had much contact with Cyneric, have you? He's not your average vamp, and I'm sure he can annoy you more than any elemental you've ever encountered before."

I suspect he's giving me a compliment in his bizarre way.

"Oh, look," Thirío says, once again smirking. "The entertainment has arrived."

When I glance toward the area that has drawn his attention, I go perfectly still. My heart might have actually thrust itself up into my throat.

Amanda is being led to Thirío. She wears only a semitransparent, billowing gown. I can discern the outline of her body and faint glimpses of her nipples as well as the hairs between her thighs. Thirío has seen her this way? What if he has admired her form while she was completely naked? Oh, but if he touched her…I will sink my fangs into him, and this time, I will drain him so thoroughly that he will never recover. Lord Thirío will be a mindless lump of flesh for the rest of eternity.

The dragon king lifts one brow at me. "Are you growling? I thought you were a vampire, not a gnome."

"You should not have brought Amanda into your vendetta against me. That will be your last mistake."

He chuckles. "I might keep you as a pet. You're quite entertaining, like the circus bears they have in the mortal world."

I might have growled accidentally a moment ago, but now I do it on purpose. "Release Amanda now. Max and Travis will take her back to the mortal world. Once she's safe there, I will allow you to do whatever you like to me."

He can't kill me. If he chooses to torture me, so be it.

Thirío rises from his throne and saunters down the steps to halt an arm's length from me. "I know exactly how to beat you into submission without laying a finger on you. In fact, you will enjoy becoming my slave."

Coldness shivers through me, stiffening every hair on my body. But the fear swiftly changes to a simmering heat that makes my whole body tense, ready for a fight. "You will not ensorcell me."

"Won't I?"

"No. My powers exceed yours."

He laughs heartily and clamps a hand down on my shoulder. "I will enjoy breaking you down piece by piece and forcing you to revel in all the depraved things I will do to you." He snaps his fingers, and Amanda vanishes only to reappear right beside Thirío, tucked under his arm. "And you will watch while I do the same things to her."

Thirío keeps Amanda tucked against his side and one hand gripping my shoulder while he begins to chant in the oldest language know to the Unseen. This is the tongue that few elementals know, the one used by the Four Winds and the gods. I sense the energies flowing around me, but I don't feel any different. Even when his voice grows louder, booming within the throne room, and I can see the magics floating in the air, I still feel no different.

Lord Thirío finishes his incantation and gazes at me with his chin lifted and his lips forming a faint smirk. "It is done."

"No, it is not. Your ensorcellment spell failed."

"That is impossible."

Max waves toward me. "Go on. Order him to do something. Make it a nasty job too, like washing your feet with his tongue."

Thirío takes three steps backward, dragging Amanda along with him. "Do what the salamander said. Wash my feet with your tongue and describe to me how good my feet taste."

"I would rather devour a gnome—including his warts and calluses."

His expression devolves from smugness to disgust and finally to rage. Lord Thirío pounds one foot on the floor the way I have seen human children do when they don't get their way. "You should be ensorcelled. The spell never fails. Never."

I shrug. "I am not like other elementals."

Travis and Max approach me, taking up positions at either side. They each lay a hand on one of my shoulders. But only Travis who speaks. "Face it, dragon breath, you have lost. Didn't count on Cyneric having mates, did you?"

Mates means friends. I have such a thing? Other beings who will assist me and join me in fighting an enemy? No matter how many times they have suggested as much, in the past few weeks, I still couldn't believe it until now.

Thirío snaps his fingers taut, releasing his talons, and touches one sharp tip to Amanda's throat. "You forget that I hold the ace in this poker game."

I glance at Amanda, who smiles faintly. Then I return my attention to the dragon king. "Release her now, and I will refrain from destroying you."

"Uh-uh-uh, that's not how this will go. You, little vampire, will do my bidding even without ensorcellment." He draws his talon across Amanda's throat, eliciting a trickle of blood. "You see, Drakon told me all about your Achilles' heel. Look at the blood trickling down her skin. I'm sure you can smell it too, that rich and savory flavor."

"Your arrogance will be your undoing, Thirío. I am not the vampire I was back when I met Drakon in his club. I have changed in ways you cannot possibly fathom." I summon Amanda to me, hugging her to my body. "Goodbye, pitiful king of a reviled kingdom."

I whisk us all away—myself, Amanda, Travis, and Max—and we emerge in the clearing that surrounds the entrance to the mortal world. With a flourishing gesture, I open the portal and teleport us directly into the garden of whimsical statuary behind the rock shop.

Max and Travis gape at me, clearly confounded by my powers. But Amanda gazes at me with appreciation.

Then she leaps at me and crushes her lips to mine.

I catch her, naturally, and devour her mouth with a ravenous hunger that has nothing to do with blood.

"Whoa, Captain Fang, this is a G-rated rock garden."

The sound of Tris's voice and his grating humor doesn't stop me. I might vanish Amanda's clothing right here and fuck her while the others watch. But she breaks away before I can do that, stepping backward a few paces. Amanda is breathing hard, and her cheeks have turned pink. Her lips are swollen too, which makes me want to sink my fangs into them.

"Well, at least we don't need to drag you off the poor woman." Tris walks up to me and punches my arm. "Glad you finally got a girlfriend. Getting your drinks by dipping into the shallow end of the gene pool isn't healthy."

I do not understand his humor.

The leprechaun turns to Amanda, holding out his hand to her. "I'm Tris, and I'm kind of Cyneric's friend. As much as anybody can be."

She shakes his hand. "Nice to meet you, Tris. I'm Amanda Nelson. And I know all about Cyneric's resistance to meeting new people."

I swerve my gaze to her. "I was not resistant to meeting you."

Tris punches my arm again. "At least you're not obsessed with my wife anymore."

Max attempts to herd Travis and Tris toward the rock shop, shouting over his shoulder as they depart. "No worries, mate. I'll make sure these two stay away from the garden and the woods." He gives me an exaggerated wink. "So you two can 'talk.' "

His attempt to make that word sound filthy has no effect on me. I don't care what the childish incubus thinks of me or what he says. The only reason women love to shag him is because of his supernatural pheromones.

I reach for Amanda.

She pulls away.

"What are you doing?" I ask. "We need to discuss your experience in the dragon king's castle."

"I don't want to discuss it."

"Did Thirío hurt you?"

She hugs herself and rubs her upper arms. "Not the way I think you mean. He didn't try to assault me, sexually or otherwise. But I was stuck in that place for what felt like days, though it was probably hours. He said things…" She begins to gnaw on her upper lip. "Things about you. What you did in the past. What you were like. I know I shouldn't believe everything he said, but I need time to sort through what's happened."

"I told you I was unattractive until Eros removed Setesh's curse."

"No, that's not what I mean."

Though I want to pull her into my arms, I hold back. She seems disturbed in a manner I can't understand, especially if she won't explain it to me. A horrible thought occurs to me, and I must fight to keep from sounding angry. "Did Thirío trick you into saying please or thank you? If you incurred a magical debt, that is not your fault. We can find a way to erase it."

"I never said those words. Why would I thank that scumbag or beg him to hold me hostage?"

"Mortals often make that mistake in the Unseen." I inch closer. "Tell me what has upset you so deeply. I will beg if necessary."

"Would that incur a debt?"

"Not in this world. But in the Unseen, yes."

She lets her arms fall to her sides, and her shoulders sag. "I can't deal with this shit anymore. It's too much."

"I don't understand. Please explain it to me." I used the P-word. I'm that desperate to keep her with me.

"Don't have the energy to make you feel better, Cyneric." She bows her head, and her shoulders quiver. "I-I went through this once before. Can't go there again. The Unseen is an evil place. I need to get as far away as I can from that world and the beings who live there."

"I do not live there anymore."

"But you're still one of those creatures." She lifts her head to look straight into my eyes. "I can't ever see you again. Please accept my decision and stay away. You know what I went through with Balder, and getting kidnapped by the dragon king just brought that all rushing back. I hope you find whatever it is you need, but I can't be a part of it."

When I reach out to touch her, she turns and runs toward the shop. The door slams shut behind her.

For a moment, I stand here as if my body has morphed into stone, like the statuary that surround me. I don't even breathe. A mortal would pass out from lack of oxygen if they refused to breathe for several minutes. But I can go hours or even days without inhaling.

Yet I can't convince Amanda to stay with me.

The door to the shop bursts open.

My heart thuds, and I swivel my head toward the building. But it's not Amanda who emerges. A weight seems to have fallen on top of me, forcing me to remain stationary while Tris marches up the hill to the rock garden.

"You okay, Cyneric? Amanda just called for a taxi to take her to the airport. We all offered to teleport her to wherever she needs to go, but she didn't want any part of that. What went down between you two?"

"Amanda despises me."

"Come on, that can't be true. She asked me and Riley to check on you now and then to make sure you're okay. She cares what happens to you."

I raise my hands, turning them palms up, and study the way they tremble slightly. What is this? I have never experienced such a sensation before. "If she cares for me, why would she run away?"

"Don't know. But we can figure this out together."

"You despise me as well. Yet you and the salamanders have assisted me."

Tris shoves his hands into his pants pockets. "Look, I know that people can change and they can have things in their past that can push them to do awful things. We all forgave Larissa for her past. And we're willing to give you the chance to prove we can trust you."

No one should trust me. Should they? Tris and his friends used to say that I'm dangerous and unpredictable, unstable too. Now they want to give me a chance to prove myself. I can't comprehend their attitude toward me.

I try to take a step but freeze as the world seems to sway around me.

Tris grasps my upper arm. "You okay, Cyneric? Don't look so hot. Maybe you should sit down on that bench over there."

"No. I do not need to sit. I need to…" My words trail off as I sway yet again, this time stumbling forward. I can't catch my breath. "I will be fine. Leave me."

"Can't do that. You need more help than you realize."

When he reaches for my arm again, I try to scuffle down the hill to head for the shop. But I make it only one step before everything around me spins like a top, and I fall to my knees, gasping for breath.

Tris kneels beside me. "What's going on, Cyneric? You've always been rock steady and sure of yourself. Now you look like you might barf."

He isn't calling me "Captain Fang" anymore. That must mean I'm in a dangerously weakened state. I do feel…not myself. I slump forward, slapping my hands on the ground for support.

"Max! Travis!" Tris shouts. "Get out here! Emergency!"

My arms give out, and I fall face-first onto the ground.

Tris rolls me onto my back. "Hang on, buddy. We'll figure out what's wrong, don't worry. Two salamanders, a former sylph, my wife, and a former goddess are all sprinting this way."

"Amanda…"

"Take it easy. We can talk about that later."

"But I must…"

A rhythmic pounding erupts inside my head, drowning out all other sounds. I clutch my head and squeeze my eyes shut while cold sweat dribbles down my temples. A sharp cry is unleashed. That can't be my voice. A pain like none I have ever felt before seizes me, and I can't stop my body from wrenching into a pretzel-like position.

And I scream.

CHAPTER SEVENTEEN

RILEY CROUCHES BESIDE TRIS. HER EYES ARE WIDE. "HE'S DYING. BUT A vampire can't die because he's immortal." She lays a hand on my forehead, where a clammy sweat sheaths my skin. "Hold on, Cyneric. We'll find a way to help you."

Nevan stands behind them, bent over to scrutinize me. "We should get him to the vortex."

The salamanders hover behind Nevan.

"Why didn't you think of that, Tris?" Max asks. "Well, come on, let's leg it to the vortex. Who wants to carry the bloodsucker?"

Nevan shoos the others away and throws me over his shoulder. The force that has twisted my entire body complicates the task of transporting me the mortal way, but Nevan manages to get there without dropping me. Then he sets me down down inside the healing vortex.

The others form a circle around the vortex, staying clear of the stone benches that serve as the boundary of the healing energies.

Nothing happens.

I writhe about even more now, and cries like none I have heard from any being emerge from me. The agony grows more intense rather than lessening. How can this be? The vortex heals. It doesn't inflict torture.

"Get him out of there!" Riley shouts. "Get him out now!"

Nevan grabs my feet and drags me away from the vortex. "What the bloody hell was that? Tris, you are the guardian of the healing vortex. Why did it attempt to kill Cyneric?"

"You think I know?" Tris stretches out an arm, waving it in the air inside the vortex. "The energies feel normal to me. I have no frigging clue what's going on. Something must be interfering with the vortex."

"Like what?" Max asks. "You're the expert on this rubbish."

Riley bites her bottom lip. "Do you think Cyneric might be cursed? Like Tris was a while back? Drakon cursed him, and now big daddy Thirío is harassing Cyneric. Seems like there must be a connection."

The agony has subsided, at least enough that I can heave myself into a sitting position. "Thirío was Drakon's uncle, not his father."

"I know. But he's the big daddy of the dragon world, right? I mean, he's the king, after all."

"Yes, that is true." I rub my neck, wincing at the lingering stiffness in my muscles.

Riley settles the back of her hand on my forehead. "You don't have a fever. Elementals run a higher temperature than mortals all the time, but now that I'm an elemental too, I can judge your temperature."

Travis has been hovering behind the others, arms crossed, observing the goings-on in front of him. "Maybe he is cursed after all. Can't think of another reason why the vortex would get itself cocked up that way."

"But I can," Larissa says. "Cyneric has a ton of inner turmoil. Can't you guys see that? He's confused and scared."

"I am not scared," I snarl. "Nothing frightens me."

"That's bollocks," Travis declares. "You're afraid of losing Amanda."

"Who is Amanda?" Nevan asks. "I've not been fully briefed on the current situation."

Travis pats Nevan's shoulder. "You actually paid attention all those times I used cop-speak. That's touching, Tarzan."

I squint at Nevan. "Why does he call you Tarzan?"

Larissa laughs. "Because Nevan used to trot around in the woods wearing nothing but a loincloth. I loved it when he was at my temple and I got to check out his almost-naked bod."

"Oh yeah, I check him out too," Riley chimes in. "Any chance you'll dig out the old loincloth again, Nevan?"

"Silence!" I roar. Once everyone has ceased their chattering, I clamber to my feet. "I should never have asked the question."

"Feeling better, Captain Fang?" Tris asks. "You don't have that gonna-barf look on your face anymore."

"I have recovered. Now, I need to find Amanda."

Larissa touches my arm. "Sweetie, maybe you should give her some time. The poor woman has been through a lot lately."

And all of that is my fault. I must explain. I must see her. I must...feel her body pressed to mine or else I will lose my mind.

Max points at me. "Uh, why are his eyes doing that?"

"Doing what?" Nevan asks. Then he leans in to stare into my eyes. His brows shoot up. "What the—I have never seen any elemental's eyes do that. They seem to be swirling with actual blood."

Travis's lip curls. "Actual blood? That's disgusting."

"We need to get Bob or Ken," Riley says. "The oracles will know what to do."

"Good idea." Travis throws his head back. "Bob! Ken! One of you needs to get your arse out here immediately."

Bob appears, though he materialized a good distance away from me.

"Can you help?" Riley asks the oracle. "Something weird is going on with Cyneric."

"Hmm." Bob moves closer but still maintains a distance from me. "The vampire is highly unstable."

"Duh, Bob."

The oracle assumes an imperious demeanor. "Do not harass me. I have come to help you, and sarcasm is entirely inappropriate in this situation. If you had let me finish, I would've told you that Cyneric is highly unstable, more so than ever before."

"Perfect," Travis says. "That's just what we need."

"Isn't Cyneric your friend now? You've gone to a great deal of trouble on his behalf."

"Yes, we want to help. That doesn't mean we can't bitch about it."

"Of course." Bob inches closer to me, seeming wary though I have never known an oracle to behave that way. "He is not cursed, that much I can tell at a glance. Neither is he ensorcelled or enchanted. But something is brewing inside him."

"He's about to spew coffee all over us?"

Bob rolls his eyes. "Don't be so juvenile, salamander. I'm trying to tell you that Cyneric is changing, and whether that will result in a better version of him or a far deadlier one, I cannot yet foresee."

"Brilliant," Max declares. "You foresaw absolutely nothing."

The oracle at last approaches me. He aims his gaze directly into mine. "Listen to me, Cyneric. You have already been warned, but I will reinforce what Janus and the Four Winds have said. You hold the power to destroy both worlds if you so choose. You must continue your quest to find Eros, for only by understanding your past can you hope to save the future of the multiverse. The choice is yours."

"Amanda—"

"I cannot advise you on how to handle a romantic entanglement."

Oracles are irritatingly vague and often unhelpful. But I need to get one answer from him. "How did Setesh retain his memories? And why does Thirío believe I am responsible for his nephew's demise?"

That might actually have been a request for two answers. Although "request" isn't the most accurate description. I growled the words.

"Your quest will reveal the truth." He snaps his fingers. "Good luck, Cyneric."

The world vanishes as I am sucked down into the abyssal tunnel, tumbling wildly until I crash to the ground. Once again, I land face-down—this time, in a slimy puddle of muck that encompasses my whole body. I push up into a kneeling position, breathing hard from the rough journey. Once I've sufficiently recovered, I stand up and stretch.

Where am I now?

Lightning lances the sky far away from here, and thunder rumbles in the distance. The storm has moved off, leaving behind puddles and mud. The scent of the rain invigorates me, though I had never experienced that before now. Either I have been dropped off somewhere near Amanda or somewhere near Eros. I do not wish to see my father, not yet. I need to assure myself that Amanda is well, even if she doesn't want to see me.

I stand within a circular area where the plant life has been trampled by an unknown force, laying the vegetation flat but in a swirling pattern. The mud puddle in which I had landed lies in the exact center of the circle. Everywhere around me, outside the circle, five-foot-tall plants fill an enormous field. Their reddish-yellow tops sway in the breeze. I might enjoy the scenery if I didn't have a mission to undertake. A quest, others have called it. Before I can search for answers, I must determine where I am.

As I turn toward the circle's perimeter, preparing to march through the field of red plants, I hear a gasp behind me. I freeze and listen, then slowly rotate toward the sound. Two human hearts are beating, and I hear their breaths as well.

"You may come out now," I say. "I know you're there."

The tall plants shiver and rustle as two figures emerge. They halt at the periphery of the area in which I stand. These creatures appear to be children. I don't like to converse with the young versions of mortals because they speak even more strangely than the adults do. These children are male. One wears glasses, while the other has a cap on his head that appears to be on backward.

"What are you doing out here, mister?" the boy with glasses asks. "You're all dirty."

"Are you in a drug cartel?" the other boy asks. "Wyatt and me saw a show about that on TV."

The child with glasses nods. "Yeah. And we saw it when you fell out of the sky, mister. Didn't we?"

Wyatt nods vigorously. "You're an alien, ain't you?"

"I have no idea what you are talking about."

"Aliens ain't British," Tyler says. "And they're supposed to be gray. If you aren't an alien, mister, why are you standing in a crop circle?"

I'm standing in a what? Mortal children are insane.

The two boys whisper to each other while pointing at my soiled clothing. Then the one called Wyatt says, "You should jump in a crick to get cleaned up."

A crick? That word makes no sense. But I decide I should get cleaned up, so with one thought, I cleanse my clothing and my body.

The boys gape at me.

"Wow, that's awesome," Tyler says. "Can you teach me how to do that?"

"No." I glance at the tall vegetation that surrounds us. "What manner of plants are these?"

"Sorghum," Wyatt says. "My dad grows it 'cause he can make flour from it, and lots of people 'round here buy that at the farmer's market."

"Where am I?"

"Ten miles west of Amarillo."

A feeling of triumph surges through me, and I straighten my posture. "Do you know a woman called Amanda Nelson?"

The boys exchange glances and both shrug. Wyatt tells me, "Sorry. Never heard of her. Do you have a name?"

"I am Cyneric."

"No last name? Like a singer or a movie star?"

"Yes." Though I have no explanation for why I ask, I do it anyway. "How old are you and your friend?"

"I'm eight. Tyler turned nine four months and three days ago. But he's not my friend. He's my cousin."

The ages of these children should not matter to me. Why, then, am I engaging them in conversation? I should go. But I remain rooted to this spot.

Wyatt tiptoes closer to me and whispers, "If you're not an alien, are you a superhero?"

"No." Whatever a superhero is, I'm certain the title does not describe me.

Tyler comes up beside his cousin. "Look at his eyes. They aren't like mine or yours. They kinda swish around."

"Swish?" Wyatt snorts. "You're such a dweeb."

The way they look at me, with admiration and awe, spurs me to do something I shouldn't. I lean toward them and bare my fangs, letting them slide out all the way. "Can you guess what I am now?"

At first, they remain frozen with their gazes glued to mine. Then they both grin.

"This is soooo awesome," Tyler says. "We met a vampire. Can you turn into a bat?"

"No. And I'm afraid I must go now."

I try to teleport, but that power still won't work. So I nod to the boys, then I race through the field of sorghum faster than any human could travel on foot. Perhaps not all children are horrible little demons who screech and unleash revolting discharge from their bodies. Tyler and Wyatt seemed reasonably intelligent.

When I reach my destination, I halt at the large sign that declares this is Amarillo. I shouldn't have wasted time talking to children, but I felt the strangest urge to converse with someone, anyone, so I wouldn't be alone. Now that I'm here, in the city where Amanda lives, I have no idea what to do next. Will she be staying in the same place where I had last seen her before the dragon king abducted her? I don't know where that would be.

Though I know it won't work, I close my eyes and pray to be sent directly to Amanda.

"Gah, Cyneric! Would you please stop scaring the shit out of me?"

The sound of Amanda's voice sends a pulse of pure joy through me. I open my eyes and haul her into my arms, kissing her so thoroughly that she seems dazed when I finally give up her mouth.

She blinks her eyes slowly several times. Then a smile stretches her lips. She grasps my face with both hands, giving me a quick, firm kiss before she…slaps me hard. "You bastard. I told you to stay away."

"But you seemed happy to see me a moment ago."

"Maybe I was, but only because you sneaked up on me. Having the power to teleport doesn't give you free rein to invade my privacy." She drops onto the sofa, slouching into it. "I'm trying to figure out what the hell I feel. You being here makes that even harder."

"Would you mind if I sit?" When she shrugs, I take that as permission to settle onto the sofa. "Doesn't the way you greeted me indicate that you know how you feel? I rescued you from Thirío and from an earthquake. How can you not love me after all of that?"

Her expression goes blank. She stares at me for so long that I begin to worry the entire world has ground to a halt. But then she rests her head in her hands, covering her face, and laughs. After a moment, she raises her head and laughs even more uproariously. Her eyes water. She eventually stops laughing and grabs a tissue from the end table, dabbing her eyes and blowing her nose with it. "Sometimes you're hilarious, though I know you don't mean to be funny."

"Will you answer my question?"

"No, Cyneric, I will not."

CHAPTER EIGHTEEN

SHE TURNS TOWARD ME, HOOKING ONE LEG BENEATH HER. "You can't ask a question like that, not after everything that's gone down lately. I need time to figure things out. And I can't do that if you're here looking like sin on wheels and smelling like the most decadent dessert in the universe. I can't think straight when you're here."

"We live in the multiverse. The universe is simply a part of that."

She rests her elbow on the sofa's back, then drops her forehead into her raised palm. "You're impossible. No matter what I say, you have some adorably confused response that makes me want to hug you."

"I would not be opposed to a hug, but I would prefer to fuck."

"Pull back on the reins, cowboy. Your horse is running away with you."

I glance around the apartment. "There are no horses here. But I did meet two young boys while I was inside a crop circle."

She lifts her head, and her brows hike up. "Crop circle? Where have you been, kid?"

"I landed in the mortal world twenty-eight minutes ago, ten miles west of Amarillo, in a field of sorghum."

"Oh. Well, that makes perfect sense." She slumps against the sofa again and sighs. "When I said I needed time, I meant more than a few hours."

"Has it only been that long? I assumed weeks would have passed, like the other times when I found you again." I desperately need to touch her, but I don't want to upset her any further. "I wish I could give you what you want and simply walk away, but I can't do that. My friends have told me that I have an obsessive nature. That's why I can't stay away from you."

"You think you're obsessed with me."

"Isn't that what you believe?"

She chews on her lip while studying me. "No, Cyneric, I don't think you're obsessed. Not sure what this is between us, but obsession isn't the word I would use."

How she can believe that, I don't know. Hasn't my behavior proved that I'm unstable? Of course, Tris and his mates have tried to help me which suggests they don't deem me to be dangerous and obsessive. But my past behavior doesn't mesh with what others believe about me.

"You don't know the things I've done, Amanda. If you understood, you would agree that I am unhinged. Everyone knows it."

"Unhinged? No, that is definitely not you."

"But you said Thirío told you things about me, implying that those were unpleasant revelations."

"Even if they were, I know I shouldn't believe anything that a dragon man tells me about you. I've seen the good in you, and I believe you care about me."

"But you don't know me. The way I was, what I turned into."

"Then show me."

Something deep inside me urges me to believe her, to do what she asks. But I don't deserve her understanding or her forgiveness. "You told me that the Unseen is an evil place and you need to escape from that world and the beings who live in it—which includes me. You need more than a few hours to change your mind."

Amanda crawls toward me on her knees, then sits back on her heels. Now inches away from me, she reaches out to lay a hand on my cheek. "Everything that's happened lately brought back all the bad memories of what Balder did to me. A little downtime helped me relax and reflect."

"Reflect on what?"

"Us. I can't just walk away from you, I know that now." She wraps her arms around me, and her lips brush my ear. "I should never have run away. But I know what I should do. Show me yourself, Cyneric, the good and the bad."

I feel my brows tightening as I stare at her. She can't want to know about my past behavior. It's abominable. "You don't understand what you're asking of me. And only a matter of hours ago, you swore you did not want anything to do with me."

Amanda pulls away just enough that she can look into my eyes. She taps my nose with one finger. "Don't be so pessimistic. Thirío wants to split us apart, so let's not allow that to happen. You have incredible powers, and even your friends don't understand what you can do. Show me, Cyneric, show me everything."

For a moment, I can't summon any words. Amanda continues to gaze at me with a sort of affection no one has ever shown me before. Eros claimed to love me, yet I never felt that bond. Ensorcellment forced me to love my father, though he did not deserve my adoration. I know that now. But how can I explain all of that to Amanda?

I have incredible powers. She told me that. Even Janus and my mates know it's true. Why can't I employ those powers to help me show Amanda what I've been through, what I've done, and how all of that has affected me? Only Janus has the power to alter time. But perhaps I don't need to travel into the past. I need only let Amanda into my memories to reveal myself to her.

She leans back against the sofa. "I can practically see the little gears turning inside your mind. What plan are you devising?"

"Not a plan, per se. But I believe I can do precisely what you asked—show you everything about myself, literally." I bow my head. "This would mean joining our minds."

"I can handle it, sweetie. Trust me."

"Before we do this, I should show you what I previously looked like. I need to glamour to do that. It means I'll use magics to alter my appearance."

She nods, and I focus on creating a false image of myself, though in this case, the falsity is not that I'm pretending to be another individual. It's that I no longer appear this way. Amanda tilts her head side to side, then leans in.

And she kisses me.

When she pulls away, I simply stare at her.

She smiles. "You assumed I'd freak out if I saw the old you. I'm not panicking, Cyneric. Beauty is more than physical. It's something inside you, a light that no one else can tap into."

"But I am hideous." I bare my teeth to ensure she sees them. "My skin is pale, almost gray, and my eyes are red. My canine teeth, my fangs, are much longer and more animal-like too. They are also discolored by all the blood I've drunk."

"I get that you expect me to cringe, but I'm not a twenty-something girl who screams when she watches horror movies on TV. I've lived a horror movie." She kisses my forehead. "You can't scare me away, hon."

Though she seems to honestly not care about my past appearance, I can't quite accept that she means it. "In all my time in the Unseen before Eros returned me and my brothers to our former beauty, I never met anyone who did not cringe at the sight of me. Some recoiled in disgust. Others recoiled in fear. But you...do nothing of the sort."

"Have you ever heard the phrase beauty is only skin deep?"

"Yes. I assumed that referred to cosmetic surgery."

She laughs. "You can be so adorably ignorant of this world. That saying means that it isn't your looks that make you who you are. It's your heart and soul."

I get rid of the glamour, returning to my usual appearance. "My heart and soul might not be as beautiful as you believe."

"Get on with it, Cyneric. Stop trying to convince me you're evil."

"As you wish." I pull her close, wrapping my arms around her. "We will not leave this room, but staying in close proximity seems like the most prudent choice. I'm not able to control my powers as easily as I used to."

"If you want to hug me, you don't need an excuse."

"Well, ah, I—"

"Take a deep breath, then relax and just do it, hon."

I follow her instructions, taking several slow, deep breaths before I attempt this feat that I have never tried to accomplish before. She rests her head on my shoulder, and we both close our eyes at the same time, though I hadn't suggested we should do that. It simply happened. Now, I let my thoughts travel back in time to the moments that I need to show her, so that Amanda will understand what I've done and decide if she wants to be with me. If she realizes she does not want that...I'll deal with the consequences later.

The contemporary world sifts away, and the past takes hold.

I stand inside the Temple of Eros, staying at the periphery in the shadows, as my father bade me to do. He likes me to watch while he defiles women, and sometimes men too, in the worst ways imaginable and others methods that no living creature aside from Eros could envision. With my father, torture always involved sex. That was his forte, after all. Eros, the god of sex and pleasure. This is the first orgy Eros ever brought me to, and I have no idea what to expect. Though I know I should not watch, I can't deny my father anything. I realize he has ensorcelled me, but I can't summon the strength to break free because the magics are too strong and I am too weak-willed.

Eros strides into the large pool that occupies the center of the room, sauntering down the steps into the deepest. Once, I had sneaked in here to dip my fingers into the pool, curious about what it would feel like. I know the water is warm and silky, deliciously sensual, as if magics flow within every molecule. Now, my father stands at the bottom of the steps in water that rises to his chest level.

He raises his arms. "Come children, it is time to feed me your pleasure."

Five women and three men wade into the pool and surround Eros. His lips warp into a self-satisfied smile as his subjects begin to perform various sexual acts on him and each other, following his edicts. When he commands them to engage in an orgy, they do it without complaint. They cannot complain, though, because they're ensorcelled like me. Do they realize that they are being abused? Or am I the only one who understands that?

As I watch the orgy going on in the pool, my cock begins to thicken. This is the first time I experienced sexual desire, and it confuses me. Yet an impulse I cannot deny urges me to stroke my erection through my clothing as I watch Eros fucking a beautiful woman. My gaze remains on her, not him. The ecstasy on her face makes my cock throb, and I want to leap across the distance between us to take her from behind while my father continues fucking her. But I don't do that. I won't do it. Yet I want it with a hunger that burns inside me.

More than sex, though, I want her blood.

After the orgy has ended, Eros leads me out of the bathhouse. "You wanted that fire-haired girl, didn't you, my son?"

"Yes, Father."

His mouth kinks upward at one corner. "You will never know the pleasure of a woman's body, Cyneric. I have ensured that."

"But why?"

"I command it, that is why. You are the reason why I fucked the fire-haired girl. She saw you this morning and asked if she could be with you." His expression twists into something more vile and angry than I've ever seen from him. "I am a god. Your god. No woman will have you above me. Do you understand, Cyneric?"

"Yes, Father."

That night, after Eros had drunken himself into unconsciousness with magically enhanced beverages and food, I sneaked out of the royal chambers and found the red-haired girl, sniffing her out with the superior senses every vampire has. I didn't want to claim her body, though. I craved something else from her, something that my father would never approve of and would probably destroy me for attempting. Until this night, I had survived on the blood of lowly elementals—gnomes, undines, harpies, whoever my father provided for me.

On this night, I sank my fangs into the soft flesh of a beautiful fae's throat and drank deeply. The flavor her intoxicated me, and I lay in bed with her afterward until the high faded.

Then I went back to Eros, who never knew what I had done.

My psyche returns to the present and the woman who lies cradled in my arms on a sofa in the City of Amarillo, Texas. "That is only the tip of the iceberg, as mortals like to say."

"That's the horrible thing you did? Sounds like teenage rebellion rather than a bad, bad thing."

"I seduced a fae girl and drank her blood."

"Yeah, I got the picture. But she wanted you too, didn't she?" When I nod, she gives me a tolerant smile. "Hon, you are punishing yourself for things that aren't vile acts. Unless you've got something worse to show me."

"I do."

"Okay. But take me with you this time."

"What?"

She shifts position to straddle my lap and plasters her body to mine once again. "I want to experience your memories the same way you do. Take me with you, Cyneric, into your past."

"I don't know if I can do that."

"You can. Aren't you the most powerful, unstoppable elemental in the multiverse?"

Perhaps I can take her with me into the memories. Why not? I've accomplished feats that no other creature has. "All right. You will come with me this time."

"Where are we going?"

"To a time long after my indiscretion with the fae girl, when Eros prepared to offer vampires to Hathor."

CHAPTER NINETEEN

Eros has summoned me and my brothers to the peristyle, his favorite spot for making grand pronouncements. I have no idea what he intends to announce today. He never tells me beforehand. My father relishes the opportunity to engender curiosity and excitement in his subjects. Now, he stands before us with his chin lifted and a smug smile on his lips.

He raises his arms. "My children, this is a glorious day. I shall give the goddess Hathor a wondrous gift that will solidify our bond and ensure that she will joyously agree to become my consort for life."

We all stand still and silent, though I know that, like me, my brothers feel a powerful joy at anything that might please our father. A few of my brothers cry. Some clasp their hands and shut their eyes as if they're overcome by the wonderful news. I react differently. I simply stand here watching, waiting, knowing I am meant to be thrilled but feeling only the barest excitement. My ability to experience sheer joy at anything my father does has waned. I don't understand why. I know only that my love for Eros has changed over the millennia since that night when I tasted a fae girl's blood. Something inside me has shifted, and nothing can reverse the change. I am different, strange, alone.

But now, as I travel back to that moment, I am no longer alone. Amanda stands beside me, holding my hand.

"You can do this," she tells me. "Show me what happened on this day."

As I share this event with her, I don't speak aloud. I know she understands what is happening, but not because I narrate the moment. No, I can feel that she hears my thoughts and I hear hers.

A bolt of lightning slams down on the peristyle, splitting it in half. Every elemental in attendance for Eros's announcement scatters away from the smoking hole the bolt has carved out. I remain in place. But Eros has been bowled over backward since he stood nearest to the strike. He springs to his feet and bares his gritted teeth, snarling like an animal.

I feel something I have not experienced before. I think I'm feeling…humor. Yes, I want to laugh at my father because he's covered in marble dust and the track of the lightning bolt scorched a jagged line across his chest. As a god, he cannot die in this manner. Still, I know I should not laugh at him. So, I contain my humor and remain impassive while inside I mock him with my thoughts. *Not the all-powerful god now, are you, Eros? You look like a child who just found out he received a block of granite as a birthday gift.*

Amanda snorts, as if she's trying not to laugh at me. "Your vampire humor needs a little work, hon. But it's adorable that you were thinking of ways to mock Eros."

"He would not have seen it that way." I wince now because I know what is about to transpire here on the peristyle. "This is the moment when everything changed."

Amanda moves closer, snuggling up to my side. "Let's watch it together, then you can tell me how this event affected you. By the way, what is a peristyle?"

"It is an outdoor area enclosed by columns in ancient Greek architecture. May we continue now?"

"Yes, absolutely."

While Eros fumes, many of my brothers gather around him to wipe the dust off his body. Then a high-pitched whistling erupts overhead, and a shape plummets toward the ground at such high velocity that I can't discern what it is. But as the object draws closer and closer, I begin to believe it is a being rather than a projectile. My suspicion is confirmed when the god Setesh touches down on the marble floor of the peristyle.

He glances at Eros and smirks. "You are quite a mess. Perhaps your vampires will bathe you with their tongues." His expression morphs into sarcastic surprise. "Oh, but then they might grow hungry and latch on to your veins. It would a terrible tragedy if the amazing Eros were drained to the point of destruction."

Eros shoves my brothers away and scowls at Setesh. "You slimy little toad. Why have you invaded my home and interrupted a ritual?"

"You really should ensorcell all your subjects. Then no one would be able to share gossip with me."

"Gossip? About what? All my subjects are thoroughly ensorcelled."

But not me. This was the moment when I knew with complete certainty that Eros did not have as powerful a hold on me as he believed. Maybe I have always been different. I don't know. But when this event occurred, I realized I had power that my father knew nothing about.

"Would you like to know who betrayed you?" Setesh asks. "It must be galling for a majestic god such as you to learn of a leak in your bucket."

As far as I know, I am the only one who isn't fully ensorcelled. But I have never gossiped with anyone.

Setesh moves closer to Eros and leans toward him. "It was your beloved Hathor. She is no longer under your thumb. But you already knew that, didn't you? She was your consort for a very long time—until I stole her away from you."

"You lie. Hathor would never betray me."

"Of course she would, for I ensorcelled her. And I shall ruin your vampires the way I ruined her."

Eros clenches his fists so tightly that blood dribbles from between his fingers. "How do you know about my children?"

Setesh laughs. "Everyone knows. You aren't very good at hiding your secret project. Occasionally, you fail to fully ensorcell one of your subjects when they arrive at your temple. Hathor heard rumors, and she shared them with me."

"I never forget. My mind is an iron trap."

Setesh laughs. "You are pathetic. It's no wonder that Hathor prefers my glorious member"—He palms his cock—"to your shriveled snake."

Eros tries to throw a punch, but Setesh catches his fist in one hand and shoves Eros hard enough that the god falls to the ground.

Though I might not be fully ensorcelled anymore, I still feel a compulsion to protect my father. I don't wish to do it, but I can't stop myself from hurrying to his side to defend him. "You will never touch the almighty Eros again."

"Almighty?" Setesh says with a chuckle. "You poor, deluded little vampire. Do you believe your creator would protect you? Of course he won't. Eros is the vainest, most egotistical being in the multiverse."

I lunge for Setesh, but he bats me away like a fly. I soar across the peristyle and plunge into the pool, sinking to the bottom before I can gather my wits enough to climb out. Once I'm on my feet again, I shake myself to get rid of the water pouring from my body and clothing. Then I rush to Eros.

Amanda whispers to me, "I know this isn't the right time, but I'll forget if I don't ask you now."

"What is it?"

"How does everyone in your memory speak English? This was tens of thousands of years ago, right?"

"It was."

She glances at the two gods and puckers her lips. "Is your mind translating whatever language they are speaking?"

"No. They use the language you hear. Elementals gave humans the seeds of many tongues, since we existed long before mortals learned to speak. The gods particularly did so."

"I get it. Go on with your memory."

The tableau before us had frozen while we discussed Amanda's question. Now, the scene comes to life once more. Setesh kicks Eros in the groin, and the god flies backward into me. I stumble but just manage to avoid being crushed under my father.

Setesh grins. "You are weak, Eros, and I will ensure that Hathor never accepts your gift."

He waves his arms while chanting in the old language, the one used only by sorcerers and fae witches. While his words echo off the columns of the peristyle, sizzling energies crawl under my skin and burrow deep into my body, twisting my nerves and tendons, gnawing at my flesh until nothing remains but a cloud of magics that seem determined to reshape me from the inside out. The process lasts only a moment, but it feels as if it goes on for an eternity.

At last, the agony ends.

I remained standing throughout the process, and now I test my new body. It feels very different. Not like me at all. In some ways, I've grown stronger but mostly I feel as if I've been forced into the skin of another being. My body feels cold, inside and out, and a hunger I have never experienced before compels me to feed. Not even that fae I tasted made me hunger for blood this much.

When I glance down at my body, I freeze. This is not me. Why do I have pale skin? My fangs have grown much longer too, which I can feel when I run my tongue over them. I shuffle over to the pool and gaze down at my reflection, stunned by the redness in my eyes. What has Eros done to me?

"Uh, wait a second," Amanda says. "Didn't you tell me that the blood of elementals can't sustain you? But you drank from a fae."

"Only since my most recent transformation have I developed an allergy to elemental blood. My mates believe my kind lost the ability to enjoy drinking blood when Eros created us, but they are misinformed."

"How did they get it wrong?"

"You will see."

Eros clambers to his feet and glowers at Setesh. "You grubby little worm. You have ruined my gift to Hathor, and you shall pay for that."

Setesh chuckles. "I have done more than make them ugly. I've made certain that my beloved Hathor will never return to you."

My father leaps at Setesh, about to wring the god's neck, but Setesh vanishes. Eros roars.

Then he turns to us. "You, my children, are no longer a great gift. If I cannot punish Setesh for his trickery, then I shall avenge myself on you, my sons. Henceforth, you will not enjoy consuming blood, though you will continue to need it to survive."

With a simple wave of his hand, he casts the curse upon us.

The memory fades away, and the apartment comes back into view. I still have Amanda held to my body. I'd assumed that reliving the moment when I had been fundamentally altered without my consent would turn out to be a terrible experience. But with Amanda by my side, I suffered no fear or anger. I simply viewed my own past the way mortals watch films in a cinema. Yes, I had entered such an establishment once, but I only saw a "cartoon." Those do not appeal to me.

"How are you feeling?" Amanda asks. "You don't look traumatized. That's a good sign."

"I feel no trauma or fear, not even anger. I believe having you with me proved essential."

"Glad I could help. Is that all? Because I'm not horrified by what I saw. Your so-called father abused you, and I can understand how that might make your mental state a touch precarious."

"You said I am not unstable."

"And I meant it." She combs her fingers through my hair in a soothing manner, and I don't mind that she does that. It feels quite good. "I said you might be a touch precarious. That just means you need some TLC. That's tender loving care, by the way."

"But you do not love me."

"I care about you, hon. I care a lot." She continues to caress my scalp, and my eyes fall halfway closed. "What we just saw isn't everything, is it?"

"No."

"Would you mind telling me about Hathor? Your relationship with her?"

I close my eyes all the way and sigh with a depth of satisfaction that I have never known before. Her touch does this to me. "I had no relationship with Hathor. It was an obsession."

"So, I wasn't the first one you latched on to."

"No. Hathor was the first. Then came Larissa, who is the former goddess Hathor, and after that came Riley. She is married to Tris, the copper fae who prefers to be called a leprechaun."

"Is Larissa married too?"

"Yes. Her husband is Travis the incubus." Though I would prefer not to do it, I know I must continue with showing Amanda my past. "Are you ready for the next memory?"

"Of course. Whenever you're ready."

With her body molded to mine, I feel as if I could do anything. But mostly, I want to sink into the warmth of her flesh and the sweetness of her scent. Right now, I must continue with my quest to prove to her that I am wicked. Why? Reliving two memories hadn't convinced Amanda of my rotten core, and in fact, she seems to like me even more now. But the worst is yet to come.

I shut my eyes. With Amanda as my anchor, I allow myself to sink into the past, into the day when I met the goddess Hathor.

Chapter Twenty

Eros leads me down a corridor where brightly painted murals on the white walls depict the goddess Hathor and her worshippers. They bow down before her, kiss her feet, and prostrate themselves in various ways. Eros might be vainglorious, but even he doesn't stoop to decorating his temple with images of himself being worshiped. Two guards accompany us to the doors of the throne room, where we must halt and await entry. The guards push the wooden doors open, then wave for us to enter.

I gaze up at the opening in the ceiling that allows the sunlight to pour into the room, gilding the space with its golden light. I have never seen a place such as this. Egyptian motifs decorate the walls, and naturally, they depict the goddess being worshiped by her devotees. In reality, they must all be ensorcelled. Our guards ferry us to the stepped dais that holds the golden throne upon which the goddess sits. I can't help admiring her body, for she displays it with an openness and casual attitude that makes her even more alluring.

She wears only a leather belt with an ornate strap that hangs down between her thighs. Her long, dark hair cascades over her shoulders, concealing most of her breasts. Hathor is incredible. Voluptuous, brazen, haughty, sensual. A thousand more words could describe her, but only one matters. She is a goddess in every way, and I am transfixed by her.

No, she cannot ensorcell me. Eros has already done that.

Hathor casually swings one foot while tapping her fingernails on the arms of her throne. She eyes us with her chin lifted, as if we are inconsequential to her. "What do you want, Eros? You may bathe my feet with your tongue, or perhaps you would prefer to simply prostrate yourself before me." She waves a hand imperiously. "Go on, then. Demonstrate your devotion to me."

I can see a muscle ticking in Eros's jaw.

My father curls his lip at the haughty goddess. "I created you, Hathor, from my own magics. You belong to me."

She huffs and rolls her eyes. "I belong to you? What a poor, deluded creature you are."

Amanda and I stand inside the throne room, experiencing this memory in three dimensions. It feels odd. I can recall this moment in vivid detail, and yet it seems as if this event happened to someone else. Does that mean I have changed? And if so, is the change good or bad?

"Hold up a sec," Amanda says. "In this memory, Eros told Hathor that he created her. Doesn't that mean she's your sister or aunt or something? Eros created you too, and you call him Father. That suggests she had an incestuous relationship with him."

"I never thought of it that way. But I call Eros my father because he told me that is what he is. Whether magics constitute a true familial connection, I can't say."

"Hmm." She clasps my hand with both of hers, threading our fingers. "I think Eros is one diabolical bastard. He convinced Hathor that she loves him and she's his lover. Then he convinced you that he's your father. Whatever he thinks will work to get someone under his thumb, he goes for it."

"Eros is not inherently evil."

"Bullshit. He's rotten to the core. Neither you or Hathor got the chance to decide for yourselves how to live your own lives." She rests her head on my upper arm. "But let's watch the rest of this memory play out. I want to know exactly how it all went down."

The way she keeps her hand wrapped around mine makes me feel that I can deal with what is to come in these memories. The darkest parts have yet to be revealed.

Eros had been angry for days, long before we made our journey to the Temple of Hathor. The goddess had been spreading rumors about his virility, rumors that suggested he was waning in that area. For a literal sex god to endure such libel is something that cannot be tolerated. That explains why we stand inside Hathor's throne room today.

"Did you want something specific?" Hathor asks, as she snaps her fingers to call in two ensorcelled servants who begin to massage her shoulders. "I have so much work to do, after all. Maintaining the adoration of thousands of elementals and the occasional mortal is truly a burden. But I bear it willingly—for my devotees."

Eros walks onto the first step of the dais, but he can't go any further. Guards rush in to bar his way. His nostrils flare. "Who has ensorcelled you now, Hathor?"

"No one. I am free."

"Impossible. You know nothing of how to survive on your own. I cared for you for many epochs, and then Setesh stole you away. After him, Kamadeva became your master. What makes you believe you can survive without one of us?" He huffs again. "No female can stand on her own. They all need a master. Who is yours?"

Hathor leaps out of her chair. "No one owns me. I am free. But you cannot believe a woman could ever escape you. Your arrogance is revolting."

Eros marches up the steps, employing his vast powers to hurl the guards away when they attempt to intervene. He halts an arm's length from Hathor. "I have brought you a gift, my love, to prove my devotion to you."

His tone of voice does not convey the emotions that his words imply. Eros has never been rejected before, at least not since I have been alive.

The goddess glances every which way, rising onto her tiptoes, and even bends over to peek under her throne. "Where is this gift? I see none. Your presence is hardly enough to qualify as a reward."

She truly is a magnificent goddess.

I suspect Eros has never seen Hathor behave in such a dismissive and sarcastic manner. He seems as if he might burst into flames at any moment, so enraged that he cannot contain his fury for much longer. But my father is cunning. And he knows how to seduce anyone he likes, even without ensorcellment.

Eros forces himself to relax and cease clenching his fists. He even manages to stop snarling, instead employing his most ingratiating voice. "My glorious gift stands behind me. I offer you my children, including this vampire and dozens more."

He is giving me up to the goddess? I might adore her, but he is my father.

"Vampires?" Hathor says. "Move aside so I might see him."

Eros turns to the side and spreads an arm toward me.

Hathor stares at me blankly for a moment. She tips her head side to side, and her brows crinkle. Then her lip curls. She recoils and shakes her head. "If that is what all vampires are like, I refuse your offering."

"This is a glorious gift. Vampires are powerful, obedient creatures who will serve you well. They boast enormous strength and agility."

"I don't care." She flaps a hand toward me. "Take this…thing away from me. He is hideous."

"You cannot reject my gift."

"Of course I can." She claps her hands and waits for her worshippers and guards to approach the dais. "Escort these two out of my temple. If they resist, take whatever measures are necessary to rid me of them."

And just like that, the god Eros is banished from Hathor's temple precinct. He could have fought to reclaim her, but even Eros understood that forcing a goddess back into his fold would only cause more strife. Besides, he had a plan for winning her back, one that would play out over the course of thousands of years. Gods and elementals can afford to wait for what they want, since we are immortal.

"That's not the end of your story," Amanda says. "Tell me what happened the next time you met Hathor."

"The goddess was no more. When I saw her again, she had been transformed into the mortal Larissa, though she retained her memories of her previous life."

My memories take over once more, drawing me back to a few months ago when I had met Larissa, though I still believed she was Hathor. I had no conception of a god becoming a mortal, so naturally, I assumed she still had immense power. This was the day when Travis and Larissa had gone to Dendera in Egypt, hoping to escape from Setesh, Kamadeva, and Eros who each wanted to claim Larissa as their prize, possibly to ensorcell her or at least lord their power over her. They all knew the goddess had become a mere mortal. This was their opening and their last chance to seize her.

Eros had brought me and my brothers with him to Dendera, and he made a ridiculous show of transforming us into attractive beings to impress Larissa. She did not want his vampires any more now than she had thousands of years ago when he first offered us to her. She didn't recognize me either, thanks to what Setesh had done. His curse gave us red eyes and pasty skin and made us all look quite similar to one another.

In this moment from the past, Travis and Larissa have just entered the main structure at Dendera, a hall with high columns that block the sun. My kind had never been allergic to the sun until Kamadeva arrived at Dendera that day and cast a new curse upon us. We burst into flames. Many of my brothers died in the aftermath, unable to get to shelter quickly enough, but I and two dozen or so of my brothers made it into the temple. My body had not burst into flames as thoroughly as the others had. I was able to roll on the floor of the temple to douse myself. So, when Larissa saw me, she was not horrified.

When she entered the temple, she held a firearm in one hand as she searched for her lover, the incubus Travis. I could see him at the other end of the hall. But once I saw Larissa, my entire world telescoped down to her and only her as she wended her way through the crowd of vampires, most of whom lay on the floor writhing in agony and smoking from the flames that had overtaken them.

I stand in the center of the hall, amid my brothers, and study my surroundings without moving. My eyes dart. My chest heaves. I scratch at my scalp, still feeling the sting of the flames that had briefly scorched me. But my gaze keeps flicking back to the dark-haired goddess who walks among us. She doesn't seem to notice my presence until she bumps into me, startling herself, then attempts to move past.

But I grasp her arm. "Please, no sun."

My voice emerged as a raspy whisper.

Larissa offers me a kind smile. "You can stay in here where it's dark. You'll get used to the change. I know what it's like to be altered suddenly. It's hard, but you can adjust."

Yes, of course she understood my dilemma. She had been transformed into a mortal only two years earlier. I remember that day in her temple in the Unseen, when she had been kind to me just as she's doing now. But the mortal Larissa clearly cares more about others then herself now, unlike the goddess who behaved horribly at times.

My transformation, from hideous beast to attractive elemental, has left me confused and weakened. Coupled with my new aversion to the sun and the fact I had been in flames moments ago, I have trouble speaking. When I speak her name, it comes out haltingly. "Hathor."

She scrunches her brows, catching her lip between her teeth.

Have I frightened her? Now I appear to be beautiful, yet she seems to fear me, or more likely, what I might do to her. I try again to speak. "No slave."

Larissa pats my arm delicately, as if she worries how I might react to the touch. "You can be whatever you want. Don't let anyone force you to bend to their will."

Hathor had not allowed Eros to do that to her. She fought off not only my father, but also Kamadeva and Setesh. If she could fend them off and learn to survive on her own, perhaps I can too.

When she moves to walk away, I seize her hand. "Protect you. Die for you."

She smiles again, but it seems partially forced and uncomfortable. Then she hurries over to where Travis is attempting to help one of my brothers.

The battle between the three gods rages on outside, but now the racket grows nearer and nearer, louder and louder. The ground shivers. Tiny bits of stone crumble from the columns and ceilings. But the real battle hasn't begun yet. I move into the deeper shadows behind the inner columns and watch as Travis conjures a gnome, then convinces my brethren to assault the gnome and feed off him. I heard their discussion about this tactic. My brothers and I needed blood to rejuvenate us so that we might take part in the next phase of the battle.

As I watched my brothers clamber up the gnome's body to feast on him, I felt a hunger growing inside me like none I had ever experienced before. I race over to the gnome and join in the feast, latching on to his ankle to drink until I can't consume any more blood. I don't enjoy it, thanks to the spell Eros cast eons ago. It satiates my hunger, though, and that's all I need right now. I detach my fangs from the gnome's ankle and recede into the shadows again.

Travis conjures more gnomes and then shouts, "Now that the vamps have full tummies, who wants to go out there and wallop a few gods who think they own the multiverse?"

"Kill Eros!" one of my brothers exclaims.

More battle cries ring out. The gnome and the vampires stampede out of the temple, and I am caught up in the melee as three gods are assaulted en masse on the steps of the temple. While I conjure a sword and begin to fight, I catch sight of Travis and Larissa on the portico above me. They join the fight as well. The details aren't critical. The important fact is that the Four Winds intervened to prevent the gods from destroying the mortal world. They swept up Eros, Kamadeva, and Setesh, taking them to who knows where. Later, I would learn they had been stripped of their powers and dumped into the mortal world to live as humans.

What happened after the battle and Dendera is the most important event to understand. Max arrived to help Travis send the vampires back to the Unseen, since the magics that lingered inside the temple complex made teleportation more difficult. They managed to wrangle the vampires.

But they missed one.

I barreled away from the crowd and strapped my arms around Larissa, whisking her away.

Chapter Twenty-One

W HAT DID YOU DO WITH HER?" AMANDA ASKS. "YOU MENTIONED that you seriously injured Larissa and Riley, at different times. So, I can guess that you stopped your memory at this point because you're ashamed of what you did to those women—your friends."

"Of course I am ashamed." I pull us both out of the memory so I can explain while meeting Amanda's gaze. "With Larissa, it was a mistake. After I abducted her, I kept her in an empty house in a place I did not know, just until I could sort out what I meant to do with her. *Protect her*, that was my only coherent thought. I knew I was doing a terrible thing. But my sudden transformation and my new allergy to sunlight had left me reeling. That is hardly a valid excuse."

"Sure it is." She begins to comb my hair with her fingers again, and I can't deny it soothes me just as much this time as the first. "Like you said, you were reeling. I felt that way when Balder took me to his lair and told me the whole truth about himself. I was reeling then, and I didn't have any-where near as hard a time as you did."

"Your experience was worse. You lost your child." I lean into her touch and let my eyes drift half-closed, but only for a moment. Then I look at her as I explain the rest. "While I pondered my next move, it turned out that Larissa was finding a way to escape from me. She ran out of the house—and straight into Travis's arms."

The memories take over one last time, and I willingly allow the past to engulf me. I need Amanda to understand. She won't leave me unless she sees how abominable I am.

We have entered the memory at the moment when I bare my fangs and try to rip Larissa out of Travis's arms. He teleports them both away. For a span of time I cannot count because my mind is in too much turmoil, I pace in the backyard of the house I had commandeered and struggle to understand…anything. I had not enjoyed drinking the gnome's blood, yet feeding had set off a chain reaction inside me. I need more blood. My veins burn with the hunger. The scent of Larissa lingers all around me, driving me madder than I already am.

Where is she? I must protect Larissa. The salamander does not deserve a goddess such as her. She belongs with me. Eros created us both, which means we share a connection no one else understand. I need her. I hunger for her. Somehow, I must wrest her away from the incubus. Am I not an elemental? I can find her simply by wishing for her. Can't I? It won't hurt to try.

I tense my entire body and focus all my mental energy on one thought: *Take me to Larissa.*

The surroundings shift. I now stand inside a hotel room. Larissa and Travis are sitting on the bed having a conversation that is clearly intimate and romantic, given that they hold each other firmly. Travis notices me first and jerks in surprise.

I ignore him and focus on Larissa. "Here to protect you. Save you."

"I don't want to be saved. Travis is my friend, not my enemy."

"But he took you."

"You were about to attack him, so he took us both away."

My gaze flits between Larissa and Travis as I struggle to comprehend the situation. My mind still whirls with chaotic thoughts, and my obsession with Larissa grows stronger every moment, as if I've swallowed a drug that has addled my brain. Nothing makes sense anymore. My brows furrow as I stare at Larissa and point at her lover. "You want him?"

"Yes. I love him."

What is left for me now? I am alone. My father did not want me, and besides, he's gone now. Larissa doesn't want me either. No one does. A weight settles onto my shoulders and spreads downward until I can't bear the weight of my own body any longer and I collapse to my knees. I have no purpose now. As the truth of that single thought penetrates deep inside me, the rest of my body crumples too, and I fall sideways onto the carpeted floor. I stop myself from smacking down face-first by planting my hands flat on the floor.

My chest heaves, and my eyes sting, blurring my view of Larissa. "But I—You are—Who am I to serve now?"

"No one," Travis says. "You're free."

Free? What does that word mean? I understand the literal meaning, but even with no master to command me, I don't feel liberated. All I can do is shake my head. "I served Eros, not willingly. Then the goddess freed me, and now I serve her, but she does not want me."

Larissa gazes at me with something between compassion and pity. "You have never served me. Why do you think you need to?"

"Because you saved me."

Larissa and Travis exchange confused looks. "I didn't save you, Cyneric. And I have never told you to protect me."

"The temple—" My head feels as if it might detach from my body and float away into the heavens. I hold a hand to the side of my head and cinch my face up in a tight grimace. I need the other hand to prevent myself from falling into a heap on the floor. "Your temple. Your energy."

Only now have I realized what I felt when I entered the temple. It was…magics. Her magics. Hathor's temple remained suffused with those energies even thousands of years after the goddess abandoned her own temple complex. Those magics have slithered into me, binding me to her even though she no longer is a goddess and has no powers. A whiff of those energies had infiltrated me, and I am changed because of it—even without what Eros and Setesh did to me and my brothers.

While my mind reels with revelations, the conversation has gone on without me.

Travis sighs, eying me where I slump on the floor. "What should we do with him? And his mates, if they turn up."

Larissa studies me. "Don't know. We can't do this alone, though."

"Don't worry. We've got family."

"I was created, not born, so I can't have parents or siblings."

Though they continue to discuss the topic of me and my brothers, my thoughts get caught on what she just said. She was created, like me. She has no family, like me. For more millennia than I could count, I had believed I did have a family—a father and brothers—but for a very, very long time I refused to accept the truth. Then I met Larissa, and later, Riley. Their compassion had taught me vital lessons, and each woman contributed to my revelation. It didn't come to me during any of the moments I have just recalled for Amanda's sake. They happened gradually, one grain of sand at a time, until I had amassed a mountain of understanding.

I have no family, therefore I have no loyalty to Eros. I am finally free—in body, mind, and spirit.

"Yes, you are," Amanda says. "Your journey into your own memories did some good after all."

"How do you know what I was thinking?" We have returned to the present, exiting my memories, and once again sit on the sofa together.

"I could hear your thoughts, hon. Loud and clear."

"But I could not hear yours."

"This little psychedelic trip into the past was for your benefit, not mine. You needed me to know what you've been through, and I'm glad you showed me."

I pick her up and set her on the middle cushion, a short distance away from me. "I have not told you about the two worst things I ever did."

"Another trip into your mind? You could just tell me instead."

"No. You need to see it for yourself."

She sighs. "If you insist. It won't change my mind about you."

I know she would not lie to me, but I can't fathom how the horrific acts I committed wouldn't affect her opinion of me.

Amanda crawls toward me and climbs onto my lap again. "Let's go."

"Not long after I left Larissa and Travis in their hotel room, I began to spiral downward into madness."

With no effort at all this time, I transport us into the memory. Amanda insists on holding my hand again, and I can't deny her touch still soothes me. But what I'm about to show her must change her mind. How can it not?

For a short while after I left Larissa, I continue to obsess over…everything. Why does Larissa not want me? I would serve her without reservation and do anything she wishes. But instead, she has gone with the incubus. My emotions have become tangled and twisted, mutating into a mixture of anger, fear, and pain. My head pounds. I grip it as if I might squeeze out my emotions and rid myself of them. But I can't. The truth will not be ignored, even in my wildly spinning thoughts.

Then one thought pierces the din. *Protect Larissa.*

I zip myself back to the hotel room.

Travis lies nude on the bed, on his back, with his hands clasped beneath his head and his eyes closed, while a satisfied smile curves his lips. The aroma of a woman's lust fills the air, and I instinctively know it originated from Larissa, though she is not in the room. But I hear noises coming from the bathroom. It sounds like water running.

Her lover is alone. This is my chance to save her.

I leap on Travis and punch him in the face, then slam my knee into his groin. A stifled cry bursts out of him. He tries to fight me off, but I employ all my physical strength and supernatural powers to keep him pinned to the mattress. He succeeds in shoving me away only because the scent of Larissa has distracted me. I tumble to the floor but spring up again.

Travis throws himself at me.

I vanish.

He stumbles into a chair, making it thump on the floor.

Save Larissa, my addled mind urges. I reappear right behind Travis and clamp one arm around his midsection while I grasp his forehead and yank his head backward. Then I punch my fangs into his throat and begin to devour his blood. He gurgles and attempts to fight, but I'm swallowing in such quick, deep motions that he has no chance to speak.

After my sudden transformation at Dendera, and my new aversion to sunlight, I need to feed more than ever before. That is my only excuse for the way I guzzle his blood with no regard for the damage I'm causing. Blood trickles down his chest, and still I cannot stop myself.

"No! Get off him! Stop, Cyneric, now!"

Larissa screams those words while she leaps onto my back in a vain attempt to stop me. I hadn't realized just how famished I was until I tasted blood again. Now, I can't make myself pull away. I vaguely notice that Larissa has climbed onto my back and locked her arms around my throat, attempting to disable me by choking my throat. She lacks the strength to slow me down and certainly can't stop me.

I shake my body to rid myself of her.

Larissa drops onto the bed.

Dimly, I wonder why I need to get rid of Travis. Larissa won't love me if I kill her fated mate. But reason has no place in my mind, not anymore.

She leaps on me again and stabs a sharp object into my neck.

Pain slices through me. I wrench my mouth away from Travis's throat and howl from the agony of my wound and the knowledge that Larissa will defend her lover at any cost, even if her efforts end in her own death.

I whisk myself away.

But I only make it to the room next door. I'm reeling from being stabbed in the neck, but mostly, I'm too high on the salamander's blood to do anything. I'd intended to flee to…somewhere far away. Instead, I'm trapped inside a vacant room in the semi-dark. I can hear voices next door, more than just Larissa and Travis, which means they must have called for help.

I sway on my feet. The room sways too. I stumble to the bed, crashing down onto it on my back, and watch the ceiling tiles rock to and fro. The voices next door grow more impassioned, more desperate. Have I killed Travis after all? Coldness rushes through me at the thought, though I can't deduce why. Am I feeling…guilt? My father never taught me about emotions.

Larissa's voice breaks through the barrier of the wall, and my heightened elemental senses kick in once more. I hear the pain in her voice even though I can't understand the words. *Protect her.* Yes, I must do that. She would never have suffered if Travis had never come into her life. That's what my mind insists on telling me.

I conjure the sword Travis had used during the battle at Dendera and teleport into the room next door.

When Larissa notices me, her grief-stricken expression mutates into fury. She turns to Max, who holds up a listless Travis with one arm lashed around his waist, and she screams, "Get out of here!"

But I am too fast and Max is too slow to react. I thrust the sword directly at Travis's chest.

Larissa flings herself into the path of the blade. The sword plunges into her chest, piercing her straight through to the hilt.

CHAPTER TWENTY-TWO

WE SPIRAL BACK OUT OF MY MEMORIES AND INTO THE PRESENT ONCE more. I feel drained this time, as if I had actually relived those moments rather than simply watching a replay. When Amanda touches my face, even I can tell my skin has grown clammy. I feel cold all over, even beneath my flesh. The chill penetrates deep into my soul—if I have one of those.

"That trip really got to you, didn't it?" she says. "I can understand why. Watching yourself do those horrible things must be harrowing."

"Do you now understand? I am horrible."

She presses her lips to mine, softly, sweetly. "No, Cyneric, I don't feel that way. I'm even more convinced that you aren't evil."

"That makes no sense."

"I've seen you under all kinds of circumstances, from your vivid memories of the past to the things that have happened recently. I understand you."

Perhaps she does. Amanda is the most intelligent being I have encountered in any world. If she believes I'm not evil, then I must believe it too. Was I ever a wicked creature? I can no longer answer that question unequivocally.

Amanda slides her hand down from my cheek to my throat. "Let's make love, Cyneric. Right now."

"No, we shouldn't."

"Yes, we absolutely should. Nothing relieves stress better than a good, hard fuck."

"But I—I might be unstable."

She drags her palm down my chest and slants her head toward me. While she kisses a path up my throat, she speaks in a sultry tone. "You are not unstable or insane or any of those other things you let other people call you. But you are damaged, and it will take time to recover."

"That's even more reason why we shouldn't fuck."

"You're wrong." She drops her hand to my waistband, then tugs my T-shirt free. Her hand glides up my belly, beneath the fabric. "Sex is exactly what you need to blow off steam. Use my body, Cyneric. You have my permission to do anything you want."

My breathing has grown heavier. Every breath ends with a soft growl. Her voice and the words she spoke have inflamed my lust for her body and her blood. But after the tale I related a moment ago, I can't understand why she would want me to fuck her, much less give me permission to do whatever I want.

"You might be ensorcelled. I might have inadvertently—"

"No, you have not done that. Trust me. I have firsthand experience with ensorcellment, so I know what it feels like."

"But if you were bespelled, you would not realize it."

She slides one leg over my thighs to straddle me. "Shut up and show me what you've got. No holding back this time. And I want you to—"

"No. I will not drink from you."

Amanda plasters herself to my body and rocks her hips to tease my cock. "I said shut up, Cyneric."

"I know what you want, but it's too dangerous."

She shakes her head while she sneaks a hand down to unzip my jeans. "We're going to undress each other the old-fashioned way. No making our clothes disappear. I want to strip for you."

"I can handle that."

"Once we're both naked"—She pulls my shirt off over my head and tosses it away, then rakes her nails down my chest—"you will fuck me while you drink me."

"Not this time."

"Yes, this time." She places her mouth on my throat and nips my skin. "Anything I want. Say it, Cyneric."

I can barely breathe now, not that an elemental needs to breathe to survive. But my pulse beats faster too, and I seem incapable of preventing the low growl that resonates in my throat—or of denying her anything she desires. "Yes, I'll drink you. While I take your body, I will devour your blood."

"No holding back."

"Yes."

She crawls backward on her knees while dragging her lips down my chest. When she reaches my groin, where the zipper of my jeans is undone, she takes hold of the halves of the zipper and yanks the pants down. "Lift your hips, hon."

I do what she asked, and she pulls the jeans down to my ankles. But my shoes block her from removing them. With a single thought, I make my shoes and socks vanish.

Amanda sits back on her haunches, her hands resting on my calves. "That's cheating. I said we'll get naked the old-fashioned way."

"This is the old-fashioned way for elementals. We've been undressing in this manner for longer than human civilization has existed." I wriggle my foot to tease her arse. "But I only removed my socks and shoes that way."

"I suppose I'll let you get away with cheating this time." She tosses my jeans and underwear away, and they land on the coffee table. "Time for my striptease."

"What is a striptease?"

She hops off the sofa and gazes down at me, licking her lips, as her attention stalls on my cock. "I shouldn't be surprised that you've never heard that word. But I guess I assumed you must've heard it since you've been seducing women all over the world."

"In two worlds—the Unseen and this one." I lie here naked while she remains clothed, but the idea of learning what a striptease is intrigues me. It also arouses me. "Show me your striptease, Amanda."

"Love to, hon." She unzips her sweatshirt, pulling it down so slowly that simply watching her do that intensifies my hunger for her. The scent of her desire grows ever stronger, proof that she loves undressing for me. She sheds her sweatshirt and begins to lift her T-shirt inch by inch, swaying her hips while she performs that task. "Damn, I've never seen a man who got hard as fast as you do. It's been a while, but I'm pretty sure Balder never got an erection that fast."

"I would prefer it if you did not discuss your former husband right now."

"Point taken. I'll focus on telling you how much I love your dick."

"That would be acceptable." My gaze follows her movements as she slowly unties the ribbon that holds her sweatpants in place. "I have traveled both realms for many thousands of years, but I have never seen another woman as beautiful and desirable as you."

Amanda shimmies out of her sweatpants, letting them fall into a heap around her feet. "Keep talking that way. I love it."

"I won't be able to keep speaking for much longer. Your striptease is inflaming my hunger for you."

"Good." She kicks her pants away and removes her socks. "I want you so turned on that you'll devour me in every way imaginable."

"Your wish will be granted."

Amanda reaches behind her back, seemingly to remove her bra, but she stops. "Why don't you finish for me, huh?"

A low growl rumbles in my throat. "Yes, I will."

She opens her mouth and drags her tongue around the periphery of her lips, letting so much of her tongue show that my soft growl becomes a ravenous one. I lean forward and grasp the center of her bra with both hands, then yank it so hard that the garment rips into several smaller pieces. Her breasts rise and fall heavily. But before I devour her tits, I must get rid of her knickers. Another swift tug sends the pieces of that garment flying.

I sit back, tucked into the corner of the sofa, and pat my lap. "Come here, Amanda. Obey my every command."

"Whatever you want, hon."

"Straddle me but remain on your knees." I watch while she climbs onto the sofa and waddles up to me. Her knees lie at either side of my hips. "What now?"

"I have only one other command for you." I rest one arm on the sofa's back and let the other drape over the edge. "Command me."

"That's really what you want? I know you were enslaved by Eros. You don't need to do this—"

I reach up to seal two fingers over her lips. "I want *you* to command me. No one else. I trust you, Amanda."

She follows the movements of my fingers as I drag them down to her chin. "Okay then. You will do what I say, Cyneric."

"Yes."

Amanda hooks a finger under my chin, urging me to look up at her instead of staring at her groin. "Shove your head between my legs and devour me."

I push my face between her thighs, and the drugging scent of her cream overpowers my senses as I grasp her arse in both hands. She moans when I begin to lick her folds, taking it slow, making sure I explore every millimeter of her slick, hot flesh. Fuck, she tastes better than any enchanted food I've ever sampled, and I can't stop myself from licking faster, scraping my teeth over her clitoris, digging my fingers into her arse cheeks.

"Oh God, Cyneric, yes." Amanda grips my head to hold me to her body and begins to rock her hips. "More, please, more."

I consume her with abandon, pushing my tongue deep inside her mouth while I shift one hand in front of her body so I can plunge two fingers into her wet sheath. She slaps her hands onto my shoulders and holds on tight as her moans grow louder and become interspersed with gasps. A need rises within me, one that I know I should not indulge, but it grows stronger every moment while I continue to ravish her flesh with my tongue, fingers, and teeth.

"Bite me, Cyneric. Please, I need you to drink me there."

I freeze, rolling my eyes up to look at her. She can't mean—No, she wouldn't want me to do what my instincts urge me to attempt. No woman would beg for that. But Amanda is not an ordinary woman. She is…extraordinary.

"Go on," she whispers. "Bite me down there."

But I still can't move, frozen by her statement. I feel my brows wrinkle. That's no surprise because I am baffled by this woman and her ravenous desires.

She ruffles my hair with the fingers of one hand. "Maybe I wasn't explicit enough. I command you to bite my clit and drink me that way."

A breath blusters out of my nostrils. A rapacious growl erupts from my throat, vibrating my lips. Never has any woman, mortal or elemental, commanded me to do such a wicked thing to her.

She fists her hand in my hair and jerks my head backward. "Do it now, Cyneric."

I let my fangs glide out.

Amanda traces her fingertips over their sharp tips. A tiny drop of blood emerges from her flesh, and I flick my tongue out to lap it up. My body reacts as if I've swallowed a fifty-gallon drum of pure alcohol. I growl yet again with even more animalistic lust as my skin grows hotter and my cock thickens even more. A bead of moisture lies poised atop the crown.

She wipes it away with her fingertip, then licks her skin to taste me. "Mm. I do love the flavor of you. Later, I'll feast on you so thoroughly your eyes will roll back in your head. But right now, I need you to fulfill my command."

"I will gladly obey you."

With my gaze bound to hers, I pull her clit into my mouth and sink my teeth into the soft, slick flesh that surrounds the head of her clitoris. The sweetest blood I have ever tasted flows into my mouth, and I groan so deeply that my throat vibrates. Amanda gasps. I watch her reactions while she watches me too, our gazes locked, our desire now a palpable energy between us. She doesn't seem to mind that my elemental nature intensifies. I haven't explained to her that blood is the element I'm bound to, just as the sylphs are bound to air and undines to water. Later, perhaps I will explain that.

Not now. Not when I have her sweet, rich blood flowing into my mouth.

Amanda clutches my head, massaging my scalp with erotic slowness and rocking her hips gently. I consume her blood in a sensual rhythm as my lips and tongue keep time with the movements of her fingers, creating a semi-trance state between us. When I thrust a finger inside her, she lets out a sharp, whimpering cry.

My cock throbs.

I need her to come now, so I can fuck her. But I don't want to stop sucking on her clit.

"Oh, Cyneric," she moans. "Don't hold back. Take me any way you want."

That simple statement pushes me over the edge. I rub my nose into her clit while I devour her blood with an intensity that sends her hurtling over the edge into a climax that wrenches a fierce cry from her. I thrust four fingers inside her to feel the contractions, the physical proof of her pleasure.

Carefully, I slide my fangs free of her clitoris and wipe the traces of blood from my mouth.

Amanda lowers herself onto my lap and kisses me. It's a long, slow, deeply sensual kiss that involves our hands too as we grope each other in an equally languid manner. When we finally give up each other's mouths, her lips are swollen and have taken on a darker shade of rose. "If there's anything you've wanted to do with me, Cyneric, but you held back, do it now. I want to feel everything with you."

"I have many ideas."

Her smile tightens her mouth in slow motion, and the slant of her lips makes my cock throb once again. "Show me."

A figure clad in only a pair of black trousers materializes on the other side of the coffee table. The waning daylight casts an eerily blood-like glow on the being who gazes at us with swirling red eyes.

The naked woman in my arms goes stiff, and her eyes grow so wide that they almost bulge out of their sockets. "How did you find me?"

Our unwanted guest sneers at her. "I have friends in very dark places."

His accent… And he has coppery skin…

Amanda huddles closer to me, though she speaks to the stranger. "No, no, go away. Haven't you tormented me enough, Balder?"

The salamander chuckles. "Not even close."

CHAPTER TWENTY-THREE

I LEAP OFF THE SOFA, BLOCKING AMANDA WITH MY BODY. THE SALA-mander standing before me is her former husband, the one who ensorcelled her so she would want him to defile her for days, even knowing what that might do to her mortal body. What sort of bastard would do such a thing?

Even I have never stooped to ensorcellment. Though I can't deny I have considered it once or twice. It would be a convenient way to silence the beings who insist that they are my friends.

"You are Balder, the wretched incubus."

He grins, but it's not a happy expression. No, his smile is suffused with anger. "Leave now, and I won't need to set you ablaze with my fire power. Then I will reclaim Amanda."

For a salamander, "fire power" is a literal term. Balder can summon flames that will engulf his body.

"You cannot have her," I tell the incubus. "Amanda does not want to go with you."

"Her wishes are irrelevant. Step aside. This is your final warning, vampire. Your kind does not do well in an inferno."

I keep my stance relaxed but ready, not wanting to tip him off to the fact that I am not a normal vampire. If he makes one move toward Amanda, I will destroy him.

Balder cracks his knuckles. "Out of the way, tiny vampire. This is your final warning."

Tiny vampire? Thirío had called me that too. But it must be a coincidence, not evidence that the dragon king and the Scandinavian salamander are colluding. How would they even have met? Thirío rarely leaves his domain. That's what I've heard.

Balder spreads his arms. Flames erupt from his skin.

While I would have no qualms about fighting this cretin, I will not risk Amanda's life. In these close quarters, Balder might cause enormous damage. That leaves me with one option.

I whisk us both away.

We land inside a bedroom of some sort. Amanda huddles against me. Moaning sounds emerge from the bed, though all I can see is some kind of creatures rolling about under the covers. A dark-haired head pops up.

And the woman screams.

Her lover shoves the covers back. "What the hell? Get out of here, perv."

I teleport again, and we wind up inside a warehouse where men with guns are speaking in another language. When they spot us, they raise their weapons, about to fire on us. On the third try, we find ourselves in the middle of a swamp. An alligator with its body partially submerged gazes at us from a dozen feet away. When the creature sees us, it swiftly swims toward us. With one more burst of teleportation, I finally bring us to an adequate location.

We stand in the garden of statuary behind the rock shop where the beings who call themselves my mates like to gather. I see no one here. There are no vehicles in the parking lot and no patrons wandering through the rock garden. Why did I bring us here? I made no conscious decision to do so. Yet I feel oddly more relaxed now that we have arrived in this location.

Amanda notices my change in demeanor too. "You say you don't have friends, but you've released a lot of tension since we got here a minute ago."

"It must be a fluke."

She pats my chest. "It's okay to admit you like these people. I wish I'd gotten the chance to spend more time with them."

"You ran away. I understand why, but you could have spent time with these people if you'd wanted to."

"True." She clasps my hand, then starts heading for the rock shop while dragging me along with her. "Come on, Cyneric. Let's meet up with your friends and maybe get a little help too."

I allow her to lead me away, down the gently sloping hill and toward the rear door of the shop. "These beings don't like me. I'm sure they will like you very much, but I'm confused by your attitude. Balder attacked us moments ago."

"Yes. But now we're safe. I can feel it in my bones."

"My bones give me no such assurances."

She smiles and laughs. "The way you talk is adorably stuffy sometimes. When we're screwing, you aren't stuffy at all—and your language changes too."

"In what way?"

"You talk dirty, hon." She halts us at the metal door that serves as the rear entrance of the shop. "I would love to hear you do full-on, no-holds-barred filthy sex talk."

"I might try that sometime. Conversation has played only a minimal role in my seduction of mortals. Until I met you."

She tips her head to the side, seeming to analyze me. "I know you're extremely ancient, but when did you have your first sexual experience? Was it with the fae girl whose blood you drank?"

"No, I did not fuck her. I consumed her blood, that's all."

"When was your first time, then?"

I avert my gaze and clear my throat. "A few months ago, when I had sex with a succubus."

Amanda stares at me. "You were celibate for hundreds of thousands of years?"

"Yes. Anthea was my first lover, though it wasn't a relationship. I, ah, shagged her to get information, to help Tris and Riley."

"Did you enjoy seducing her?"

I still can't look Amanda in the eye, and my skin has begun to itch. "Anthea was ensorcelled by Drakon. But as a succubus, she would have engaged in intercourse with anyone, anywhere, with or without magical inducements. I did not care about the, ah, moral aspects of what I'd done, not at the time."

"But you regret it now."

"Yes."

"Good. That means you've changed." She kisses me. "You are not the same vampire you were before. So give these people a chance to get to know the real you, the version that emerged after all the trials and tribulations you've been through."

The door bursts open.

Amanda jumps and sidles closer to me.

"What are you doing out here?" Nevan asks. "We could see you two on the security cameras, and we expected you to come inside." He waves for us to enter the building. "Don't dillydally. The gang is waiting."

Since we seem to have no choice in the matter, we walk into the shop and follow Nevan to the sales counter. His wife, Lindsey, sits on a stool behind the counter and holds their young son on her lap.

She smiles when she sees us. "There you guys are. It's a slow day for customers, which means this is the perfect time for a meeting."

"Meeting of what?" I ask.

"The gang, of course." Lindsey pulls in a large breath and shouts, "Come on out, guys! The meeting is about to convene."

I see no one else in this building, only me and Amanda along with Nevan and Lindsey—and their child.

Several figures materialize.

Max, Travis, and Tris have teleported here along with their wives—Harper, Larissa, and Riley. Janus is among the group too, and so is a being I would never have expected to see taking part in such a meeting. It's the raven shifter, Brennus. Since he rarely speaks, I can't imagine why they invited him to this gathering. Then the oracles arrive, and I know something terrible must be coming. Bob and Ken prefer to remain in their lairs.

"Who wants to go first?" Lindsey asks. She waits for someone to speak up, but no one does. "Come on, people. Don't make me do this every time. It's somebody else's turn to take the wheel."

Travis steps forward. "All right, I'll do it."

Lindsey winks at him. "I knew I could count on you."

"You mean you knew you could guilt me into doing this."

"Same thing." She flaps a hand toward him. "Go on. The floor is yours."

We are all standing on the same floor. But I assume that's another mortal saying that I don't understand.

Travis rolls his shoulders back. "Here's the situation. The most powerful beings in the Unseen have all sensed a storm coming, the likes of which no one has seen before. That storm is called Cyneric."

"I am not a storm elemental. I am a vampire."

The incubus rolls his eyes. "It's a metaphor, mate. May I continue without your sarcasm?"

"It wasn't sarcasm. I stated a fact."

Although Travis clearly wants to argue with me, he has the good sense not to do that. "Moving on. The metaphorical storm has been brewing for a long time."

"Storms do not brew," I tell him. "They gather. That's what mortals like to say. 'The gathering storm' is the appropriate cliché."

The salamander squints at me and flares his nostrils. "Maybe I won't bother trying to save you after all."

"I do not require saving. My power exceeds yours."

Just as Travis opens his mouth to speak, Amanda does so first. "Calm down, boys. We're all adults here, right? Cyneric doesn't understand mortals and especially our sayings. Let's give him a pass, okay? It sounds like this gathering storm is more important than your petty squabbles."

"Yes, it is," Bob says. "But convincing these creatures to stop harassing each other is nearly impossible. You, child, have done the impossible. Good job."

"I appreciate the compliment. But I'm not a child. I'm fifty-three years old."

His lips tick up at the corners, and he leans forward to wink at her. "I'm at least ten thousand times older than you."

"Oh. You're almost as old as Cyneric, then."

"He is a child compared to me, pet."

Travis claps his hands. "Quiet, everyone. Getting back to the matter at hand, we need to talk about the huge honking apocalypse that's looming. No one can complain about my metaphors this time because it's not a metaphor. The oracles, the fae witches, and many other varieties of creatures from the Unseen have sensed the approach of this apocalypse in recent days."

"That's not much lead time," Lindsey says. "Why did it take so long for anyone to notice the gathering st—the coming apocalypse?"

"Bob, why don't you explain this bit?"

Ken huffs. "I could explain it just as well."

"Don't get shirty about it. Bob, go on."

The oracle grasps the lapels of his suit jacket. "Something changed in the last few weeks, and every being with any sort of foresight knew a terrible event might occur soon. But the specific signs eluded us. A power like none we have ever seen is rising, and it will annihilate both worlds."

"How did this power come to be?" Larissa asks. "And why did it rise now? What changed?"

"Not what, dear. Who."

The oracle swerves his attention to me. "You changed, Cyneric, and the darkest powers in the two worlds have aligned against you."

"Why? Who are these beings?"

Bob folds his arms over his chest. "You have met them all before. These vengeful beings harbor intense ill will toward you."

"Tell me who they are before I tear your throat out."

Amanda pats my chest. "Cut him some slack. Cyneric is adjusting to a lot changes lately."

Bob shakes his head. "Yes, I know all about his travails."

"Please tell us who these dark powers are."

"They are Thirío, Setesh, and Eros."

I think I must be gaping at him, for I feel a draft coming in between my lips. "But Eros and Setesh were disempowered."

Bob sighs. "You are correct. But Thirío has amassed enough power of his own that he can re-empower those gods. He has begun the process with Setesh, which I know you saw when you met him in Australia. Eros has not yet been reactivated by Thirío, so we have a small window in which to stop that from happening."

Eros. My father. The god who enslaved and betrayed me.

He is coming for me.

"What about Kamadeva?" Travis asks. "He got power-stripped too."

"Yes, but he has adjusted to his new life much better than the other two. Still, he could be sucked back into his old life as well. We aren't certain of his fate yet."

"You said you aren't sure of the others either. Only Thirío is definitely involved in this plot, though his motivations are unknown."

Bob returns his attention to me. "Are you all right, Cyneric? You seem a bit...twitchy."

I glance down at my hands and realize they have indeed begun to twitch. My whole body feels as taut as a rope stretched to its limit, and I struggle to maintain even breaths. My skin grows warmer every moment, though I haven't started to sweat yet.

Amanda lays a hand on my cheek. "Take it easy, hon. We'll handle this together. And you've got friends to back you up too."

"Balder." I can only eke out that one word. My teeth are too tightly clenched.

"Don't worry about him."

I haul in a deep breath and attempt to release it gradually, but I fail. The breath gusts out of me. "But he tried to harm you."

"We don't know what he wanted."

"Ah, hold on a minute," Max announces. "Bob seems to be getting a transmission from the other side."

We swerve our gazes to the oracle. His eyes have rolled back in his head, and his mouth has fallen open.

"Is he okay?" Amanda asks.

"Oh, yeah, he'll be right as rain," Max declares. "Oracles do the trance thing once in a while, especially if they're getting a whopper of a vision."

Bob goes still, and his lids shut. After a moment, opens his eyes and grasps his lapels. "Did someone mention Balder the salamander? Yes, of course you did, pet."

"Whose pet are you referring to?" Travis asks.

"I was speaking to Amanda. Balder is her husband, after all." He focuses on me, and his eyes glow faintly. "This was a powerful foresight. Circumstances have changed, and the entire scope of the apocalypse is realigning."

"What caused the change?" I ask. "Was it me?"

"Not precisely. Balder was not meant to participate in this event, but somehow Thirío must have gotten wind of him and decided he could exploit your greatest weakness—Amanda."

"She is not a weakness, not for me."

"You misunderstand. Thirío believes she is a weakness for you. The more you bond with her, the less the chance that his plan will work."

"I don't understand any of this."

"Neither do we," Larissa says. "But something awful could happen if we don't prevent it. And I think Bob is saying that you're the key to stopping the apocalypse from ever getting started."

"Correct," Bob says. "And Ken agrees with me."

Janus steps forward, coming up to the front of group. He ambles over to me. "I warned you that you must find Eros. At the time, I did not know about this impending catastrophe. With that knowledge, I now realize that I must assist you in whatever manner is appropriate."

Amanda gives him a cool look. "And what does that mean? Seems like everyone is piling the blame on Cyneric."

"He nearly killed Larissa and Riley," Tris pronounces. "Is anybody here sure that we can trust him to save the worlds?"

"I do not need your help," I snarl. "Amanda is my concern and no one else's. I will risk my own destruction to protect her."

Chapter Twenty-Four

EVERYONE IN THIS SHOP BESIDES THE TWO OF US GAWPS AT ME AS IF I've declared that I want to ally with Thirío and his mates to bring about the total annihilation of every world in the multiverse. Do they believe I might do such a thing? Maybe I have been suffering from recurrent memories that take over my mind and trigger earthquakes. I don't even know for certain that I caused those disasters.

Amanda gazes up at me with a soft, sweet smile on her lips. "I know you will protect me no matter what, and you have no idea how grateful I am for that. But I'd rather you not get annihilated by my ex and his new friends."

Ken makes a peevish face. "Why do you keep referring to Balder as your ex-husband? You're still married to him. Doesn't anyone else remember that? Eh, Bob?"

"I was trying to break the news to her gently."

Amanda puckers her lips. "I am not married to that bastard anymore. I got a divorce."

Bob approaches her and sets a hand on her arm. "In what sort of ceremony were you wedded, child?"

"The kind with vows and rings."

"Yes, but what sort of vows did you recite?"

She shrugs. "I don't remember the details. Balder wanted a New Age ceremony with incense and other garbage, and I wanted to make him happy."

"Were the vows in English?"

"Partially. Balder claimed to be from Norway, and he wanted part of the vows to be in Old Scandinavian. He said that was a tradition among his people."

Bob warps his mouth into a slanted expression as he peers into Amanda's eyes. "I can't tell yet. Would you mind if I reach into your mind briefly to hear what words you spoke during the ceremony?"

She looks at me, a question in her eyes.

"You can trust him," I say. "Bob is an oracle, and thus, a force for good in the multiverse."

Unlike me. I will, apparently, destroy two worlds.

Amanda smiles hesitantly, but I can tell she believes what I said. So, she turns to Bob. "Go on. Do whatever you need to do."

Max and Travis lift their brows.

They shouldn't be shocked that Amanda trusts me. But with salamanders, I never can figure out what's in their heads—if anything at all.

Amanda closes her eyes, and Bob does the same. He doesn't chant or wave his hands about like a seer in a Hollywood film. The oracle simple stands there with his one finger resting on each of Amanda's temples.

He opens his eyes and drops his hands. "I'm afraid you are still married to Balder. The incantation you spoke during the ceremony was not a wedding vow. It was a spell to bind you to him forever."

"What?" Amanda flattens her lips and makes a noise not unlike the way I growl when I'm angry. "Oh, that bastard. How do we cancel his cute little spell?"

"Removing it will take a great deal of magics. We will need to travel into the Unseen to accomplish the task."

"Then let's go there."

"Cyneric should remain here. His instability will be far more of a problem in a world that teems with supernatural energies."

"Absolutely not." Amanda snaps her spine straight and stares directly into the oracle's eyes. "He goes where I go and vice versa. No arguments. This is nonnegotiable."

Ken comes up beside Bob, and the two exchange looks that I cannot decipher. Bob nods to Ken, who nods in return. The oracles have clearly reached a decision, but about what, I can't tell.

Bob faces us. "We agree. Cyneric and Amanda should both enter the Unseen." He grasps both of Amanda's hands. "But you will need to be extremely careful, pet. The Unseen has rules, the sort with severe consequences. Has anyone explained that to you?"

She shakes her head.

"Cyneric, why don't you take Amanda out to the falls and tell her about our world. The rest of us will follow you shortly."

I nod and lead Amanda out of the shop building. As the door clicks shut behind us, we make our way up the hill and through the garden of statuary, then follow the dirt path toward the falls. We hear the rumble of the cascade before we can see the waterfall, though only I can smell the distinct scent of the water, the damp earth surrounding the pool, and the various plants and flowers that populate the forest.

We halt at the wooden railing that surrounds the pool.

Amanda gazes up at the twenty-foot curtain of water that crashes down into the pool, churning up white foam on the surface and releasing mist that rises halfway up the red sandstone cliff. "This is beautiful. I can see why elementals want to travel into the other world this way."

I crook a finger under chin and urge her to face me. "We do not choose the manner in which we access the Unseen. We have no choice in the matter. Water is the gateway to our world, and we must find a natural source. I can't give you a bucket of water and tell you to jump into it. The portal will only open if you enter through a waterborne gateway."

"Why water?"

"No one knows. The Oversoul must have arranged it this way for a reason, but we aren't privy to the reasons."

"Oversoul?"

I gaze into the churning pool as I try to explain. "The Oversoul is that which created the Unseen and which oversees everything that goes on in that world. I've heard the Oversoul compared to God in the mortal world. But I don't understand what God is either."

"Skip that discussion, then. It's too complicated, and we have more immediate problems."

"Yes, we do." I rest a hand on the wooden fence, turning toward Amanda. "Here are the rules of the Unseen. You must never speak the words please, thank you, or sorry. Any sort of gratitude will trigger a debt between you and the other party that will give them enormous power over you. Never attempt to bargain with any elemental. They know the rules of bargaining, and you do not. But even if I outlined for you all the intricacies of bargaining, it would be too dangerous for you to attempt such a thing."

"I understand."

"No, you do not." I grasp her upper arms and pull her closer. "This is not a game, and you won't get a second chance to reword your statements. Mortals are used to speaking those words to express their gratitude or regret. Once we are in the Unseen, you must consider every word carefully before you speak. If you trip up, the consequences could be disastrous."

I pray my tone of voice and my expression convey the seriousness of the situation. Though I have never worried about debts or bargains, there is one simple reason why. I consider every word before I speak it. I've lived in the Unseen for countless millennia, and I have navigated the land mines of debts and bargains for just as long. But will Amanda remember the rules if we're attacked? Or if we should get separated?

My gut churns at the prospect. I cannot lose her.

She pulls in a deep breath and exhales it slowly. "I understand everything you said. I won't break the rules. Well, I suppose the only promise I can reasonably make is to say that I will do my damnedest not to break the rules."

"I know you will do that." I kiss her forehead. "The Unseen is a strangely beautiful world, but it holds many dangers."

"You know I've been there before, twice. But I never really got to see anything since I was a prisoner or ensorcelled." She slips her arms around my waist. "Now I have you as my tour guide."

"This is not a holiday. It is a treacherous journey into a hostile world full of beings who will take any opportunity they can find to trick you into becoming their slave."

"I will follow your lead. Don't worry about that."

How can I not worry about everything? For the first time in my entire existence, I have fallen in love. That realization stops me for a moment, and a lump forms in my throat that I cannot rid myself of by simply swallowing it. Do I even know what the word love means? My father pronounced that he loved me above all others, yet he treated me as if the opposite were true. No other being, elemental or mortal, ever cared for me the way Amanda does.

"You okay, hon?" she asks. "You seem a little pale."

"I am...reasonably well." No, I can't tell her that I believe I'm in love with her. Not yet. Perhaps never. What if I'm wrong? This feeling might represent something else entirely.

"Don't take this the wrong way, but you don't seem 'reasonably well' to me."

"I had a strange thought, that's all."

Fortunately, the oracles and the salamanders arrive to interrupt us. I won't need to discuss my confusing revelation any further. I might be the son of a literal sex god, but I know nothing about romance. I have no experience with friendship either.

Nevan appears next, though Lindsey has not come with him. Tris and Riley arrive after the sylph. Neither Larissa nor Harper has attended this gathering, undoubtedly because they, along with Lindsey, have children to care for and wouldn't want to risk their families. Harper has a baby, and Larissa has her adopted daughter to consider.

Babies confound me even more than adults.

"Now that the gang's all here," Tris declares, "it's time to talk strategy. Cyneric, I assume you've told Amanda about the rules that will take effect once we walk through the portal."

"Of course I have. Do you think I'm an idiot?"

"No comment, Captain Fang. Let's move on to strategy." Tris scans his gaze over each of us in turn, then lets his focus land on me. "While you and Amanda were getting cozy, the rest of us mapped out how this should go."

"I will consume Thirío's blood until he has none left, then I will tear Balder to shreds and punch my fist through Eros's heart."

The leprechaun raises his face to the sky and shakes his head, sighing with no small measure of melodrama. "We need to get to the dragon king's castle before you can do any of that. Thirío has wards, right?" When I nod, he sets his hands on his hips. "Okay, then. Step one, we teleport to the creepy woods that surround the castle and the basin it lies in."

"If you had been here the last time we tried that, you would know the salamanders and I were captured. Thirío's henchmen must have sensed us coming."

Bob clears his throat. "It's more likely that his oracle sensed you coming, long before you arrived in the Unseen."

Max raises his hand. "Ah, I thought oracles were independent contractors. That's what you keep telling me."

"Yes, most of us are independent and serve no master. But Thirío somehow gathered enough power to ensorcell my good friend, the oracle Dickenwahnashitz."

No one speaks for a moment. Then, as one, everyone except for Amanda and myself bursts into uproarious laughter.

Bob purses his lips and narrows his gaze. "What is so bloody funny about the oracle's name? You people are children."

Gradually, everyone stops laughing. Max wipes his eyes dry with the palm of his hand. "Are you serious, mate? Your friend is called Dickenwahnashitz? That's hilarious. What's his nickname? Dicky Pooh?"

"No, he is simply Dick. May we move on now? And I appreciate that you, Cyneric and Amanda, both refrained from making fun of the oracle's name." Bob tugs his suit jacket down and regains his regal demeanor. "What you need to focus on is the fact that Thirío has amassed an extraordinary amount of power thanks to having an oracle on his side. It is unprecedented."

"Tell me where to find this oracle," I say, "and I will eliminate him."

"He is not the enemy. Dick is a prisoner."

Travis folds his arms over his chest. "We can't trust Cyneric to do the right thing. If he sees blood, he'll gobble it up no matter whose throat he has to sink his fangs into. I've sort of decided he might not be completely evil, and maybe he's even kind of a friend, but he can't fight his true nature. Just ask Larissa and Riley. The blood lust overpowers everything else."

"Not true," Amanda tells them. "Cyneric has been drinking the blood of mortals for months without hurting them. He drank from me too, more than once, and he never hurt me."

Everyone except Amanda swerves their attention to me.

I know Amanda is trying to help, but I doubt her proclamation will convince these beings to trust that I won't lose control. I did that when Thirío attacked us. Or did I? The details have become hazy. I've also begun to feel weak.

Amanda lays a hand on my cheek. "You need to feed, don't you? I thought you were looking a little pale."

But I fed from her clitoris just a little while ago. How can I be hungry again? I don't feel peckish, though, and that can mean only one thing. "Someone used dark magics to drain me of energy, so that I've grown hungry much earlier than I should have."

Ken and Bob approach me and walk in a circle around me, seeming to analyze every inch of my body. Then they halt and exchange glances that tell me nothing.

Bob speaks to me. "Your aura was partially shielded from our perception, which is why we didn't notice the change immediately."

"I have not shielded my aura. I wouldn't know how to do that."

"Not consciously. But your subconscious has been protecting you from whatever pain and fear you have been hiding inside yourself. Will you allow me to do a full reading?"

"Do what you like."

Bob sets a hand atop my head and closes his eyes. For several minutes, no one speaks or moves, and the only sounds I hear are birdsong, the wind rustling the leaves on the trees, and the rumble of the waterfall. Then the oracle opens his eyes and removes his hand from my head. "The apocalypse will happen—unless you can overcome your fears."

"I fear nothing."

Tris huffs. "Bullshit, Captain Fang. We've all seen the way worry about Amanda and the way you wanted to protect Larissa and Riley. You went about it ass-backwards, but I can't deny you were trying. And you've definitely changed lately."

Travis nods. "He's right. You aren't the same bloodthirsty moron with a German accent that we all met and wanted to kill at Dendera. I don't feel at all like ramming an endued sword through your chest."

Max rolls his eyes. "How sweet. You and the bloodsucker are besties now."

Nevan strides up to me, staring straight into my eyes. "I was once bound by magics to do Skeiron's bidding. I know what it feels like, the fear and the self-loathing. Lindsey helped me move on, and if you let her try, I believe Amanda can do the same for you."

Chapter Twenty-Five

"NO ONE SHOULD EVER WANT TO CRAWL INSIDE MY MIND, FOR ANY reason, and certainly not to remove my fears." I don't wish to discuss this with anyone, not even Amanda, but I know these beings are trying to help me. Perhaps I do feel better, stronger, when I'm with Amanda. But I have lived for far too long to believe I can easily overcome my issues, as mortals like to say. Still, I find myself asking, "What would you have me do?"

Nevan tips his head to the side. "You already know the answer, don't you?"

"I wouldn't ask if I knew."

Bob waves for Nevan to step aside. "There is only one logical course for you to take. You must go back to where it all began."

No, he can't expect me to do that. The oracle must have something different in mind, because that is the last thing I should ever do.

The oracle leans closer. "You need to go back to the Temple of Eros."

I cling to Amanda as the world around me spins. When I stagger backward, she refuses to let go of me and uses her body to keep me upright. That has never happened to me before. No one helps me. No one cares enough to do that. Yet everyone here today has vowed to do whatever is necessary.

The very thought of returning to my birthplace, to the Temple of Eros, makes my skin crawl and everything inside me turn to ice.

You were my first son, and I shall always love you above all others.

My father's voice resounds in my mind, full of regal power and a distinct lack of affection. I had never noticed that before. Whenever I hear Eros in my head, he has always sounded this way. Would a father who loves his son speak in such a remote and godly manner? I think my friends are right, and I do need to return to my beginnings.

Still, my chest heaves as I struggle to catch my breath.

Amanda slings one arm around my neck and combs her fingers through my hair in the slow and steady rhythm that always calms me. "Shh, sweetie, you're safe. I will always be with you, and your friends will do everything they can to help you. No matter what, I'll be here with you."

My breathing normalizes, and my eyes drift half-closed. I feel...at peace.

"Holy cow," I hear Tris declare. "She's the vampire whisperer. I've never seen Captain Fang look so serene."

Am I serene? I suppose I must be. Having never experienced a sensation like that, I couldn't recognize it until someone else gave it a name.

The woman who has introduced me to peace and serenity kisses my cheek. "Time to face the past, hon."

I open my eyes and gaze at the beings gathered before us. "Will we all go to the Temple of Eros?"

"No," Bob says. "This is a journey for you and Amanda to take together, just the two of you."

Travis glances at the other men, who all nod in agreement though no one has spoken. Then he looks at me. "The rest of us will wait at the training ground."

Amanda's brows draw together. "Training ground?"

"It's a place we created where the vamps could learn how to behave like relatively normal, non-psychotic bloodsuckers."

"Cyneric has already done that."

Travis eyes me with deep interest. "Yeah, maybe he has."

Ken claps his hands. "No time to waste, people. Let's head for our designated destinations."

Tris grips my shoulder. "Don't worry, Captain Fang. If it comes to it, we'll bring in the cavalry to fight off these jerkwads who want to annihilate the worlds. We've done it before, like, five or six times. It's kind of a hobby for us."

I assume he intends that statement to be encouraging. Despite the fact these beings call themselves my mates, I still can't understand them.

Everyone except Janus disappears.

He strides up to us. "I have enabled every portal in the Unseen so that each will remain open to all of us for as long as we need. If you must effect a swift escape, simply teleport to the nearest portal and rush through it. No one else will be allowed to travel between the worlds until after this matter has been settled. May the Oversoul bless you with success in your search."

The god vanishes.

And I whisk us away to the place I have avoided for months, the place where I was born and ensorcelled and forced to do my father's bidding.

We land in the portico, where giant marble columns line the front portion of the temple. The roof is constructed of marble too, and it rises so high above our heads that we can't tell where it ends. Since we stand sideways to the closed wooden doors, I can see the peristyle below us and the columns that surround it.

I am home.

Amanda still clings to me as she rotates her head to take in the surroundings. "Holy cow. This is even more intimidating that I thought it would be. Even the most impressive architecture from ancient Greece couldn't compete with this gigantic structure."

"It was designed for a god. Mortal architecture would not suffice."

"Should we go inside?"

"Yes. I'm sure Bob and Ken intend for me to do so."

Amanda grips my hand as we approach the wooden doors, which tower above us as if they were designed to accommodate a giant. Eros is not of gigantic stature, but his persona and powers make him powerful beyond what his physical size would suggest.

"Here we are," Amanda says. "What do we do now? You need to confront your past with Eros, right?"

"Yes."

"When were you last here?"

"I have not entered the temple since the day I walked away from Eros."

"You walked out on him?" She turns toward me so that she might look me in the eye, but she doesn't let go of my hand. "What encouraged you to do that? There must have been a powerful reason."

"Indeed. My transition from devoted follower to traitor began on the day when Eros, Kamadeva, and Setesh descended on the temple at Dendera. They were determined to battle each other until one of them had destroyed the others and claimed Larissa for his own."

"You aren't a traitor. Eros betrayed you."

"I know that now." As I disentangle my hand from hers, I begin to shuffle toward the doors that tower above our heads. I halt an arm's length from the wooden barrier. "At the time, I believed I was the worst sort of traitor. How could I turn on my own father? But he did nothing to stop me or my brothers from being scorched by the sun so badly that many of them could do nothing but writhe on the floor inside the temple."

"Larissa cared, though. I saw that when you took me into your memories."

"Never could I have imagined that the goddess Hathor would become a mortal who cares about others. If she could overcome her past..."

"Then you could too."

I nod because I can't speak anymore, not with these doors looming in front of me. I've waited long enough. It's time to confront my past once and for all. Amanda curls her arm around mine. I know she wants to support me, and I appreciate that more than she could know. But this is something I must initiate on my own. I pull away from her and set both hands on the ornate wooden doors. An image of Eros himself is carved into them.

And I shove them open.

In slow motion, the doors swing inward to reveal the temple's interior. My pulse accelerates more with every inch that is revealed until, finally, the doorway is completely open. Sucking in a deep breath, I grasp Amanda's hand and lead her into the temple. Nothing has changed, though that shouldn't surprise me. It has been only a matter of months since that day at Dendera.

"Talk to me, Cyneric. Tell me what you're feeling."

"I don't know how to describe it."

As we wander across the open interior of the throne room, the solid walls that surround it block our view of the portico that encompasses the entire structure. The royal chambers remain hidden behind a concealed door. Friezes high up on the walls depict devotees worshiping Eros—with sexual acts, yes, but also by washing his feet or spreading sacred oil on his skin. Eros might have been a god worshiped by the ancient Greeks in the mortal world, but in the Unseen, his devotees were elementals, ensorcelled to do his bidding.

The great throne of Eros lies near the rear of the temple. Its platform consumes three-fourths of the width, and the seat itself lies ten feet above our heads. A series of steps lead up to the throne. How many orgies had I witnessed in this temple? I'd grown accustomed to hiding in a corner to avoid the depravity going on around me.

Finally, I answer Amanda's question. "To be here again... I know I should feel anger or resentment or something similar. But all I feel now is a sense of disappointment. Eros never deserved my love or respect. I gave it to him without reservation, but I will never do that again."

"He still has a hold on you, though. Just thinking about seeing him again makes you very anxious. Eros might be out there now plotting to annihilate the worlds. How does that make you feel?"

"I want to hunt down Eros and squeeze his neck until the bones shatter, then rip his head off his body."

Amanda does not seem stunned or revolted by my statement. She simply lifts her brows. "That's not an answer to my question. You told me what you want to do to him, but not how you feel about Eros."

My hands have begun to tremble and ache, and I abruptly realize I've been clenching them hard enough to cause pain. Warmth trickles between my fingers. When I glance at them, I see blood seeping out.

"Take a deep breath, Cyneric. Let it out slowly, and flush out all the anxiety and fear. That's right. Keep breathing slowly and deeply."

Amanda's voice calms me, but when she holds my hand to her chest, the turmoil within me quiets. I can hear her heart beating and feel the warmth of her skin. The sweet scent of her envelops me. I close my eyes and let her presence soothe me until I feel that I can continue with my journey to understand and come to terms with my past.

When I look at Amanda again, she's smiling. The expression is soft and gentle, full of emotions I can't decipher.

I lead us up to the steps that lead to the great throne. "On the day I was born, Eros commanded me to climb the steps and bow down at his feet."

"That's not a very loving thing to do."

"No. I realize now that a parent who truly loves their child would never behave the way Eros did. Being forced to genuflect to him moments after I was created does not suggest he loved me. Still, he enjoyed flouting his love in words." I stare at the throne that towers above me, resisting the impulse to clench my fists again. "No one has ever loved me."

Why did I say that? It does not matter.

Amanda pulls me into her arms, wrapping them around my neck while her body is pressed to mine. I can't stop myself. I slip my arms around her waist and tug her closer. She rubs her cheek against mine.

"You're wrong, Cyneric. You are loved."

Does she mean that she... No, she can't mean that.

Amanda rises onto her toes, leveling our gazes. "I'm in love with you, Cyneric."

I am in love with her too, but I can't manage to speak the words.

When I part my lips, ready to attempt to tell her how I feel, she seals my mouth with her fingers. "You don't need to say it, sweetie. I know. Right now, you need to focus on dealing with your emotions where Eros is concerned."

This woman loves me. Never in all my existence has another being cared for me at all, much less with the depth of feeling Amanda has expressed. Am I not a monster after all? Could I find the sort of relationship that Travis and the others have?

I can't think about that right now. Thirío and Balder are out there, and they might well have recruited Eros and Setesh as well. I need to focus on that. I've confronted my past here in this temple. But now, we must all focus on the present and the future. But to do that, I must complete one more task.

Giving up Amanda's hand, I mount the steps that lead to the throne. My feet don't want to do it, but I summon all my willpower to complete my journey, drawing ever nearer to the seat upon which, for countless millennia, Eros had sat and proclaimed himself to be the greatest god in the multiverse. At the second last step, I halt and gaze at the throne. I take three deep breaths, then march up to the marble chair.

You were born of my blood, of my flesh, of my powers.

I had never doubted what my father told me, not until now. Am I truly the son of Eros? Did he create me from his own blood and flesh? I don't know if I will ever have definitive answers to those questions.

"May I come up now?"

I glance over my shoulder at Amanda. "Yes, I want you to join me."

She trots up the steps and stands beside me. We both face the throne. Its ornate design features images of satyrs and other wicked beasts.

"You should sit on the throne," Amanda says. "That would be the last step in separating yourself from Eros. Don't you think?"

"Perhaps." I sit down on the seat, lowering myself cautiously. Then I rest my arms on the chair and lean back. "Eros told me that he created me from his own blood and flesh. Do you believe that is true?"

"No idea. Travis mentioned that you used to speak with a German accent, which seems odd."

"I did speak that way until shortly after I met Riley. Then, the Unseen changed my voice, just as it did for Max and Travis. Tris's accent also changed."

"But why did you sound German? Eros is a Greek god."

The instant Amanda spoke those words, something within me awakened and paralyzed me with a hard chill, as if I had turned to ice. Now, a tingle of something that resembles excitement rushes over my skin. Why hadn't I considered this before? After a virtual eternity with Eros, I should have considered the ramifications much sooner. But then, I'd been ensorcelled. Even after I was free, I never thought about it. Can it be? No, it's impossible. Because it would mean...

"Eros is not my true father."

Chapter Twenty-Six

"D ID ALL YOUR SO-CALLED BROTHERS HAVE GERMAN ACCENTS too?" When I don't respond after a long moment, she moves to stand directly in front of me at the foot of the throne itself. She waves her hands in my face, yet I still cannot respond. "Wake up, Cyneric. Snap out of it."

Since the moment I spoke those words, proclaiming that Eros is not my true father, I have become immobilized by the shock of my revelation.

Amanda leans over to smack my face. "Wake up right now, or I'll punch you in the stomach. If that doesn't work, I'll knee you in the balls. You have five seconds to snap out of this trance."

She counts down the seconds, but I still do not respond.

I want to move. I want to speak. But for the first time in all of my existence, I can't do anything except stare vacantly at nothing in particular.

Amanda smacks my face.

Still, I cannot move or respond.

But when she lifts her leg, about to knee me in the balls, I finally rouse from my trance. I catch her knee before it can contact my groin. "That will not be necessary."

"Good. I'm not sure I could have actually hurt you that way, but I'd rather not risk it."

"I appreciate that."

"Mind if I sit on your lap?"

Despite my near coma a moment ago, I smirk and pat my thigh. "You are welcome to sit here. I relish any chance to feel your body pressed to mine."

She climbs onto my lap and wriggles until she's tucked against me with her arse on my right thigh. Her calves hang over my other leg. She kisses my cheek. "I'm glad you're feeling good enough to tease me."

"This throne is too bloody enormous even for a god like Eros. But he has always enjoyed lording his power over everyone else."

"Are you going to explain what you meant? A German accent means you were never really the son of Eros? I don't understand."

"I know Eros created me only because he told me so. I did not exist until the moment I awakened in this temple, fully grown and already ensorcelled." I slide an arm around her waist, resting my hand on her hip. Perhaps I need the comfort of her body and her scent. "How could I ever know for certain in what manner I came to exist? Even if I found Eros and he remembered who he is, I doubt he would explain."

"Don't know unless you try. Bob did say you need to go back to where it all began." She suddenly snaps upright, her eyes large, and swerves her head toward me. "I think I get it."

"Get what?"

"The thing Bob said. He didn't mean that you should find Eros, not yet. Bob was telling you what to do in explicit, literal terms." She clamps her hands on my face to hold me in position. "Back to where it began."

"But I am where I began."

"You just admitted that you only know Eros created you because he told you that's what happened." She moves her hands in a manner that causes my head to shake slightly. "Don't you get it yet? You had a German accent. Eros is Greek. Where it all began must mean…"

I stare at her, unblinking, as the truth dawns on me like the rising sun, growing brighter every moment. "Maybe I came not from the Unseen, but from the mortal world. I might have been forged instead of created."

"What is 'forged'?"

"It's a method certain elemental tribes use to create more their kind. Travis and Max were both forged, and that is how they became salamanders. Max was originally a Roman soldier." I stand up while still holding Amanda, cradling her in my arms. "The forging is performed when a mortal is on the verge of death, a hair's breadth from expiring."

"So, you might have been created in that way."

"Yes." A realization slams into me, and I set Amanda on her feet. Then I sigh and bow my head. "But gods don't forge mortals, as far as I know. They attract followers with their charisma and their powers."

"Just because no one else has ever tried it doesn't prove that Eros never did. Or maybe he ensorcelled another elemental to do it for him."

"Eros is too vain to call me his son if he actually coerced an elemental to do it for him. He craves power and control over every aspect of his domain."

I glance back at the throne, on which my father had squatted since at least the age of dinosaurs on Earth, possibly longer. He had been ancient already when I came into being. How can I determine whether I am the son of Eros? I would need to investigate my origins, yet I have no idea how to do that.

Might Eros have left a clue somewhere in this temple? If so, it would have been inadvertent. The god would not want anyone to know he had done something as lowly as forging a mortal so he could call that being his son.

"I can see the gears turning in your mind, Cyneric. What have you figured out now?"

"Probably nothing. But I need to scour this temple to find out if what I suspect might be true." I claim her hand, leading her down the steps. "Eros was always arrogant. He insisted that he had never made a mistake because gods never suffer from such mundane problems. I learned through my experiences with Tris and the others that hubris is the greatest weakness of powerful beings. They underestimate others and overestimate themselves."

"That's for sure. I can help you search the temple. It would go faster if two of us are looking at the same time."

"I would appreciate that."

She leans against my side. "I assume the word appreciate is safe to say in the Unseen, since you just used it. But the P- and T-words are verboten."

"And the S-word."

"Yes. I won't screw up and blurt out one of those words, cross my heart."

Amanda is far too intelligent and mature to make a mistake like that. The one thing I no longer worry about is that she might accidentally indebt herself. But I fear what might happen to her if Thirío, Balder, Setesh, and Eros find us.

We begin our search of the temple, starting at the main doors and splitting off in opposite directions from there. The bas-reliefs on the walls high above us contain nothing but sexual imagery, which hardly seems helpful. Eros did not create me by impregnating a woman. In every frieze, Eros is depicted as the greatest lover in the multiverse, the god who has the biggest "equipment," as mortals like to say. None of the imagery shows the vampires he created. That's no surprise. He never brought us into the fold, not genuinely. We were his toys, and therefore undeserving of a place in the permanent artwork of the temple.

"Over here, Cyneric!"

Amanda's shout echoes inside the cavernous temple.

I sprint over to her faster than any mortal could run. She doesn't seem at all surprised by how swiftly I moved, but then, she has seen me perform similar feats before. I'm not in the least winded when I reach her. "What have you found?"

"Look up." She points a finger straight up toward the ceiling. "I think that might be something."

"You want me to see what is on the ceiling."

"That's right."

I tip my head back as far as I can, squinting up at the ceiling. There is indeed something of interest there. "That appears to be Eros with three of his devotees attending to him. They have dark hair and olive skin, like the god. But there is another figure in the background who seems to have...pale skin."

"Not conclusive evidence. But if we could somehow get up there to examine the frieze up close…"

"We might find more clues."

"Can you jump that high?"

I lift one brow.

"Dumb question, right?" Amanda pats my cheek. "Sometimes I forget you're a vampire with incredible powers. You seem so…normal most of the time."

"Normal? Only you would describe me that way."

She points at the ceiling. "Can we get up there or not?"

"I believe I can jump that high and possibly remain there if I could find a handhold. But it would be difficult to study the imagery while clinging to the ceiling."

"You do the clinging. I'll study the images." She puckers her lips, which I've come to know means that she's thinking. "Now, if I had my cell phone I could take pictures of the—"

I conjure her phone, holding it flat on my palm.

She stares at the device, then laughs and kisses me. "Great trick, hon. You conjured it, right?"

"Yes. Now you may take pictures while I hold us in position."

"The perfect team, eh?"

"Indeed we are." I turn away from her and bend my knees. "Climb onto my back."

She follows my instructions, wrapping her arms around my neck and her legs around my waist. I bend my knees even more deeply, suck in a full breath, and blow it out as I launch myself into the air.

Amanda whoops.

I latch on to the ceiling, grasping two sections of the raised frieze with my fingers. "I'm not sure how long I can keep my hold. Take your photographs quickly."

She snaps a series of pictures in quick succession, then flips through them on her phone to ensure they are not blurry. "I think we've got enough. You can take us back down to the floor."

I release the handholds and haul in a deep breath and hold it as we plummet toward the floor. When we are nearly there, I gust out that breath to slow our downward trajectory. We land with only a slight bump.

Amanda slides off my back.

Breathing hard, I need a moment to regain my equilibrium. Once I've done that, Amanda crushes her mouth to mine. Our tongues twist and glide around each other like serpents, and my cock begins to rouse. When we separate our mouths, her pupils have dilated.

"Damn, kid, that was the most amazing feat I've ever witnessed." She kisses me again, thrusting her tongue between my lips. "The way you did that, it made me so horny. I need to fuck you right now. Ride you like a bucking bull, that's what I want to do."

"I am also growing aroused."

"What should we do about that?"

All the blood in my body has flooded into my cock, and it begins to throb with the need to take her body and sink my fangs into her flesh to drink of the most delicious flavor in the multiverse—Amanda's blood. The aroma of her lust for me permeates the air, sweet and musky, redolent with her cream.

She grasps both sides of my jacket and drags me closer, pasting her body to mine and hoisting herself onto the tips of her toes. Whiles she speaks, she rolls her hips into my groin. "Maybe this temple is affecting us both, but I have never felt this horny in my life. I can feel my cream soaking my panties, and my breasts are so sensitive that I could almost come just because of the way my nipples are rubbing against my bra."

"I also feel an intense need to fuck you." My voice has grown rougher, infused with the lust she always inspires in me, but with greater intensity than ever before. "I have witnessed many erotic acts in this temple, yet I never wanted to join in those activities. But being here with you... If we do this, I can't guarantee I won't lose control."

She grasps the lapels of my shirt and rips them apart. Buttons fly away, ticking on the marble floor. "Don't care. Lose control, Cyneric. Show me all your sensual power, here in this temple."

My breaths come in heavy gusts that flutter her hair. My skin has grown hotter than usual, and my senses are heightened. The intoxicating scent of her seems to fill the entire temple. I have seduced many women since I abandoned Eros, but only one has ever turned the tables to seduce me. Amanda has never feared me. She wanted me, even after she knew the truth about me. Now, we are alone in the most erotic place in the Unseen, and I need to do what she suggested. I need to unleash my passion and inflame hers until neither of us can hold back any longer.

I vanish our clothes. They now lie in two neat piles out in the peristyle, near the columns, along with her phone. "You can show me your photographs later. It's time I made you mine in every way."

"You can do anything to me. *Anything.* I need to be yours, body and soul."

"I haven't shown you everything I can do."

I spread my arms and shut my eyes, breathing in the scent of her but also the sensual magics that live inside this temple. They suffuse my body and slither out to tease Amanda's flesh, diving under the skin to penetrate every part of her. The way her tits heave, I know she experiences exactly what I'm feeling too.

"How many women have you done this with?"

"None, until now." I saunter toward her, halting just close enough that I can touch her. "My previous lovers enjoyed my seduction, but I worried that I might injure them if I unleashed my full potential. But with you, I know that will never happen."

I set my hands on her shoulders, making sure my palms barely brush her skin. Then I skate them down her arms gradually, letting her feel every minute sensation, and my cock twitches when she sucks in a sharp gasp. Her nipples have stiffened into a rich, rosy shade that reminds me of succulent berries I had once seen in the mortal world. I drag my fingers ever downward until their tips brush the backs of her hands. She shudders, but I know it's from the heat of desire and not a chill.

"Oh God," she murmurs. "This feels…unh, so good."

Her lips have turned a darker shade of rose too, and I want to devour them. But not yet. I move my hands to her hips and slide them around to her arse, then skate my hands up her back while letting my fingertips dance along her spine. She gasps again, and her breaths come faster and shallower. With a single thought, I reposition myself behind her so I can trace my fingers over the curves of her arse cheeks while I lower myself onto my knees. I spread my palms over her arse.

Then I graze my lips over those cheeks.

A soft cry emerges from her. But when I flick my tongue out to delicately taste her flesh, Amanda jerks and stumbles. She nearly falls down but catches herself. I can't risk her getting injured, so I change my tactic. "Lie down, love. On your stomach."

She obeys my command without even a split-second's hesitation.

"Your cream and your blood belong to me." I lay my body atop hers, whispering into her ear. "And it's time I devoured you."

CHAPTER TWENTY-SEVEN

I CATCH HER EARLOBE WITH MY TEETH AND FLICK MY TONGUE OVER it. My breaths flutter her hair. She flattens her palms on the floor, but her fingers curl when I nibble my way down her neck to the soft flesh of her shoulder. Her nails scrape on the marble. I slither down her body inch by inch, tasting and teasing her, with my fingers and my lips, my teeth too. She can certainly feel the hardness of my cock as it's dragged down her spine, leaving a hint of wetness in its wake.

"Drink me, Cyneric. I want to feel your fangs in my flesh."

"Soon, love, soon."

I push up on my elbows just enough that I can slide my cock between her arse cheeks and rub my length up and down. She moans, her nails raking the floor again. With one knee, I push her thighs apart. Now, every time I push my cock between her arse cheeks, it also glides down the length of her cleft. Her silky cream coats my flesh, and the aroma of it inundates my senses, but I will maintain control—for now.

My voice has become a harsh growl. "You belong to me, Amanda. This will end with more than orgasms. I will claim you as my mate, branding you forever."

"I want that. No one else could ever make me feel this way." She twists her head around to see me. "But it goes both ways, hon. You'll be mine forever too."

A thrill races through me, something I have never felt before. "Yes, I will be yours."

I rub my cock up and down while she bites her lip and slaps her palms flat on the cool floor. Her eyes have narrowed to slits, and she gasps with every thrust. I haven't even penetrated her yet, and already I can tell she's teetering on the edge.

No more gentle teasing. I can't hold back now.

"Roll over, Amanda."

She obeys me once again, without hesitation, placing her legs at either side of me. A wicked smile curves her lips, and she lifts one foot to hook it around my hips and rub it against my arse. "Bite me, Cyneric."

"Not yet."

I take advantage of her position and hook both her legs over my shoulders, pushing them forward until her knees touch her chest. But I still do not thrust into her body. I want to do it, need to do it, but I sense that claiming her will require far more than a simple sexual act. It will demand…everything.

So, I crush my mouth to hers and plunge my tongue between her lips as I had done before, except that now I take possession of her tongue in the most literal sense. I coil my tongue around hers so that she can't respond in kind. She can only moan while I devour her tongue with slow sucking movements. I rest my arms on the floor, pinning her legs in place, while her moans grow deeper and go on for longer. The sound drives me mad, yet I refuse to succumb to the need.

I have other plans for her mouth.

While she grips my biceps, I sink my fangs into her tongue delicately, piercing it only enough that I can drink from the artery there. Amanda moans more softly, as if the sensation of me suckling her tongue to taste her blood makes her even more aroused. Her fingernails sink into my flesh. She can't hurt me this way. My skin is too thick.

I slide my fangs free of her tongue and lick it to seal the wounds.

She licks her lips in a leisurely manner. "Mm, that was hot. Don't stop now."

"Don't worry. I have no intention of stopping yet."

I shimmy backward just until my face lies directly over her tits. I keep her knees pinned to her chest, using my hands to do that. When I glance up at her, she gives me a lazy, sensual smile. I know that means she wants more, so I swallow her nipple, pulling in the entire areola too, and flick my tongue over it again and again until her breaths once again become shallow and quick. I won't bite her there, so instead, I suckle that peak while grazing my fangs over the tip repeatedly until she thrashes her head and release wordless cries.

"Bite me again, Cyneric. I need to feel you inside me, your teeth and your dick. I love it when you do that."

Fuck, I want to do that. The husky tone of her voice drives me half-mad with the need to give in and do what she asked. But I'm not ready yet. I need to go further and take her with me into the erotic abyss.

I shimmy backward even more. Then I lower one of her legs until it lies flat on the floor, and I hook her other knee over my shoulder. This is the perfect position for what I mean to do. I thrust into her sheath so hard and so deeply that she cries out and arches her back. For a moment, I simply stay in this position, reveling in the molten heat of her body surrounding my cock and the knowledge of what I will do next.

"Oh, yes. Don't hold back anymore, Cyneric. Make it wild and hot and hard, like something out of a Greek myth."

I rest my hand on the floor and turn my head to the side. My lips now graze the inner thigh of her leg that's resting on my shoulder. I wet her skin with my tongue, using languid strokes to excite her even more, and then I do it. I sink my fangs into her inner thigh and drink.

Amanda writhes beneath me and slaps her hands on the floor over and over. I begin to fuck her in earnest, gently consuming her blood while I thrust in and out of her body, keeping the rhythm slow and steady until I feel she's ready for more. Then I increase the pace, plunging into her while simultaneously drawing on her blood. My cock thickens even more, and deeper growls rumble out of me. Amanda thrashes and cries out.

Something stirs. Is it inside me? Inside her? No, it's something else. The temple itself seems to have awakened because of what we're doing. The more intense our passion becomes, the more I sense the magics pulsating inside me. I had never thought of supernatural energies as erotic, but I should have known they could be under the right circumstances.

"Cyneric, do you feel that?" Amanda massages her breasts and shoves her hands into hair, biting her lip. "Shit, this is—Don't stop. When I come, it'll be—"

I withdraw my teeth but go on pumping hard and fast. "So powerful it will blow you apart, I know. But magics are, ah, gathering around us."

"Don't care. Take us to the climax."

I wrap my arms around her and lift until her chest is plastered to mine. Her legs encircle my waist. All the while, I keep fucking her. The magics continue to heat up and expand, spiraling out into the center of the temple in slithering waves that are now visible. The tongues of energy lick at our skin, but that only heightens our lust. While sparks of green and red burst and swirl above us, I teleport us directly onto the throne with Amanda on my lap. She rocks her hips into me, gripping the back of the throne with both hands, and throws her head back in ecstasy. Her cries reverberate through the temple.

She is so bloody beautiful, a goddess in control of both our bodies.

"Drink me again, Cyneric. Make me yours completely."

How do I claim her as my mate? I told her I would, yet I've never known precisely what that involves. All I can do is keep going and let the magics within this temple guide me.

I grasp Amanda's hips, then slide my hands up to her waist. As I lick my way up her belly, she throws her entire body backward, forming a graceful arch that accentuates every sensual curve. I glide my hands up her lower back so I can tilt her toward me just enough to do what I suddenly know I must do.

I lean forward and sink my fangs into her carotid artery.

The rush of sweet blood intoxicates me, and I crush her body to mine even while her spine continues to arch backward. She comes within an instant, her inner muscles clenching me fiercely as she screams. I roar as my cock spasms, and I know I will come in a matter of seconds. But an impulse I had never experienced until we entered this temple compels me to do something else.

I lift Amanda off my cock, though her knees are still straddling me. "Use your hands to make me come. Do it now, love."

She falls forward, her forehead touching mine, and we gaze into each other's eyes while she pumps my cock with her hands and my release sprays onto her belly and chest.

Amanda collapses against me. Her head lies on my shoulder, and her breaths bluster over my ear. I run my hands up and down her back, soothing us both while we wait to regain our breath. Over her shoulder, I can see the magics winding down, growing dimmer, retreating into the recesses of the temple.

I nuzzle Amanda's ear. "Are you all right, love?"

"Yes. Felt like my heart might burst out of my chest, but yeah, I'm okay." She lifts her head to smile at me. "Actually, I've never felt this good in my entire life."

"Neither have I."

"Did you claim me?"

I cup her cheek with one hand. "We claimed each other."

She grins. I grin. And then we both start to laugh.

Once we've stopped doing that, I whisk us out of the temple and straight to the reflecting pool—into the water. It feels cool and silky on our skin. We enjoy the pool for several minutes, until we finally must restart our quest for answers concerning my true origins. Amanda insists on hoisting herself out of the water rather than allowing me to teleport her or lift her myself. She does, however, let me dry us both off with a puff of air.

I might not be an air elemental, but I know how to borrow a bit of that power whenever necessary. Other elementals do the same thing, so I'm not an air thief.

Amanda laughs when I tell her that. "Air thief? That's cute, hon. But you are a thief. You steal my breath away every time we make love."

"You mean when we fuck."

"That's also called making love." She lies on a chaise alongside the pool, her delectable body more beautiful than that of any goddess in the multiverse. "Do you know what the word love means?"

"Not entirely. Mortals and elementals alike use the term, and Eros used to say he loved me. But I still don't understand."

Amanda climbs onto my chaise, nestling her body against mine. "That word is a hard one to define. It means you have deep feelings for another person—or another being. But honestly, love is something you just know when you feel it."

"You have said you love me. But how do you know that's true?"

"Because I feel it in my soul. When I'm with you, I know that no one else could ever give me this warm, glowy sensation." She lays a hand on my chest, then taps one finger on it. "Your heart will tell you when you're in love. No one could give you a concrete explanation because it's about what you feel in your heart."

"I have thought... But I can't be certain."

"Nothing is for certain. Go with your gut."

"Then I believe my gut tells me..." I swerve my attention to the pool, despite knowing that won't make this any easier to say. I shut my eyes briefly, then meet her gaze. "I am in love with you, Amanda."

"No kidding. I never would have guessed."

"You are being sarcastic."

"That's right. Couldn't resist. I love the cute little dimple that forms between your eyebrows whenever I say something that confuses you."

I doubt I will ever fully understand mortals, but I would very much like to spend eternity learning to understand Amanda Nelson. "How did you know that I love you? I didn't speak the words until just now."

"A woman always knows. We have great intuition."

"I see." Perhaps I don't actually understand, but explanations can wait. I conjure Amanda's phone. "Show me the pictures you took in the temple."

She fiddles with the device, then tilts its screen toward me. "Here you go. Just swipe left to see the next one."

"I have heard mortals talk about 'swiping' before. But I assumed it meant they wanted to steal the belongings of another person."

Amanda laughs, but it's a gentle, affectionate sound. "You know the older kind of swiping, but not the newer one. Now that might be even cuter than the dimple between your brows."

With her advice and instruction, I manage to view the photographs she had taken while I clung to the ceiling of the temple. Most of the imagery involves various beings gathering around Eros to worship him and perform sexual acts with or for the god. To get a better look, Amanda uses her thumb and forefinger in a pinching gesture to make the images larger.

Her brows rise, and one side of her mouth kinks upward. "Does Eros really have a dick that big?"

I growl. "Does it matter? His cock is not important to our quest."

"Take it easy, hon. I don't care if Eros really does have the most enormous rod in the multiverse. Size isn't everything."

"During my time in the mortal world, I've heard women talking amongst each other. They often say that size does matter, though they deceive their lovers by saying it doesn't."

"I honestly don't care about that." She pulls her head back. "Did you just call it 'our' quest?"

"Yes, I believe I did. I don't expect you to stay with me throughout—"

She holds two fingers to my lips. "Can't chase me away. You're stuck with me, hon."

I relax.

Amanda whispers into my ear, "Your dick is the only one I want."

We go back to exploring the images, "zooming" in and out with our fingers to get the best views. Yes, I've learned another word and another skill. I know how to "swipe" and "zoom."

"Wait," Amanda says. "Go back to the left a little bit. I think I saw something."

I hand the phone to her, and she zeros in on an image that had been hidden in the shadows. We hadn't noticed it before this. But now, she taps the screen several times to light up the figure in the background.

"How did you do that? It must have been magic."

"I upped the brightness and contrast, that's all." She hands me the phone. "Don't worry about it. You've got forever to learn all the new technology and jargon."

But I won't have eternity with her. She is mortal.

I have no time to consider that terrible thought, because we need to examine the figure she had brightened.

Amanda's eyes go wide. "Do you see what I see?"

"Yes. I'm looking at the same image."

"No, I meant—Never mind. Just zoom in a little more, then pan to the left."

"Pan? How will cooking help?"

She raises the phone directly in front of my face. "That figure. It's you."

CHAPTER TWENTY-EIGHT

I STARE AT THE IMAGE ON THE SMALL SCREEN, THE ONE AMANDA CLAIMS looks like me. No, what she actually said was that it is me. As I scrutinize the figure, an odd tingle sweeps down my spine. The figure has dark hair and blue eyes as pale and bright as mine. But most tellingly, he has two long, sharp teeth. "This image must have been created shortly after Eros brought me into being. It does not provide any new insight."

"Are you sure about that?" Amanda moves the image up and down, left and right, until she apparently finds the correct angle. "Look at this. It's a symbol etched on the vampire's chest."

I slant my head forward and down, scrutinizing the symbol she pointed out. "That appears to be three interconnected spirals. I don't understand the significance."

Amanda taps the screen. "I saw this symbol once in a documentary on TV. It's called the triskelion, and it's a very ancient symbol that was prevalent throughout Europe." She prods me with her elbow. "You said you used to speak with a German accent."

"Germanic is a more accurate description. I lived long before the country of Germany came into existence."

She taps her finger on the screen with even more vigor. "Look hard at this image, Cyneric. It's you. And the triskelion symbol implies you have a connection to the ancient cultures of Germanic Europe. That would mean you are not the son of Eros. If he had made you from his own flesh and blood, you would be like him. You'd have a Greek accent."

"I have wondered about my true ancestry. But I'm having difficulty accepting what you say, despite feeling that it is true."

"We need to talk to your elemental friends about this."

"Yes, the oracles may be of some assistance." I conjure our clothing onto our bodies and leap to my feet while holding Amanda. "I have learned all that I can from the Temple of Eros. It's time to leave."

I teleport us directly to the training ground. Everyone is here waiting for us, even Janus.

The god walks up to us. "You have done what you needed to do, yes? I could sense the change even from a distance."

If he could see what Amanda and I did…

"Don't worry, Cyneric. I am not a peeping god." Janus spreads his arms. "I used my vast powers to ensure no one would interrupt you and Amanda. So tell us, what did you learn about your past?"

Janus must already know the answer, or he would not have asked. But I assume he wants me to tell him so that the others will hear it. Amanda shows Janus the image on her phone, though he seems almost as baffled by the technology as I was. Then she passes the phone to Max, and it makes the rounds among our mates.

"What is it?" Travis asks.

"A triskelion," Nevan tells him. "I saw that symbol often when I was a warrior in ancient Ireland, before I died and was reborn as a sylph."

"But what does it mean for Cyneric?"

"The symbol suggests that he came from an ancient tribe in Europe or the British Isles."

"Germanic Europe is most likely," I say. "Eros claimed he created me from his own flesh and blood, yet I spoke with a German accent. The triskelion symbol we found in the Temple of Eros also seems to suggest I was not from the Unseen and therefore not the son of the god."

"You told me earlier," Amanda says, "that you figured you must have been born a mortal and forged into an elemental vampire. Do you still think that's the case?"

"It seems like the most plausible explanation."

Max chuckles. "Plausible? Since when did anything about the Unseen become believable? Mortals deny we exist."

"There is but one way to be certain," Janus pronounces. "Cyneric must travel back in time to the day of his creation. If Eros did indeed create him, then he will know immediately upon reaching his destination. If Eros is not Cyneric's father, then he will also know that immediately."

"You're letting him travel through time?" Max says. "He might have another earthquake seizure and destroy the multiverse."

"That is highly unlikely." Janus raises one arm to point his hand at me. "You must learn the answer. Now."

Everything goes black, and for a moment, I cannot see or hear or feel anything. Then the abyssal tunnel telescopes open, dragging me through the darkness to spit me out into bright sunshine. I hit the ground face-down. I need a moment before I can move, since the journey through the tunnel is rarely easy and never pleasant.

"Cyneric? Are you there?"

Amanda's voice rouses me, and I leap to my feet to search the area for her. She is not lying on the ground beside me. Trees and bushes proliferate here, making it difficult to hunt for Amanda. "Where are you? I can't see."

"Look up."

I tilt my head back.

"Higher, Cyneric."

Leaning backward from the waist, I at last catch sight of her. "What are you doing in a tree?"

"I thought it would be fun to climb up here and wait for you to find me. What do you think? That damn tunnel flung me here."

She sounds irritated, but I can't blame her for that. I attempt to conjure her into my arms, but it doesn't work. I was able to conjure while in the Temple of Eros, but now my powers fail. Perhaps being in the past has something to do with it. Since I can't do this the easy way, I leap into the air and touch down on the branch beside the one where Amanda lies, clinging to the limb. I pluck her off the limb and jump back down to the ground.

"Thank—" She flattens her lips. "I meant to say that I appreciate your help. Do the rules about gratitude apply to wherever we are now?"

"I do not know. This would seem to be the mortal world, but I can't tell for certain. If we're in the past, I have no idea whether the Unseen's rules apply here."

"Guess all we can do is explore to figure out where and when we are."

I set her on her feet. "That seems the most prudent plan."

We wander through the forest in search of clues to our location, the current time period, and answers to the most important question. Was I born here? I can't understand how time travel will solve that mystery. I do not know where I might have lived or how I died. My own past has always been somewhat of a mystery, since Eros would never divulge any details. But now I have become a living mystery, uncertain of everything about myself.

I know I am an elemental vampire. But that is all I know.

Eventually, we emerge from the forest and find ourselves at the edge of a large valley, where we can see a settlement in the middle of that area. Houses and other sorts of structures are gathered there. Smoke drifts up from chimneys. This does not appear to be a Stone Age settlement, but I'm hardly an expert on the history of the mortal world. Perhaps this is a later time or an earlier one.

As we head down the slope of the valley, I decide to ask a question. "You are a native of the mortal world. What time period do you believe this is?"

She makes a derisive noise. "I'm not an archaeologist. That means I don't know enough about the past to answer your question."

"Did humans in the distant past live in buildings like the ones in this valley?"

"I guess that would depend on how distantly we've gone into the past. And also whether modern historians have gotten the facts right."

She is correct, of course. Only people of the past know precisely what life was like in this period.

We amble across the grassy fields that surround the little village, but we halt far enough away that no one will be likely to notice us. Our clothing will not match with the way people here dress, I'm sure. But I won't know how they do dress until we approach the village.

So, I stop us and turn toward Amanda. "I will need to glamour for both of us, to ensure our attire doesn't cause confusion among the locals."

"Good idea. But I assume these people won't speak the same language that we do. How will we communicate? Do you have a speech version of glamouring?"

"No. We will need to, ah, improvise."

"Winging it doesn't sound like a great idea. No offense, hon, but you aren't the best at improvising."

She has a point, and I can't deny that I lack the finesse of other elementals. I can seduce women. But convincing strangers that I pose no threat to them? I'm far more likely to frighten them so much that they want to murder us both.

I wince. "Perhaps you should do the talking."

"But these might be your people. I really think you should talk to them."

She tightens her features in a manner I've heard mortals call "scrunching." I never understood that term until now. Yes, Amanda is scrunching her face.

"Then again," she says, "you might get annoyed and let your fangs come out, which would terrify everyone."

"You are not helping."

"I guess not." She straightens and takes a deep breath. That always lifts her breasts and draws my attention to them. "Why don't we just dive right in? Let's wing it."

"What does 'wing it' mean? I assume you aren't suggesting I should fly. I'm not a dragon shifter."

Amanda shakes her head, and her expression is one I've seen before. It seems to indicate that she thinks I'm being overly literal, or perhaps adorably confused. She has called me both of those at various times. Then she grabs my hand, leading me toward the village. I glamour us into what I believe clothing of this time period would look like, though I am not a historian. Various types of animal skins would seem the most likely option. The closer we come to the settlement, the more I begin to feel as if I am being drawn toward a familiar place, where I will be welcomed. But that's rubbish. I have no foresight, like the oracles. Yet the feeling grows stronger every moment.

When we reach the periphery of the village, I see small huts that have thatched roofs and walls constructed with something that resembles modern plaster but must be a different material. I ask Amanda what she believes they are made of, and she takes a moment to consider her answer.

"It might wattle and daub. I'm no expert, but I've watched enough documentaries to know that wattle is a kind of woven wood and daub is, I think, mud and straw."

That sounds odd to me, but then, I'm from another world. In the Unseen, we don't need to bother with devising construction methods. We use magic to do that.

We pass by the first hut, since it seems to be vacant at the moment. A well-worn path leads us closer to the center of the village, and we pass by a large boulder that has various pagan symbols painted on its surface. I notice more wattle-and-daub houses that all have thatched roofs as well. Still, we see no sign of living beings. Yet someone inhabits this village. Might they be hiding from us?

At the center of the settlement, we find a few larger structures that I suspect are not homes but gathering places instead. The buildings are longer and wider, with walls made of wood planks. The roofs are thatched like all the other structures we've come upon so far. Crude wood fencing closes in paddocks that hold livestock. I recognize cows, but only because of my experience with the shotgun-wielding man in Texas.

"What are those other creatures?" I ask Amanda. "I haven't seen any like them before. They have a great deal of fur for such small animals."

"I assume you're talking about the sheep."

"Sheep? That is a strange name. I've seen cows before. Are these creatures meant to be killed and consumed?"

"Yes and no."

Before she can give me a more informative response, a figure emerges from the largest building in the village. We stand directly in front of that structure. The being who saunters toward us appears to be a man, based on the person's long blond beard and lack of breasts. He wears crude leather trousers and a shirt made of woven fabric as well as leather boots.

The stranger halts a short distance away. "Who are you? Why have you come to our village?"

I can understand the words he spoke. How, I do not know.

"We walked here," I tell the man. "And we are seeking knowledge about this village and the people who live within it. I believe I might have been born in this place."

Perhaps I shouldn't have blurted that out. But if I want answers about my past, I must ask questions.

The man gives me a quizzical look. "How could you not know where you came from?"

"I assume I was taken away from my parents."

He steps closer but still keeps a distance between us. "What is your name?"

I glance at Amanda, but she only shrugs. Neither of us knows how to handle this situation. So, I face the man again. "I am Cyneric."

The man stares at me. His eyes gradually widen, and he takes one step backward. "You cannot be Cyneric. Only one male of that name has ever been born in the village, and he is with the gods now."

"'Which gods? Perhaps they would know more about my past."

"The gods are in the sky. You can't speak to them." He stalks closer, stabbing a finger into my chest. "Never again invoke the name of Cyneric."

"But it is my name."

He clenches his fists, and his body begins to tremble with what seems like rage. Then he shouts over his shoulder. "Come out now! Come out and spit upon the invader who has invoked Cyneric's name."

Men and women pour out of the building behind him, each holding some sort of weapon, everything from knives to spears and other items I have never seen before. Everyone stays behind the blond man, though one woman comes up beside him and clasps his hand.

Tears shimmer in her eyes. "How could anyone do this? They must have invoked black magics to recreate him. It's vile and evil."

"Indeed it is," the man says. "We should execute these two at once."

"Wait," Amanda says. "Don't you want to hear us out before you lop off our heads?"

The man squints at her. "Say your piece."

She moves closer to me, gripping my hand more firmly. "Cyneric is not a demon. We have reason to believe he was born in this village, and we simply want to talk to his parents, if they're still alive."

"They live." The man veers his gaze to mine. "But my son died many years ago. This must be a demon impersonating him. Cyneric is no more."

A chill like none I have ever experienced freezes me as surely as a blast of frigid air might do. This man just said… He implied that…

These are my parents.

Chapter Twenty-Nine

MY MIND REELS FROM THE REVELATION OF KNOWING THAT MY parents believed I had died, and that it means Eros is not my father and never created me. Not in the way he made me believe, that is. But since gods do not forge mortals into elementals… He could not have played a role in my creation. Since I am still frozen, unable to do anything except stare at the man who might be my true father, Amanda speaks for me.

"Cyneric isn't deceiving you," she says. "He only recently discovered that he's not who he thought he was. His memory must have been erased when he became…something else."

"What does that mean?" asks the man who claims to be my father. "Our son was murdered. This man is not Cyneric. Perhaps his eyes are the same extraordinary shade of blue, but he cannot be our son."

Is he correct? How do I know which of us is wrong? I wouldn't know what to do with a family if I suddenly acquired one, so it might be best if I accept this man's assertion that I am not his son. Yet I wish for this couple to be my family. Amanda has shown me that I am not a monster at heart, incapable of caring for anyone, bound for destruction.

"Maybe it would help if we introduced ourselves," Amanda says. "I'm Amanda Nelson, and this is Cyneric. But you already know that."

The man gazes at her steadily, but his brows gradually furrow, and finally, he sighs and relaxes. "I am Germund, and this is my wife, Sahsa."

"It's wonderful to meet you both." Amanda curls her arms around my bicep. "Cyneric and I have been anxious to find you ever since we learned that he might not be the son of Eros."

Germund stiffens. "Eros? He is not a benevolent god, but a demon hiding within the guise of a deity."

Sahsa clings to her husband. "Germund, please, don't blame Cyneric for what Eros did. We lost our son once. I cannot lose him again."

They don't want me, do they? Of course not. I am a demon, just like Eros. Sahsa might wish to uncover the truth, but her husband is skeptical. The chill inside me has grown even colder, and I have trouble taking in a full breath.

Amanda smiles at Germund and Sahsa, portraying compassion and kindness in that simple expression. "We want nothing more than to find out if Cyneric came from this village, and if so, whether you two really are his parents. He was snatched away from his family and lost his memories of them. Won't you let us try to find out?"

Germund looks at his wife and lays his hand over hers on his arm. "You should decide, Sahsa. The one who gave birth to our son would know him best."

"I need to learn the truth. Please, we must try."

He nods and kisses the top of her head. "Then we shall."

Relief surges through me so swiftly that I lose my balance and stumble into Amanda. She slings my arm across her shoulders to support me, and we follow Germund and Sahsa away from the large building, heading toward one of the smaller wattle-and-daub structures that's clearly designed as a home. Smoke curls up from the chimney.

Inside the house, Germund and Sahsa invite us to sit on the chairs around the table where they eat their meals, I assume. The chairs appear to have been fashioned from small tree branches that still have most of the bark on them. I settle onto the seat beside Amanda. My potential parents sit opposite us.

"How do we find proof?" Germund asks. "This man might resemble our son in many ways, but he is clearly different in others. How can we ever know for certain when he claims to have lost his memories?"

"Give him a chance, please," Sahsa pleads. "There must be a way to know."

While they continue to discuss the problem of me, and Amanda offers possible options, I scan the room in hopes of seeing something that might trigger a memory. Nothing seems familiar. If I had lost my memory during the forging process, I don't know how I might reclaim it.

"Do you recognize anything?" Sahsa asks. "Perhaps you should walk through the house."

"That's a good idea," Amanda says. "Anything might trigger a memory. Would you like me to walk with you, Cyneric?"

"No, I will do this alone."

I rise and begin my survey of the small house. It has only three rooms as far as I can tell. One is the large area in which we now stand. The other two appear much smaller, and they have no doors. As I approach the nearest room, I can see that Germund and Sahsa must sleep in there. Clothing and shoes lie lumped in a corner, and the bedsheets look slightly rumpled. I continue past that room and step into the doorway of the other.

This one looks as if no one has slept here, not recently, not even in the recent past. It has been kept in meticulous order. Why would anyone do that? If they had lost a child, I suppose they might want to preserve the room. But it seems like a morbid thing to do. I can't explain why, but I trudge into the little room and sit down on the bed. It fits me, but that hardly proves I lived in this house.

I close my eyes and attempt to relax, taking slow, deep breaths. My elemental senses kick in, and I can hear the respirations of the three individuals in the main room. I hear their heartbeats too. The only aroma that wafts into this room belongs to Amanda, and the scent soothes me. I allow my perception to reel back into me as I imagine what this room might have looked like in the past, when a young man slept here. A human being. Someone's son.

Please don't let him die. Save my son.

My eyes fly open. My heart beats faster. The voice in my head sounded like Sahsa. Is that proof she is my mother? Of course not. I have no idea if I experienced a genuine memory, but if I have, I can't explain what it means.

I lie down on the bed and shut my eyes.

Healer, I beg of you, spare my child.

I jerk upright. My skin has begun to burn and prickle, though only in one spot. I rip my shirt out of my waistband and hold the fabric up to see the area where the pain originates. It's my tattoo. The one Eros gave me. I probably shouldn't believe everything he said, but I can't think of a reason why anyone else, not even myself, would tattoo my skin.

A woman cries out.

I leap off the bed.

Sahsa stands in the doorway, eyes wide, one hand resting on her chest. Amanda and Germund come up behind her.

"What is wrong?" Germund asks his wife. "Sahsa, you are pale."

She stretches out a hand to point one finger at my lower abdomen. "He—He has the mark. The one our Cyneric had."

"What? The healer's mark?"

"Yes. Look, and you will see for yourself."

Germund strides up to me. "I must see your mark, to know if it is true."

I have no reason not to oblige him, so I lift my shirt.

"Would you mind undoing your pants? The mark goes below your waist." He seems to abruptly notice something. "How did you change your clothing? This is not what you were wearing a few moments ago."

I must have lost my hold on the glamour while I was experiencing those memories. But if I confess the truth, he will no longer believe anything I say. Still, I have no choice. "I glamoured so that you wouldn't be shocked by the way Amanda and I dress and the way I look."

Germund swerves his attention up to my face. His eyes widen now too, just like Sahsa's had done a moment ago. "Your skin, it's not like ours. It seems to shimmer with a faintly golden color. And your eyes are..." His eyes bulge, almost as if they might fall out of their sockets. "They were an unusually bright shade of pale blue before, but now they are frighteningly pale with a faint glow."

"Yes, I know." My throat feels tight as I unhook my pants and roll the waistband down just enough to reveal the rest of my tattoo. "Is this what you needed to see?"

Germund nods. He moves closer, bending forward to peer at the circular pattern on my lower belly. Then he whirls around to face his wife. "Sahsa, this is—It must be—*He* must be—" Germund shakes his head as tears gather in his eyes. "He must be our Cyneric."

Sahsa shrieks and races up to me, hugging me so hard that I would probably lose consciousness if not for the fact that I'm an elemental. She hoists herself onto her toes to cover my face with kisses. Tears roll down her cheeks. "Cyneric, my son, you have come home at last."

Memories assail me, and I stumble backward as the torrent pulls me deep down into the past.

I'm lying in bed while my mother and father stand at the foot of the bed, watching and waiting. Sahsa clings to Germund, her lips trembling and unshed tears glistening in her eyes. The healer sits beside me. She has just finished etching a circular mark onto my lower abdomen, and now, she raises her arms to chant an incantation.

I had been unwell for some time, unable to eat more than a few bites or drink more than a few swallows. My strength had ebbed after I was injured during a skirmish with another tribe. The injury festered until I grew too ill to even get out of bed. But the healer had saved my life. She employed magics and herbs, even her healing touch, to eradicate the illness.

My perception returns to the three people gathered around me. Sahsa sits on the bed beside me while Germund has his hand on her shoulder. Amanda stays behind them, clearly aware that my parents need time to recover from the shock of learning that I am their son. But can I be certain? Only an oracle would be able to certify that what we all believe is indeed a fact.

Oracles, the sort who have genuine powers, exist only in the Unseen.

I do not want to leave Sahsa and Germund, not yet.

Before I leave this place, I must know how I became an elemental vampire. Who forged me? Why? Was Eros involved?

Sahsa hugs me fiercely while small sobs hiccup out of her. "My darling boy, I have missed you so much. Vow you will never leave us again."

I can't make that vow. Yet I suddenly realize I want to give her that promise. It would be a lie, though. Amanda and I do not belong in this time, and I can't abandon my friends who are relying on me to stop whatever apocalypse is about to occur in the twenty-first century.

A force I cannot describe seizes me, and I'm compelled to gently peel my mother away from me so that I can rise to my feet. "I need to know what happened to me after my illness was healed. Will all of you come with me? I have an intuition that I cannot ignore, and I believe it will lead me to the ultimate truth."

Sahsa throws her arms around me again. "Of course we will come with you, Cyneric." She releases me, only to seize Amanda. "I am grateful beyond words that my son found a woman like you. I can tell you're good, strong, and loyal."

Amanda bites her upper lip. "You don't mind that I look older than Cyneric? He's immortal, so technically much older than I am."

"I don't care about anything except that I have my son back."

Once my mother lets go of Amanda, I lead us all out of the house. "I believe I know where it happened."

"Where what happened?" my father asks. "Are you going to tell us what this is about?"

"Yes. I am taking us to the place where I was forged and became an elemental vampire."

CHAPTER THIRTY

AMPIRE?" GERMUND SAYS. "WHAT IS THAT? I HAVE NEVER HEARD such a word before, so I can't understand what an elemental vampire would be either."

"Let me show you." I stop and turn toward my parents and Amanda, then I allow my fangs to slide out. My eyes will have begun to glow and swirl too. Once they have seen enough, I retract my fangs. "Elementals are beings who live in another world known as the Unseen. Each type of being in that world is bound to a specific natural element. I am bound to blood."

Germund and Sahsa both seem stunned by my admission. I can't blame them. It must sound horrific that I must consume blood to survive, but before I try to convince them that I am not a monster, not anymore, I first need to understand how I became a vampire. With no evidence to guide me, I'm relying on my instincts and the memories that have begun to surface in my mind.

While I march onward toward an unknown destination, Germund questions me. "You drink blood? Does that mean you…injure people?"

"Yes, I consume blood to survive. But I have never made the conscious decision to harm anyone, mortal or elemental." I am trying to sidestep the issue because I don't want to tell my parents that I nearly killed two women. The explanation of how that happened and how I've changed will need to wait. "Please, follow me and all will be explained, I hope."

I spoke the P-word. But we are in the mortal world, so it won't incur a debt. The fact that I said the word at all provides evidence of my desperation. I need to know how I came to be. The answers lie ahead of us, in the forest, I know they do.

Amanda walks alongside me now, holding my hand.

Occasionally, I glance back to make sure my parents are still following us. But otherwise, I try to avoid even thinking about them. I must keep my mind open and free of noise. Only then might I find the place that I seek.

"Slow down," Amanda whispers to me. "Your parents are starting to look tired, and you don't want them to collapse. I know you're anxious to get answers about your past, but please just ease up a little. Okay?"

Though I don't want to slow down, I realize she's right. And I accept her advice.

It takes us longer to reach our destination than I would've liked, but when we at last get there, my parents don't seem exhausted at all. My heart is pounding, but I doubt that has anything to do with the journey to reach this place. I feel excited and afraid, two things I had never experienced before I met Amanda.

"This is it," I say, turning to face Germund and Sahsa. "This is where I was forged and became an elemental vampire."

We stand on the bank of a river, where it widens into a deep waterhole. I cannot see the bottom, that's how deep it is. The water flows from the pool into the river.

Germund shuffles closer to the bank's edge and gazes down at the murky water. "I don't understand. How did this river make you a vampire?"

"It didn't, not directly. But water is the portal. In every place on earth where water naturally flows, there will be a portal to the Unseen at the bottom." I kneel to study the pool and the swirling eddies within it. "I want to show you how I became what I am today. This will not be pleasant to watch, but I believe we all need to see it."

"If you think it will help, we will watch."

Amanda crouches beside me. My parents cling to each other as they move closer to the edge, halting beside us.

The time has come. I empty my thoughts and allow the memories that had lain dormant within me for millennia to come to life before our eyes. The scene plays out like a film in an outdoor cinema.

I see myself swimming in the pool with a pretty young maiden. We have our clothes on, having removed only our shoes, and now splash each other while laughing. I leap up to grab onto a low-hanging branch, then swing back and forth while making silly noises. The girl laughs. Emboldened by her reaction, I swing even more vigorously and attempt to jump onto the bank. But when I release my hold on the branch, it catches on my shirt. The limb cracks and falls with me still caught on it. The weight of the branch drags me down into the murky water.

The last thing I hear is the girl screaming. Then silence descends.

I can't even hear my heartbeat. Nor can I see the bank above me. I'm trapped between the branch and a large rock, unable to break free. My lids drift closed.

A pair of large hands hoist me out of the pool, tossing me onto the bank.

Only later will I realize the beast that rescued me was an undine, a water elemental, and that he served Eros. As a human with no knowledge of the other world, I believed I was being rescued from certain death.

The undine backs away from me, and I notice that another being stands beside him. That creature is a salamander, a fire elemental, but I don't understand that yet. Both creatures are males. The two seem like polar opposites, yet I am about to learn a lesson that the god who called himself my father would never have wanted me to learn.

A figure emerges from the shadows of the forest, sauntering up to me where I lie limp and half-dead. The massive, muscular being gazes down at me with an impassive expression, as if he were examining a slab of meat to determine if it would make a good meal. Eros tips his head this way and that, seeming mildly interested in me.

"You are sure he is the right one?" Eros asks. "I do not wish to waste my time on a weakling."

"He is the one," the undine says. "We have watched him and tested him, though he was oblivious to our machinations. This one will make an excellent addition to the ranks of the elementals. You will be admired universally when the other gods learn that you have created an entirely new category of creatures."

"Do you think I care what my fellow gods think? They are pathetic." Eros kicks me in the side. "If this one survives the forging, he will soon have brothers, and I shall gift them to Hathor. She will surely return to my fold when she realizes what a magnificent offering I have given her."

"As you wish."

Eros backs away from me. "It is time to prove that a hybrid elemental is possible. Use your unique powers to forge this pitiful mortal into a wondrous vampire."

The undine and the salamander seem less than convinced that the god's plan will work. But they know he will destroy them if they don't succeed. The two creatures kneel at either side of me and begin to chant in the old language, the one rarely used except to cast powerful and dangerous spells. Orbs of glittering white light dance around me, then dive down to envelop me with energies that nip at my flesh and devour it molecule by molecule. The scalding heat of the transformation rends fearsome screams from my throat as the magics melt me from the outside in, plunging deep into my flesh and bones.

Once the old Cyneric has been obliterated, the new me rises. But the resurrection process is neither easy nor painless. To create a hybrid being, the salamander and the undine must invoke the most powerful magics of all to meld the characteristics of both beings into one living thing.

My screams echo through the forest.

Then, at last, blessed relief comes. The pain dissipates. And I am reborn.

Eros flips me onto my back and studies me. "You will do, provided I can train you to serve me. But I will handle that once we return to my temple." He waves toward the undine and the salamander. "You may go. The ritual is completed."

Those two beings vanish.

Eros lifts me into his arms and whisks us away to his temple, straight into his bedchamber, where he lays me down on the plush bed. "I cannot allow you to remember how you came to be. But you will be much happier without the memories of your former life, trust me."

I am still too dazed from my transformation to comprehend what he said.

The god spreads his arms and recites the spell that will ensorcell me. I instantly forget everything that occurred before this moment, and that is exactly what Eros wanted.

He grasps my chin. "Tell me who you are and from whence you came."

"I do not know."

The god smirks. "Excellent. You came from nowhere, my son. I am your father, and you are Cyneric, my greatest accomplishment. I created you, and henceforth you shall adore me above all others and do everything you can to make me happy. Do you understand?"

"Yes, Father."

The memory crumbles away.

Germund and Sahsa gape at me for what feels like hours but is only a matter of minutes. Then they both fling their arms around me and cry.

My mother wipes away her tears and touches my face. "I have my son again."

Suddenly, Amanda and I are whisked away.

The journey through the abyssal tunnel is never pleasant, but this time, we cling to each other as we ricochet against the invisible boundaries of the tunnel, crashing into them so hard that my mind starts to whirl. Amanda cries out and clutches me as if she will die if she lets go. I wrap my entire body around her to protect her from the melee. A screeching like none I have ever heard in all my existence deafens us.

We are ejected from the tunnel, plummeting through the air until we slam down onto the ground. I had flipped us around in midair to ensure my body would strike the earth instead of hers. I lie here somewhat dazed for a moment. Then I regain enough of my wits to remember that I need to check on Amanda. She appears dazed too, but a hands-on inspection of her body assures me she hasn't broken any bones.

Everywhere around us, I hear the horrendous racket of a cataclysmic battle raging.

Amanda and I get to our feet and absorb the situation, holding each other as we realize the scope and intensity of the war going on around us. There is no doubt it is a war, though nothing like any I've ever seen before. A rumbling, whirring, screeching, clattering, wailing jumble of noises echo around us. I glimpse objects flying through the air, but then realize those are not mere objects. They're living creatures.

Which world are we in? Mortal or elemental? I can't tell.

The bluish-black sky makes it difficult to see, even with supernaturally enhanced vision. Fingers of crimson snake across the dark sky, and bolts of shimmering silver lightning lance the heavens and the earth. Creatures are intermittently disgorged from the abyssal tunnel, streaming forth even while other beings are sucked up into it. Harpies race across the sky while shrieking as if the world is ending.

Perhaps it is. But have I caused this tumult?

Amanda clutches me even more tightly. She needs to shout to be heard above the commotion. "What is going on? Where are we?"

"I have no idea."

Four figures materialize in front of us. Travis, Max, Nevan, and Tris wear expressions I have never seen before, not from them. I can only describe it as horror. Despite their fear, which I do not blame them for experiencing, they remain resolute and relatively calm.

"Where are we?" I ask. "It seems like the Unseen, but something isn't quite right."

Travis shakes his head. "We are in the mortal world."

Impossible. That's what I want to say, but I know all too well that nothing is impossible. "What is happening?"

"Isn't it obvious?" The salamander throws his arms wide. "Welcome to the apocalypse, mate."

The hairs at my nape stiffen, and a chill races up my spine. "How did this come to be? Have we been gone for years?"

"It's only been a few hours, but that was long enough. The dragon king got tired of waiting and decided to just go for it."

Hours? That's all that it took for Thirío to initiate an apocalypse? Something must have triggered his anger, though I can't imagine what. So, I need to ask my mates. "When did this begin? What pushed Thirío over the edge?"

"I don't think there was an edge for him to tip over. He just got bored of waiting to destroy you." Travis turns his palms to the sky and raises his arms higher. "The dragon king is having one whopper of a tantrum."

Nevan nods. "And he's dragging us all into hell with him."

"Where precisely are we? What location in the mortal world?"

The sylph glances at Max and Travis, who shrug. "As best we can tell, it used to be a city called Amarillo."

"How could Thirío know I was ever here?"

Max rolls his eyes. "Because he's a wickedly powerful elemental. Duh."

"Take Amanda away from here, to a safe place. Then we can deal with the dragon."

"Can't do that. There is no safe place anymore."

An enormous shadow distends over us. The thwapping of wings rushes closer, and we have no time to glance up and prepare for what might come next. A dragon touches down directly in front of us. Perhaps it's my imagination inflating everything, but I would swear this dragon is larger and more muscular than any I've seen before. It towers over us like a monster in a horror film with saliva dripping from its peeled-back teeth.

"I have caught you at last, little vampire, and you won't escape me this time. There is nowhere to go." Thirío ducks his head, thrusting it in my face. "No one will escape the apocalypse."

CHAPTER THIRTY-ONE

WE ALL STAND HERE GAWPING AT THE BEAST THAT CROUCHES BEFORE us, as if none of us can comprehend the situation or convince our minds to function and help us devise a plan. Thirío couldn't wait to destroy me. But he can't do that, no one can, and he must realize the attempt is futile. His tantrum is illogical. But I suppose all tantrums are. I am hardly an expert on the nature of elementals or humans.

Max raises his hand. "Ah, just wondering, Lord Fire Breath. What's your big plan? If no one will escape the apocalypse, that means you'll die along with the rest of us."

Thirío flares his nostrils but doesn't breathe fire. "You, little salamander, will be the first creature I roast and devour."

"Awesome. I love being first in line. But I'm still wondering, what's your plan? If you want to die, just hit the big annihilation button and have done with it."

Travis shakes his head. "Yes, let's all die. What a brilliant idea."

"At least we'll take him with us."

The dragon king snaps his wings out and snarls, "Silence, you filthy whores. I care nothing for what salamanders think or say. Only the vampire will speak."

Travis raises his hands, palms out, and shrugs.

I release Amanda's hand while I take three steps toward Thirío. "Tell me what I must do to stop this apocalypse."

The dragon king stretches his neck out until his snout is inches away from my chin and his eyes glare straight into mine. "This will end in just one way. You will suffer and die. Then, perhaps, I'll cancel the war."

"Do what you like to me, but end the chaos now. Bind me with enchanted chains, ensorcell me, I don't care."

"Cyneric, no," Amanda shouts. Peripherally, I can see Nevan holding her back as she struggles to get to me.

I ignore her cry. I have to, or I'll never be able to do what must be done.

Thirío studies me intently, tilting his head side to side, squinting his slitted eyes. Then he lifts his head to gaze at the beings behind me. When his eyes narrow once again, I know his attention has stalled on Amanda. His dragon lips peel back in a strange approximation of a smirk as he returns his attention to me. "I will end the chaos, on one condition."

"What are your terms?"

"You and Amanda will come with me."

"No. I will go alone. She remains free."

Thirío rises to his full height. His eyes burn an incandescent shade of red. "There will be no negotiation. Do as I say, or I will annihilate the multiverse."

"You can't do that. The multiverse is too vast."

He chuckles. "And I am vastly powerful. Shall I demonstrate?"

Thirío puffs up his chest, sucks in a deep breath, and unleashes a torrent of fire that blows my friends to the ground and causes me to tumble over backward too. The fire engulfs the trees at the periphery of the open area. Beings in agony scream, wail, and roar. A whirlwind latches on to the flames, funneling them up toward the portal to the Unseen.

A shape hurtles out of the opening, and the portal telescopes shut with a grinding racket.

Janus lands beside me and dusts himself off, then aims a steely look at the dragon king. "You have annoyed me and caused my clothing to become dirty. Angering a god is ill-advised."

Thirío thwaps his tail on the ground, causing a minor tremor. "You don't scare me, Janus. I can reopen the portal whenever I like, and you will not be able to stop me."

"You are alone. We are not. The odds seem not to fall in your favor."

The dragon sniggers. "Even a god can be a fool."

He snaps his scaly fingers, and two beings appear behind him. He snaps his fingers again, and an army of dragon shifters fill the clearing. I recognize the two beings who are not dragons. Balder and Setesh take up positions at either side of Thirío.

Balder grins at his fellow salamanders. "I cannot wait to fuck your women after I've torn you both apart so thoroughly that no magics can reassemble you. Naturally, I will ensorcell them so they'll enjoy being debased and abused."

Neither Max nor Travis responds to Balder's taunts. Neither does Nevan. Amanda, on the other hand…

She wrenches free of Nevan's grasp and comes up beside me. Then she spits at Balder. "Go screw a harpy, you sick son of a bitch. I will never get naked with you ever again."

Amanda spits again, with more power, and the spittle lands on Thirío's face this time.

But another being interests me more. I cant my head at Setesh. "I was right, wasn't I? Thirío found you and unraveled whatever spells the Four Winds had cast to strip your powers and your memories. You are Setesh once more, not Seth Gamal."

He shrugs. "Perhaps Thirío did free me from my life in the Outback. But I had found ways to pass the time until then."

"You mean you became a mass murderer. I saw the bodies in your house. Those mortals had been tortured and slowly killed."

Setesh grins. "Yes. Wasn't it a beautiful tableau?"

He is the evilest creature I have ever met. I doubt even a harpy would attempt the things that Setesh brags of doing.

Thirío peers around me and smiles with wolfish delight. "There you are, little leprechaun. You will watch while I defile your woman and also the women belonging to your sylph and incubus friends, then I shall destroy you." He glances at Balder and waves for him to come forward. "But I gift Amanda to you, salamander. All I ask is that you let me observe when you ensorcell and debauch her. Perhaps I should keep Cyneric alive until after you do that, so he can watch too."

I clench my fists.

Above us, the apocalypse rages on, despite the portal having telescoped shut. It shouldn't be able to spread into the Unseen, not completely, but the mortal world remains at grave risk. We can no longer trade sarcastic taunts. It's time for war.

I conjure my sword. Though I haven't spoken a word, my mates conjure their weapons too. I also provide a weapon for Amanda—a long, sharp, endued knife that appears in her hand. She smiles with grim satisfaction. Riley and Larissa materialize, both wielding swords of their own, which I'm sure are endued. None of us will enjoy killing, but we know it must be done.

A horde of beings appear. Most of them are dragons, but they've brought a contingent of harpies too. The dragons all bear swords, large and glistening ones that I'm certain have been endued. Even Janus has conjured a weapon. At least the stakes are even now. One god for us, one for Thirío.

The dragon king raises his sword high. "Let the battle commence!"

Dragons and harpies descend on us, and I suffer an unprecedented but brief moment of panic. I pull Amanda close.

Travis throws his head back and shouts, "Open the portal, Janus!"

What is he doing? The portal will allow the apocalypse to run rampant in the Unseen.

Janus hoists his sword high and chants in the old language.

While the dragons descend on us, I keep Amanda beside me, holding onto her, while I fend off the beasts with one hand. Metal clashes against metal. Sparks erupt from our blades. In the darkness of the bluish-black sky, I can see the flashes of other blades colliding. I lost track of my mates, more concerned with protecting Amanda than knowing where the others are. They can take care of themselves.

The portal telescopes open. Fairy lights pour out of it to brighten the battlefield for us, tumbling out of the opening in the sky to hover in the air or spill across the ground. Then an army of gnomes leaps out of the portal, immediately engaging the enemy. Gnomes are on our side? I had no idea.

Shouts and screams and clanging swords ring in the air. I glance around but it seems as if none of our mates have been struck down. The bodies on the ground belong to harpies and dragons. When I search the area, I can't see where Thirío, Balder, and Setesh have gone.

I suddenly realize I am no longer grasping Amanda's hand. Spinning around, I scan the battlefield in search of her. I don't see Amanda, but I locate the tallest dragon on the field, whose head rises above the others. He hurries along the periphery, heading toward the portal.

Thirío must have Amanda.

A primal roar explodes out of me with enough volume that even creatures on the other side of the large open area pause to glance in my direction. I bolt through the crowd, taking down harpies and dragons along the way. Blood soaks my clothing and my hair. None of that matters. Nothing will stop me from reaching the portal before Thirío can abscond with Amanda.

Just as I come within a few yards of the portal, about to leap onto Thirío from behind to tackle him, a harpy latches onto my back. The creature drags me to the ground. She sinks her talons into my flesh, gnashing her teeth in a manic attempt to bite my neck. I flip over and ram my elbows into the harpy.

She loses her grip.

I leap up and thrust my blade straight into the harpy's heart. While the destruction process begins, I race toward the portal.

Thirío has Amanda in his grip, her legs thrashing and her arms pinned by his much stronger ones. He vaults into the portal.

"No!" I roar. "Amanda!"

Then I summon strength I didn't know I possessed, vaulting across the distance and up into the portal just as it shuts.

And I touch down in darkness. The twin moons have turned a deep shade of crimson. I stand within the small clearing around the portal, but I don't see Amanda or Thirío. So, I stop and listen. Crunching. Grunting. Hissing. The sounds are distant, but I can hear them.

"Let go of me you son of a bitch!"

That was Amanda, and her cry echoes through the forest. She might be shouting so that I can more easily track her. But she needn't have bothered. I have caught her scent, and nothing will stop me now.

I run faster than I ever have before, my footsteps barely making a sound because my feet barely touch the earth. Amanda's unique scent drives me onward, but it's the call of her soul that leads me toward my goal and spurs me to sprint even faster. I leap over bushes and veer around trees.

Why hasn't Thirío teleported? Whatever Janus had done to the portal must have circumvented teleportation. I can't whisk myself away either.

At the edge of the dragon forest, I slow down to tiptoe toward the figures I can see ahead of me. They wait at the rim of the basin that houses the dragon kingdom. I want to hurl my sword into Thirío's back, but I might hit Amanda by accident.

Thirío whirls around, holding his blade to Amanda's throat. "Come out, little vampire, or I will slit your woman's throat."

I can't risk her life. My own doesn't matter. So, I march out of the shadows and straight to the dragon king. "Release her. I am the one you want to punish."

He laughs. "Yes, I want to destroy you. But my vengeance would not be complete without your friends—the leprechaun and his girl, as well as the salamanders. They all participated in murdering Drakon." Thirío's eyes widen, but only for a moment. "So, Janus helped you find us, did he? He saved me the bother of summoning you one by one. Excellent. I will need to conduct only one destruction ritual for all of you."

I glance over my shoulder. Travis, Max, Tris, and Riley do indeed loiter behind me. But behind them, a small army of sylphs stands ready to fight.

Thirío leaps backward. He rolls over in midair, still clutching Amanda, and soars across the basin toward the castle.

While my mates battle the dragons, I do the only thing I can.

I leap off the cliff.

"Cyneric, what are you doing?"

The voice of Travis echoes behind me as I drop lower and lower even while I soar forward. Will I make it to the castle? If not, I will run the rest of the way even if I have many broken bones. Fortunately, I'm wearing my leather coat, so I let it flap around me like a cape. The coat provides just enough lift to keep me from crashing to the ground.

Thirío dives through the cylindrical opening in the ceiling of the castle, vanishing from view.

A current catches me, and I struggle to keep my trajectory level. But as I descend, I lose control and wind up hurtling downward wildly. I crash into the edge of the opening and ricochet off the walls. When I slam into the floor, for a moment, I can't move. Only when I've caught my breath do I manage to push up onto my knees. A shaft of white light shines down through the opening above us, but the bluish-black sky still roils.

Thirío sits on his throne, wearing his robe, with legs crossed and one foot swinging. "You have arrived at last."

I scramble to get to my feet. "Kill me, but let Amanda go. She is innocent."

"She won't be innocent anymore once I've had my fun with her."

I conjure my sword. "We will fight to the death."

"No, we will not." He claps his hands. "Bring her."

A dragon soldier drags Amanda out into the throne room, where she is forced to stand beside Thirío's monolithic chair.

The king rises and stretches, then conjures a large black sword into his hand.

I bend my knees just enough to be ready for his assault.

Thirío turns toward Amanda and thrusts his blade straight through her heart and out the back of her body.

"No!" My cry echoes inside the throne room and vibrates the walls.

The dragon king yanks the sword out of Amanda's body and tosses it away. "See? I don't need to fight you. Killing her accomplishes the task in a much cleaner way. You will mourn her forever."

He throws his head back and laughs.

A roar explodes out of me as I hurl myself at Thirío. We tumble to the ground, wrestling for control of our swords. The soldier does nothing to intervene and help his master. The second I see an opening, I seize it. My fangs drive deep into Thirío's throat and my weight pins him to the floor. At full strength, he could overpower me. But the dragon king is growing weaker by the second.

Balder appears and tries to wrench me away from Thirío, but he fails. When Setesh materializes, the two bastards combine their strength but still can't pull me away.

I drink until I'm full and keep drinking, sucking out every last drop of anything resembling blood or liquid of any sort. By the time I retract my fangs and rise to my knees, the dragon is no more.

He is a desiccated body on the floor. No magics will resurrect him now.

An explosion cracks overhead, above the castle, echoing throughout the land of the dragon shifters. The bluish-black sky becomes bright blue. The beauty of the sky matters nothing to me. I have but one task to accomplish.

I turn toward Setesh and Balder, grasping my sword in both hands.

They are staring down at their dead master, whose flesh desiccates more and more and soon will crumble to dust.

I swing my sword once, severing their heads before they even realized I still had a weapon. Their bodies slump to the floor, atop the pile of dust that once was the dragon king. I kick their heads out of the way as I stride over to Amanda.

Her eyes are open, yet she does not breathe.

I kneel beside her, but I can't hold myself upright. I slump onto my arse and pull her onto my lap so I can cradle her in my arms. The sounds of Setesh and Balder being destroyed can't even penetrate my mind.

"Oh, bloody hell, no."

Travis's voice barely registers in my mind. I kiss Amanda's lips, but she still does not rouse. With her body pressed to my chest, I bury my face in her hair.

"What should we do? We can't leave him like this."

Is that Max? I don't care who it is anymore.

"Oh no, not Amanda. Were you guys just gonna let him sit here like this?" A hand shakes me. "Snap out of it, Cyneric. We need to get her to the healing vortex. Come on, get up."

I lift my head.

Tris tugs on my arm. "Wake up. We can still save her." He reaches for Amanda. "Just let me take her. I'll go straight to the vortex, and you guys can follow. Okay?"

Let go of her? No, I can't do that.

"Damn, I can't even teleport her out of your arms." Tris kneels beside me. "I know you love her and you want her back. I can't make that happen unless we get her to the vortex right now. Time is running out."

Travis settles a hand on my shoulder. "I know what you're going through, believe me. The vortex is the answer."

Reluctantly, I hand her over to Tris. He disappears with Amanda in his arms.

A moment later, I stand at the periphery of the healing vortex behind the rock shop. Max, Nevan, and Travis stay at my side while Tris consumes two large chunks of copper. He's powering up the vortex. Nothing happens. He waves his hands over Amanda, but still nothing changes.

Tris bows his head. "I'm sorry. It won't work. This makes no sense. I mean, the vortex heals everybody."

But not Amanda. Not the woman I love.

I collapse to the ground and pass out.

CHAPTER THIRTY-TWO

Is he awake yet? I can't tell. I mean, the bloke is a vampire, so maybe he never has a pulse. But did anyone check for one? Oh, no, don't point at me. I'm not going to be the one who gives the bloodsucking fiend a shake, especially after what he's been through."

"Man up, Max. You're such a dufus."

The voices I hear sound far away at first, but gradually, they draw closer until I no longer feel as if I'm floating in outer space. That was Max talking to Tris, I believe. My mind hasn't quite roused fully.

"No playing possum, Captain Fang. We know you're not conked out anymore."

Is the leprechaun speaking gibberish? It sounds like that to me. Groaning, I rub my eyes and force my lids to open.

Tris, Max, Travis, Bob, Ken, and Janus all hover around me. I lie on a bed that I don't recognize in a room that I don't recognize. The covers feature a flowery pattern of pink, lavender, and yellow. No, I would never sleep on a bed like this, not willingly.

Yawning, I sit up and stretch. "Where is Amanda?"

They all stare at me. Tris clears his throat and cautiously pats my shoulder. "Uh, you don't remember, do you? There was a battle, with dragons and harpies and all that shit."

I freeze. My heart pounds. "Amanda—"

"Think he remembers now." Tris gives my shoulder a squeeze. "She's not dead. Well, she was dead, but we fixed that. Took a hell of a lot of research and help from a dream team of powerful beings, but we finally figured out why the healing vortex didn't work."

I leap up. "Take me to Amanda. Now."

"Don't need to take you anywhere." Tris takes a step backward. "Time to show yourself before Cyneric starts mainlining our carotid arteries."

A figure materializes beside the leprechaun.

For a moment, I can't believe what I see. Is it real? Am I hallucinating? But no, this is not a figment of my imagination. I haul Amanda into my arms and hug her so tightly that she must not be able to breathe. So, I force myself to loosen my grip. "You're alive. I watched you die, but—How is this possible?"

"Two oracles, a god, some fae witches, and one snarky leprechaun." She smiles. "Don't you want to kiss me now?"

"Better hold off on that," Travis tells us. "I have a feeling you two will be at it for days once you get started. Let us explain first."

"Make it fast."

Bob pushes past the others to reach us. "Amanda already knows the story. But here's what happened. She did indeed die, and the healing vortex would not work for her. But the fae witches placed her in a state of suspended animation while we searched for the problem. Do you remember when Amanda was hospitalized and was very anemic, despite transfusions?"

"Yes, of course."

"Balder had injected her with a magical poison. It was slow-acting and meant only to keep her weak until the dragon king could complete his plan. Then, Balder believed Thirío would give him Amanda as a reward for aiding him in his apocalyptic plot. The salamander wanted to father more hybrid children with Amanda as the incubator."

I still have my arms around her, and I glance at the woman I thought I'd lost forever. "This is true? You are not ill?"

"That's right. And you did not make me anemic. It was all the fault of Balder and Thirío."

Knowing that I never harmed her, even unintentionally, lifts a weight off my chest that I believed I deserved to bear. But it wasn't my fault. I still have questions, though. "But how is Amanda alive now? You healed her, Tris?"

"No. She was way past that option. So we, uh, went a different way."

I squint at him and bare my fangs.

"Nice try, Captain Fang, but I'm not scared." Tris shoves his hands into his trouser pockets. "Bob talked to Miriella, and the Four Winds agreed to transmute her into an immortal human. For a lot of complicated reasons, they couldn't make her an elemental. She couldn't be a normal mortal either, so transforming her into an immortal and invincible human was the only way to go."

"She is…like me? Not a vampire, but unkillable."

"Bingo."

Nevan clears his throat. "We have another surprise for you."

My mates step aside to make way for two newcomers.

I gawp at the couple who just entered the room. "Germund? Sahsa? I don't understand. How were you brought here?"

Germund hugs me. "Call me Father. You are our son, after all. We don't fully understand the situation, but we will live wherever you and Amanda are. We've been advised that adjusting to this world will take time and patience."

Sahsa hugs me as well. "Please, call me Mother. I have waited so long to hold you again."

Amanda and I spend the rest of the morning with my parents, getting reacquainted and starting the process of becoming a family once again. My mates had conspired with Janus to bring Germund and Sahsa here—permanently—so that I might regain some of what I'd lost because of Eros. My father asks if I would prefer to live in the Unseen, but I assure him that Amanda and I would both prefer to remain in the mortal world. It has become my home. The Unseen harbors too many bad memories.

As it turns out, no one in this world knows anything about the apocalypse. Several gods and the most powerful elementals had joined forces to erase the memory of the cataclysm in the mortal realm, strictly to protect this world. Only a select group will remember.

In the afternoon, Nevan and Lindsey invite my parents on a nature walk. My mates have another surprise for me.

We are in the rock garden with Bob and Janus.

"Now that you've had a chance to bond with your mother and father," Bob says, "we need to tell you about Eros. Like Kamadeva, he was not part of the dragon king's plot. Thirío had intended to reactivate Eros, but he never could find him."

Janus nods. "Indeed, he failed to track down the god. But Eros is still alive and in the mortal world. He has no memory of his previous life. And as far as we could determine, he has done nothing more nefarious than working as a gardener."

"He will not harass me again?"

The god shrugs. "We cannot say for certain. Only time will tell."

I don't care about Eros anymore. All that matters to me now is that I have a family and a woman who will be at my side for the rest of eternity.

But Amanda needs closure of her own, the sort only a god can provide. One day, we are "cuddling" on the sofa together while my parents are away. Travis, Larissa, and their adopted daughter Dani have taken Germund and Sahsa on an outing to explore more of this world. I have just pulled Amanda closer, intending to kiss her.

Janus materializes in front of us. "I have news, if you wish to hear it."

"Tell us or leave. I need to shag Amanda."

"Yes, I know. This news is for Amanda." Janus crosses his arms over his chest. "We have found your son."

"What?" She jerks forward, her eyes large. "Is he—Does he want—" She lays a hand on her chest and takes two slow, deep breaths to calm herself. "My God, I never imagined this would happen. I don't want to upset his life, but could I at least get a peek at him?"

"You may have more than a peek. I will escort you to him and employ my vast powers to cloak the three of us."

I rise and help Amanda up too. "May she meet him? Amanda suffered greatly to bring her son into the world."

She rests her cheek against my upper arm. "I don't want to turn his world upside down."

"You cannot meet him," Janus declares. "Not yet. We need to smooth the path before that may happen. When you gave up your child, the Four Winds bound his powers. He knows nothing of his true parentage or his true nature. Be patient, and one day soon you will meet him."

"I understand. Can't deny I'm disappointed. But after all the horrible things I've been through, I owe it to my kid to make sure he wants to know me, rather than forcing the issue."

Janus whisks us away to the backyard of a house in a small town—where, he won't say—and we observe a cheerful young man who is playing a game with his father. Baseball, I believe it is called. Amanda's son is twenty-four years old, Janus informs us. The young man has joined the military as a pilot in the Air Force, which I learn means he flies a "jet." I don't understand that term, but Amanda will explain it to me later.

My life is unrecognizable these days. An awkward, unstable, confused, and lonely vampire has become a contented man. I have mates, a woman who loves me, and the freedom to do whatever I choose.

That's all the redemption I need.

Did you love
CYNERIC?
Visit

ANNA DURAND IS A BESTSELLING, MULTI-AWARD-WINNING AUTHOR OF contemporary and paranormal romance. Her books have earned bestseller status on every major retailer and wonderful reviews from readers around the world. But that's the boring spiel. Here are the really cool things you want to know about Anna!

Born on Lackland Air Force Base in Texas, Anna grew up moving here, there, and everywhere thanks to her dad's job as an instructor pilot. She's lived in Texas (twice), Mississippi, California (twice), Michigan (twice), and Alaska—and now Ohio.

As for her writing, Anna has always made up stories in her head, but she didn't write them down until her teen years. Those first awful books went into the trash can a few years later, though she learned a lot from those stories. Eventually, she would pen her first romance novel, the paranormal romance *Willpower*, and she's never looked back since.

Want even more details about Anna? Get access to her extended bio when you subscribe to her newsletter and download the free bonus ebook, *Hot Scots Confidential*. You'll also get hot deleted scenes, character interviews, fun facts, and more! Plus you'll receive the short story *Tempted by a Kiss* and mutliple bonus chapters in both ebook and audiobook formats.

VISIT ANNADURAND.COM TO SIGN UP.